Immaculate

Anna McGahan is the author of *Metanoia* and a collection of poetry, *Skin*. She is an actor, playwright and screenwriter, and has written essays and poetry for *The Griffith Review*, *The Guardian* and other publications. Anna lives in Meanjin (Brisbane), with her two daughters.

Immaculate

Anna McGahan

This is a work of fiction. Names, characters, places and incidents are products of the author's imagination or are used fictitiously. Any resemblance to actual events, locales or persons, living or dead, is entirely coincidental.

First published in 2023

On p. 371, 'The Little Match Girl' by Hans Christian Andersen, translated by H.L. Braekstad, published by The Century Co., New York in 1900.

Allen & Unwin
Cammeraygal Country
83 Alexander Street
Crows Nest NSW 2065
Australia
Phone: (61 2) 8425 0100
Email: info@allenandunwin.com
Web: www.allenandunwin.com

Allen & Unwin acknowledges the Traditional Owners of the Country on which we live and work. We pay our respects to all Aboriginal and Torres Strait Islander Elders, past and present.

A catalogue record for this book is available from the National Library of Australia

ISBN 978 1 76106 799 0

Set in 13/17 pt Adobe Jenson Pro by Bookhouse, Sydney
Printed and bound in Australia by Pegasus Media & Logistics

10 9 8 7 6 5 4

The paper in this book is FSC® certified. FSC® promotes environmentally responsible, socially beneficial and economically viable management of the world's forests.

In loving memory of Tim, Andrew and Margy.

For anyone who has ever missed a child.

This book was written on the unceded lands of the Jagera and Turrbal people, Meanjin, where storytelling has been established for millennia. I pay my respects to Elders and acknowledge that some of the experiences explored in this book are inarguably endured with greater urgency and injustice by Aboriginal and Torres Strait Islander people, whose stories and processes are their own to tell.

Part One

The Book of Mary 1:1

God.

Dog should've ripped off his limp little dick while he tried to find his fly.

Hot piss. *Beer* piss. In my mouth. My hair. Down the sleeping bag.

Dog is useless. I wipe my face on him, and he licks the piss off my eye.

The sleeping bag is soggy. I reckon I can get my belly out – okay nah, I'm stuck.

It's like being born all over again. Fuck.

The Gospel According to Frances 1:1

I wash them all off me. It's a rainwater showerhead. We bought it so the house plants could feel like they were back in the subtropics once a week. Lucky them, they get an illusion of home. I like it for its sound. For the white noise.

I tiptoe out of there, past the king-size bed. I don't look at it. I don't want to wake whatever sleeps there. The bed has remained made for two years, the sheets bleached in a failed attempt to remove the memories they once absorbed.

I dry myself. Bodies are easily cleaned. Skin doesn't stain. Isn't that a little miracle?

I bandage the cold with a t-shirt. I find socks. I grab a mandarin in the kitchen. It's shrunken, peppered with dusty green mould. The food I buy turns bad so quickly.

I hover at her door. The linen screams at me to come, to hold her. She must be freezing tonight. It's a cool snap. I need to be outstretched into her space. To move the air around, warm the sheets and smell the clothes. Kiss the head of the sleeping child, count her breaths, watch her chest rise and fall. I could. I could go in and calm her – she's crying, it's a nightmare, she *needs* me. I'll just hold her, quickly. Gulp her in like air.
Find her. Eat her. Keep her.
But she's not here.

I'm so *hungry*.

Text messages from Lucas Harkin to his ex-wife Frances
Kocsmáros, 3 November 2020

I'm out front. Can you pack her togs, please. Also a spare pair of clothes. (09.42 am)

One missed call. (09.45 am)

Frances I'm in a hurry. (09.50 am)

I would like to put in writing that your behaviour at handover was entirely inappropriate and aggressive. (09.59 am)

The Book of Mary 1:2

Do you have any spare change? *(No, sorry)*
G'day, mate, can you spare a couple of dollars? *(I've got no cash)*
Hey – (. . .)
Excuse me – (. . .)
Hey, sis, I'm just trying to get a bite to eat, I'm pregnant – *(Little slut)*
Hey, I'm only five dollars short of a bed tonight – *(We both know that's not true)*

Just want a hot meal, for me and my dog – *(Oh my God, that poor puppy)* = $4
(Is that a dog? Here you go, love. What's his name?) = $2
This is my pup. Yeah, she's, um, pregnant – *(Keep that little mama warm)* = One McDonald's Happy Meal.

(Hey)
What?
(We have soup and sandwiches, if you're hungry)
I've had Macca's.
(We have showers)
. . .
(. . .)
Okay.

The Gospel According to Frances 2:1

I walk to the door of Spice Den with a beanie and baggy jumper on. For some reason, the more I look like a teenage boy the more authentic I feel. Femininity does not enter as a client; femininity waits inside to be purveyed. This thinking is laughable, knowing Celine, but I let my body lead. I am paying for the privilege to let it, after all.

I press the buzzer on the black door and wait for Sharon to usher me in, which she does with a matronly smile. Sharon reminds me of a high school teacher. Straight-talking, trustworthy, but will call your mother if it's serious. You don't fuck with Sharon, in any sense of the word.

I like reception – it feels like an upmarket hotel. Somewhere to rest after a really long day, week, month, year, life. It is sturdy, grounding, with no air of sexual transaction, until Blair suddenly slips out from a door behind the manager, wearing a G-string, fake-lashes and nothing else.

'Is that my Uber eats, Sharon?'

'Nope. Tell Celine she's up for an hour.'

Blair sees me holding the paper bag of food and rolls her eyes, disappearing back into the mythical girls' room like a sylph into the mist.

Sharon writes up my booking, charges me for the hour and takes me to Waiting Room 4. I know it well: she brought me here my first time, too. It has sleek black leather armchairs, a small vase of flowers on a black glass coffee table, and a twenty-four seven reel of terribly uncomfortable-looking porn on a wall-mounted television. My first visit eight girls came in for intros, one after another. An audition of sorts. *Hello, my name is* __________.

What are you looking for? What do you need tonight? Would you like to pay for this additional offering? They entered with a practised elegance, all high-heeled and straight-backed – some immaculately made-up and wearing lace lingerie, some in robes with conspicuously dishevelled hair, straight out from the last booking.

Celine was one of the first few to intro with me. I remember her face contorting as she eyed me sitting on the tall black armchair, my hunched shoulders dwarfed by the masculine longing of it all.

'What do you want?' she asked me, unsmiling.

'I want to find the clitoris.'

'On me, or on yourself?'

'Maybe both?'

She allowed a small smile then. Gently levelled with me, perching on the other armchair.

'Honey, you're about to find the fucking multiverse.'

I had to speak with the others as a matter of course: Blair – Amazonian, tanned, who mostly did lesbian sex in two-girl bookings for guys; Sara – cute, ex-corporate, wearing a lot of pink; Danika – eighteen years in the business, fucking exhausted and uninterested in emotional chat; Tahlia – almost jaw-dropping in her beauty, baffled by my presence but professionally polite. All of them astute, empathetic and alluring in their own way. Businesswomen. Everyone wanted the booking, but only Celine knew how to get it.

I don't do intros anymore. I just wait for the familiar plod of boots against tile, my tummy grumbling, hairs standing up on end across each of my thighs.

Tonight, Celine opens the door and nods at me to follow. I do. We wind through a corridor to Room 5.

Celine is not male-gaze feminine. She's wild and large and tattooed, with cropped hair that she gels into this delightful 1920s kiss-curl and a septum piercing that hovers over purple lipstick. She wears a leather harness with silver studs, covering pectoral muscles instead of breasts. She wears platform Doc Martens to her knees. She smells like myrrh.

Celine closes the door behind us. The room is like an inner-city hotel: lush, low-lit, not a crinkle in a bedsheet. The glass of the shower glistens with water, recently used. Celine sits on the bed and starts to remove her Docs, revealing a pair of thick bed socks. She stretches, then reaches for the paper bag of food, grinning at me. I take her in: the whole, sexual persona of her own creation. Her armpit hair, her shaved undercut, her heavy exhalations. The flex of her thigh and the sharp diamond of muscularity in her back. She reminds me of an acrobat. A stuntwoman. A pilot. An athlete. That primal marriage of dominant power with the watchful feminine wisdom to know how to use it.

I settle onto the bed with her, shoes off but clothes on, silently indicating I don't need a medical check tonight. After learning a couple of things about the clitoris (through a dental dam, no less), suction vibrators and strap-ons, I have now embraced true lesbian kink: cuddling in front of Netflix while eating takeaway on a Friday night. So, unless either of us is feeling particularly ovulatory, that's what we do.

Celine opens a Pepsi Max and slurps the little bubbles in the rim. 'Banh xeo?'

I pull the food out, water condensing on the lid.

'Com tam.'

'You hot bitch, get it in me.'

We lie back on the bed and Celine pulls a blanket from somewhere. She switches the television from cyclical adult films to a streaming rental site. I log in. We watch episode three again because I fell asleep twenty minutes before it finished last time, and Celine wants to see the end. She absent-mindedly plays with my hair, the beanie left at the door.

'I hate that guy. He's like a British Hitler.'

'What, Winston Churchill?'

We eat our food. The show has gunfire and bombs tonight.

Celine bristles. 'Did you see action?'

I squirm, unsure what she's talking about?

'You were in the army, right?'

Oh fuck.

'I think that's what you told me. A soldier?'

She watches my face shift in avoidance, and laughs. 'I get my daylight identities mixed up sometimes, too.'

'No, no . . . I forgot I mentioned it.'

'I'm being cheeky. I just wanted stories. Gossip about guns and bombs and heroes who are actually just little boys with complex post-traumatic stress disorder.' She rearranges her body around mine, doesn't take her eyes off the television. 'I get those guys in here a lot.'

'And those girls.'

She raises an eyebrow at me.

'If you're ex-military, you're nothing like them.' Celine eats, pauses. 'But there's always something weird behind the eyes. Like they've seen too much of something that should never be seen. And you've got that.'

She's right, of course.

'Did you have to shave your head?' she asks, my plait loosening in her fist.

'No . . .'

'You don't have to talk about it. We can just watch.'

But she has stiffened a little. Her hand is no longer stroking my hair and the myrrh is dulled just slightly. It's transactional, but it's not. You can't watch the same shit TV side by side and not catch feelings.

I do not miss Lucas, except when I come across one of our television shows. Is that all our relationship can be distilled down to? *We ran out of conversation at the same time each day. We laughed at the same jokes, we held our breath at the same cliffhangers. We sat together at 8.30 pm on a Sunday night. We were together. And now we are not.*

Celine offers me the paid experience of a familiar, peripheral loneliness.

The fight scene rages onscreen, and I look at her, trying to open.

'I came into it all later, but my ex signed up as a young kid. His grandparents were part of it. Parents, brothers, everyone. It was a generational expectation.'

'Took on the family business?' scoffs Celine. 'Many wish I did the same.'

She laughs, pirouetting deftly off that tender pressure point.

'I was really enamoured by the discipline and community of it. I took the oaths, did the training, learned the language of it. It's deeply immersive, exclusive, protective of its own. So many people have been in it since they were kids.'

Celine shakes her head, horrified. 'Like child soldiers?'

'More like cadets? They instil the values early. Honour. Purity. Loyalty. You learn to value discipline and sacrifice and warfare and victory. You learn not to fear anything. You believe the battle is already won, because you're fighting for righteousness. You're the heroes, not the villains.'

'And you believed in these ideals?' She is equally repulsed and fascinated. I wonder how far I will take this.

'Yeah, I guess I did.'

She curls into me, tentative but intrigued. Myrrh.

'So you would have seen people killed, huh? Maybe killed them yourself?'

I don't answer that. I close my eyes. *Not here. Not right now.*

Celine is not finished, however. I can feel the sweat on her hands. The tick of a clock somewhere inside of her. An urgency.

'Did you ever feel like it was kinder to let someone die than to keep them alive?'

I cannot look at her. Not because I do not know the answer.

I will never admit it. I will never submit to it. I will never accept it. Do not ask me to. She is searching for something, and I will not let her find it in me.

I pretend I am asleep as she strokes my hair, bombs and British accents in my ears, musky scents filling the gaping hole in my life. Our breathing settles back into sync, until I have finally faded into the furniture.

Website: www.thespiceden.com.au/celine/

THE SPICE DEN – Legal Brothel – Open 24/7

BOOK HERE: phone or email

Image description:
A picture of Celine's torso and arse in red leather lingerie
A tattoo of a cockatoo on the side of her left butt cheek

Playmate: Celine
She/her

Curvy, powerful, dom or switch
Tattoos + piercings
Experimental or gentle
Queer femme explorations
Couples bookings + double bookings
Girlfriend experience for men and women

Australian
Size: 14
Age: 35
Bust: A
Hair: Cute short dark hair

About: Wild, passionate, intimate – Celine will have you eating out of her hand.

Bank statement of Frances Harkin *née* Kocsmáros, 12 August 2022

— Bao Vietnamese Takeaway: $47 – 10.17 pm
— Celine Riot, Expert Consultancy Services: $270 – 10.31 pm
— Apple Rental (Digital Streaming) – Episode 7, Season 1 of *The Crown*: $6 – 10.35 pm

Letter from Frances Harkin to the congregation of the Eternal Fire Church, 15 June 2020

To the valued and loved congregation of Eternal Fire:

As you may be aware, I have recently stepped down from full-time service in our street outreach program. I have also stepped down from any ministerial, pastoral or teaching roles. It is with deep gratitude that I thank the congregation and leadership team for their ongoing support and love as I traverse the next season in my faith and focus my energy on motherhood. I acknowledge with sadness Lucas and I have decided to end our marriage, and I ask that you keep us in your prayers.

Lucas Harkin will continue as teaching pastor, and I wish him all the best in this endeavour as we continue our parenting journey together.

Blessings,
Frances

The Gospel According to Frances 3:1

The psychologist hasn't met my eyes yet. I have decided to come here a maximum of three times. This is the third.

She has framed stock images from Kmart on her wall and wears bad jewellery. I don't trust anyone who thinks a photograph of a succulent is art.

'I want to check on the homework from last week.'

She's looking at me now, pen at the ready.

'Ah, yeah, I emailed the questionnaire.'

'And you were going to contact the support group, I think?'

'Yeah. I haven't done that.'

She looks disappointed.

Woman, I live to disappoint. Just ask my Hungarian mother.

'They would be an incredibly useful resource regarding the next stage, be it treatment or remission. You can talk to other parents.'

'We only had the latest scans a week ago. It's just one day at a time for me.'

I can see her eyes drift to the clock on the wall, her patience faltering. I am reminded she has squeezed me in on a Saturday afternoon. Maybe she's meant to be at a party, or a soccer game, or her own support group.

'I really think you –'

'Lucas already goes. So I can't.'

She nods, processing. Concedes.

'I've actually been meaning to ask – how have you managed to balance your separation with your Christian faith?'

I lunge at my own mind, grabbing for ideas in the dark.

'Um, it's been difficult.'

'I can imagine. Do you feel supported by the community?'

I laugh so hard that I actually snort, and cross my legs so as not to wet myself. *Do I feel supported?*

She leans in, curious.

All right, lady.

'There are some people in the church community who see marriage as the outward manifestation of your faith, you know? So if you're getting married, you're kind of climbing the ladder to heaven. If you're married with kids, you're even closer. If you're single, God must be working on your character. If you're infertile, you're having trust issues. If you have marriage problems . . . well, someone's living in sin, because the covenant *is* your salvation. Even if staying feels like self-betrayal or abuse, it's the most important thing. Leave your spouse and you might as well have left God. And once you've exited the institution of marriage – which is the bedrock of the church's survival, because if you can't control people with sex you can't control them at all – once you've left the system, you just don't fit into its trajectories anymore. You've done the forbidden thing, the unforgivable sin. You've eaten the apple. You know too much.'

'So you feel guilt for leaving?'

'No. I feel punished and abandoned.'

She cocks her head and tuts in an attempt at sympathy.

'Your ex-husband worked for the church you attended, didn't he?'

'We both did. He was a teaching pastor. I worked in their street aid department. They had a program. I was a case officer.'

'Like a social worker?'

'Like a chaplain.'

'I see. And you quit that job?'

'It was complicated. I was dismissed quietly. He's still there.'

'Right.' She takes notes. 'What about joining a more progressive, open-minded church?'

'I don't want to. I don't need Sunday anymore. I have other people I can talk to about spiritual or emotional things . . .'

'Who?'

You? Celine? I don't even consider telling her.

'I mean, I have work. And bad TV. Baking a cake. Dancing. Watering plants. Buying cereal. Dreaming. Parenting. That's church for me now.'

'Dreaming?'

I didn't mean to mention that. People don't do Freud anymore. It's hard to explain.

'I have dreams, at night. Significant dreams.'

'Like nightmares?'

'No, dreams that have meaning. Dreams that show me what is happening. I used to think they were God trying to talk to me. Then I thought they were anxiety-induced. But they keep happening.'

'What do you think they are now?'

'A weird gift. A burden. The only mystical thing I've got left.'

The psychologist nods.

'Does the shift in your faith change how you feel about Neve?'

'No. Why would it?'

I can feel myself heating up.

'In terms of her prognosis. Her eternal home. The possibility of your own impending loss.'

Eternal home? Fuck, is she a Christian?

'It doesn't change how I feel about Neve. I love Neve exactly the same. It changes how I feel about other things, though. The one thing the Bible was really effective at was redirecting our thinking, forcing us to accept that God was always *good*. It meant you saw everything through that lens. Poverty – he's still good! Failure – he's good! Cancer diagnosis – he's good enough to heal it! Death – well, off to your eternal home then, because he's *good*. But without that structure, that spiritual bypassing, the question just floats there. Who let this happen? Who decided? Who could have stopped it, and didn't? Nothing about this is good. And if God is present and lucid, I feel terribly disappointed that someone I trusted could possibly sit there, watch that happen to me and my kid, and do nothing.'

'You sound unsure about what you believe. That's understandable.'

'Sometimes I think I can still feel God watching me. You know how people like David Attenborough can watch a lion kill an elephant calf and just stand there, refusing to interrupt the 'natural way of things'? Or maybe he's just kind of lurking, collecting evidence to use against me, like my ex-husband hacking into my iCloud and reading it all. He's there, sure. He's taking it all in. Commentating. I just don't know if he's *for* me. If he likes me, or if I like him. I certainly don't trust him. I don't know if I want to start up a conversation with someone who took so much and gave so little back.'

The psychologist nods, scribbles some more notes.

'Do you think God has some attributes of Lucas, in your mind?'

'No, I think Lucas is a perfect example of a man who believes God's got nothing to answer for.'

She breathes in, nods.

'Do you sometimes think Neve's illness is your punishment for doubting?'

'Yes.'

'And what is your instinct when faced with that fear?'

'To kill God.'

My body feels heavy. I've said way too much. She's going to cancel our sessions. She's going to tell me to journal or meditate. Medicate. Or *exercise*. She doesn't know what to do with my mind.

'That's all the time we've got for today.'

Psychological notes from session 3, Dr Mia Hutton with Frances Kocsmáros, 13 August 2022

> Seems to be going through significant deconstruction. Highly critical lens.
> Potentially in a depressive low?
> Grief a major factor. Defences up. Self-censoring. Lucas a trigger. God (?) opens her up.
>
> Reconstructing identity. Too far in the other direction?
> Magical thinking/dissociation a risk.

The Gospel According to Frances 4:1

I put on my work clothes. It's a uniform, I suppose, but not in the same way as before. It has a sensuality to it – theatre blacks. I am myself, but I represent a larger whole in my participation with the darkness. I feel very close to the darkness, and the way the theatre descends into it, like falling asleep before the dream begins. I usher them into their seats, as they so naively allow their bodies to be put under the influence of *story*. The similarities to church baffle and compel me, but the differences are stark. I would usher them into church, too, and they would sit under the bright lights and hug their neighbour and stand to sing together. They'd participate in a soaring coming-together of purpose with the performance, before settling in to be fed. Always that same word – fed. *Fed* the ideas they should be believing, loosely justified by the *Word*: just the equivalent of blogs and texts from ancient homies who wanted to start a podcast.

Church always invited some kind of immersive participation. A call and response. *How will this change you? What will you do to implement this story?* Theatre doesn't do that. It doesn't preach – at least, not if it's good. It just asks that you listen to the story. Listen, thank the storytellers, and leave. Take it home to marinate it and rave about it and hate it and be kept up late at night by something you didn't fully understand. The stories are not explicitly true. Sometimes they're politicised. Sometimes they're indulgent. Sometimes they're abominations. But sometimes they are like a sharp line of sunlight hitting a mirror, and in a sudden blinding rush I see my own humanity cowering naked on stage. I remember what it means to learn truth, and it makes me want to stand up with every other person in that audience and sing the same strange song in response.

I put on my blacks and I put on the eyeliner that has come to be a part of the uniform. I never wore make-up before – I mean, not young people make-up. It felt too invitational. Too mutton. Now, it makes me feel strangely singular in the sea of people. The truth is, I have regained my singularity. I am no longer a wife. I am no longer a mother, fifty per cent of the time. I am able to be here, and you are able to ignore me as you walk in with your champagne, or you're allowed to look at me, ask of me. And if you do look at me, you'll never *know* me. You'll never guess what I once was. You'll only see a woman in blacks. Her eyes distinct, hawkish. A midwife to your theatrical dreaming.

When I walk into work Cress doesn't avert her gaze from the till. She's counting tubes of coins, and waves at me like I'm a fly.

'Can you please check row three for a brown leather wallet? It's the hour call and a man has been ringing in all day insisting it was left here. Cleaners saw nothing.'

Cress, like most of the people who work here, is a failed actor. Not that she would put it that way. She would call herself an independent theatre maker. She loathes everything this company puts on but runs their front of house with a defiant bravado which seems to accept that any theatrical experience is better than none. At the age of forty-seven she is a cut copy of every strong, Greek mother-to-cute-kids in a Telstra ad – brown hair in a ponytail, high cheekbones, great fake smile and a concerned furrow. She writes bootleg blog reviews of the city's shows under the alias 'Theatre-Mama'. Everyone knows it's Cress, but it doesn't stop her from being utterly scathing. She worships at the church of thespian ecstasy and, though jaded as fuck, is still waiting for her big main-stage break.

'Are the actors warming up in there right now?' I ask, a little nervous about interrupting.

Cress shudders – she doesn't like the new play. It's 'new writing', and half the cast are interstate hires brought up from Sydney. (*'But why? We have the talent!'*)

'Probably. Don't let them bother you. You have every right to be in there, doing your job.'

I never realised how much actors hated other actors until I came to work in a theatre. It's not their fault. They're flung into the industry like cocks in a fighting ring, just trying to stay alive.

I buzz myself through the security-locked stage door and walk into the studio theatre. The seats stretch around the stage in a circle, the perspex box platform in the middle artfully raised and lined with a neon LED set design reminiscent of a dance game from Timezone. It flashes blue and purple while a lone figure gyrates in the middle, lost in a world of their own.

I keep my gaze down, Cress's voice in my head. 'Don't look actors in the eye – not in the middle of an *exercise*.'

The theatre is abnormally dark for pre-show, save for the light box, and I pull out my torch. Time to find a wallet.

I scan below each seat. The silhouetted actor moves freely in my periphery, twisting under the lights in complete silence. He – is it a he? – must have earbuds in. Underneath the seats, my phone lights up shadow monsters, theatre ghosts and forgotten crumbs of contraband-snacks-past. It reminds me of working in cinemas as a teenager. Will I find a used condom? I get to the end of row three: no wallet. Just as my torch swings out of the metal chaos, the light catches something. I stop, lower myself again to look. So strange, it looked like . . . absolutely not. No. But there . . .

It is a ring, sitting idly on the carpet. A tiny, rose-gold crown of thorns.

Impossible. Not after so long. We never came here.

I reach out for it, and just as my fingers brush the precious metal there is a shocking explosion of sound. The theatre erupts into some of the most obnoxious pop music I have ever heard. The actor on stage screams in satisfaction, pulling out their earbuds and flinging their body around like a monkey in a tree. I realise now they might be female, their jaw fine and their hair cropped tight around their neck. They don't see me.

I look under the seat again, and the ring is gone. Ghosts, huh?

The music pumps and thrusts and pulls me back into the theatre. My adrenaline is high, too high, I'm engorged and hot with it. I stand in the aisle and let it run through my body, exorcising the memory. This music is *intense*. This actor is intense. They're going to be too tired for the show. I watch them from the shadows of the seating bank, unseen and tempted. I lift my hands and start to push the air around like I'm fighting. I punch to the music. I spin away from every thought. I cut up the darkness like I am made of knives. I fall like water. I shake my hair, it's everywhere, it's filling up the theatre –

'HEY.'

They are right there in front of me. A strange, familiar face. Once young and smooth, now covered in crinkled lines and piercings. Thinner than before. But the same eyes.

'Frances?'

They are staring at me, incredulous. Perhaps I am the theatre ghost.

'I thought . . . I never expected to see you here.'

I realise I'm mute. I could still get out of this. Deny I remember. Give a different name. They'd be so apologetic. Say that I look like someone they once knew. An old friend they haven't seen in years. They think she might have become a born-again Christian and vanished off the face of the earth. Married with a kid, or something. So sorry for the mistake.

But I take a step backwards, and let the little crinkle in their eye touch that seventeen-year-old self who remembers liking it, very much.

'Hello, Ruairí.'

And like that, the blessed darkness is struck by a too-bright light. Exposing, betraying, removing the moment.

The house fluorescents flicker on, the music is gone, and somebody here knows way too much.

YouTube comments on 'The Grief of Job' – a sermon by Frances Harkin for Eternal Fire Church, 28 February 2020

This was not biblical. Her references are just flowery poeticisms and not actual preaching. God does not giggle. Where in the Bible is there reference to such a naive, adolescent and reductive version of Yahweh?

—

I know she's had a hard time, but this is heretical. We're not here to take a front seat to her deconstruction. Find some comfort in the Word of God, love, don't throw the baby out with the bathwater.

—

Well, I think we all knew this was going to happen eventually. Pastors' kids and the later-life zealous converts always go rogue. Don't have the fuel to actually run the race to the end. Not interested. Please reconsider who you ask to preach.

—

She can go jump into the pits of hell along with Glennon Doyle and Rob Bell, but I'm staying over in biblical truth.

—

I felt quite encouraged by this talk. Thank you.

The Gospel According to Frances 5:1

It's almost 4.30 pm. I feel my body beginning to tense, knowing what it is about to endure. I fumble my keys while unlocking the door, the adrenaline beginning to glitch my system. The house is a mess because I haven't been there, I've been Jekyll and Hyding that shit, forging another version of existence for myself. Mum thinks I should be spending my off days cleaning and preparing for the on days. I can't exist in that kind of preparatory waiting. The house remains untouched for the few days since Neve was last in it, and I only become that person again at exactly 4.30 pm, when she walks through the front door.

I panic a bit at the kitchen – there is porridge caked on the ceramic, and the floor is layered with food and dust. I don't want to spend our days together cleaning, but I know that part of me did this on purpose, and always does. That I am so overwhelmed by her presence I cannot hold the tension of offering her my undivided attention that long. That cleaning will mediate the disorganised emotions which are about to pull into the driveway.

A message. *We're running ten minutes late.*

Cunt. How dare he. We don't have ten minutes to lose, and he knows it.

The missing is a cliff and I am constantly dancing on its edge. I fall at that moment. Like busting to wee as you drive up your own street, the fact they're close only makes it worse. I might burst, I might break, I might die from the proximity.

The urgency is familiar: hospital feels the same. We take turns on the recliner beside her bed, and at every handover into my care I come into the ward at seven in the morning like a parched dog, rabid with need, hoping he has ducked out for coffee. The smell of the hand sanitiser lets me know I am close, and I've been conditioned to find it beautiful now. *You're clean, you can almost touch her, you will almost be whole again, almost.*

Rounding the corner of the final corridor of the ward I lose my breath, I'm so frantic with hunger. When I see her I'm worried I might crush her. I don't know how to make up for the separation. I forget words, my system freezing from the stress, and often I simply grab her and don't let go until she says, 'Mummy, off.'

Time is so limited. So horribly, acutely finite. I stare at families on the street, both parents ambling along utterly oblivious, not knowing what it feels like to spend a single night away from their children, let alone imagining a world in which they do not live forever. The only survivable perspective in parenting is magical thinking. *I love you, so nothing bad can ever happen. I love you, and therefore you are eternal.*

There is a scuffle on the front porch. I start and move towards it, hate and love bubbling among one another in my throat.

I open the door.

Neve stands on the top step, grinning. She knows the gift she is. She knows she's going to get a true reaction every time. She is a shooting star, she is a rose, she is the first bite of a summer peach. A swirling mix of her mother and father, and yet entirely herself: a fluffy nest of hair, green eyes and a smile larger than her face. She is puppy fat and piercing questions. Tutus and Matchbox cars. Stubbornness, sass and softness.

Behind her, the bag of meds dangling in his hand, Lucas retains a neutral expression, avoiding eye contact. Fair – he has to leave without her.

I don't let him linger; I swoop in and grab her little body, drink in her scent, let her hair touch my cheek.

Lucas drops the bag of meds beside us.

'Bye, Nevie, I love you. Can I have a hug?'

Ugh. Just leave already.

'Neve, do you want to hug Daddy goodbye?'

She dutifully embraces him and I flinch.

He walks off, looking back every couple of steps. I usher her inside and close the door, and finally – *finally* – I am able to breathe again.

Letter from Dr Roberta Nguyen, general practitioner, to paediatric oncologist Dr Simon Yates, 12 January 2020

Dear Simon,

I am referring my patient Neve Harkin (2 years 2 months) to your urgent and immediate care due to the diagnosis of hepatoblastoma (right lobe of liver). Please see the imaging attached.

I know this family. Parents have tense dynamic, potentially at risk of separation. A beautiful child.

Initial tests indicate late staging.

Thank you for taking care of them.

Respectfully,
Roberta

iPhone notes from Frances Kocsmáros to herself, 14 August 2022

— email lawyer back
— Send hours to Cress – swap Thursday shift
— Dr Yates 2 pm Tuesday (16/8)
— Fill med diary
— Swimming lessons
— Ballet lessons fees due
— Call BUH 'Make A Wish' line back

—

'A picture of Mummy and Neve and there is a colourful, colourful wind and it comes around us and carries us away.'

'A picture of Daddy and Mummy and Neve and we're a family again and there is a fire.'

'A picture of Neve and God and God gives me chocolate with sprinkles.'

'A picture of a poo and a dog and a lot of poo with sprinkles.'

'A picture of hospital and Mummy and Neve, and all the grumpiness leaving Mummy's heart.'

—

— Meds × 2 repeats
— Mandarins
— Cucumbers
— Rice x 3
— Paper towel
— Stickers for chart
— AAA batteries
— Chocolate and sprinkles

—

DO NOT call him back. Do not reply within 24 hours. Take notes on all provoking behaviours.

–

Cancer Council Support Group, Meanjin (Brisbane): 1800 99 780
LGBTQI+ Parents Support Group, Meanjin (Brisbane): 07 3841 7381

–

Tuesday night: I dreamed and saw a vision of this money buried in the ground, and out of it grew a tree. And on the tree were little Christmas decorations or something. Consumerism? I picked them all off and gave them to my family. I was still with Lucas, and he didn't like his. Neve stole them all and made them into a nativity at church. Except they were weird – not normal nativity shapes. She said it was a nativity about all the babies in the world, not just Jesus. Dream-Neve says things I think Real-Neve might say one day.

Thursday night: I dreamed of a giant pool or river or something inside the hospital. Neve went in but she couldn't swim, so we both went in naked, and I didn't feel embarrassed. When I got out, I was cold and she was screaming. Woke up and she was screaming in her bed and my blankets were all off.

Sunday night: I dreamed about a girl I saw in Coles who was buying the place out of cucumbers and tonic water – a trolley full of both – and just kept laughing to strangers who looked over: 'I'm not crazy, I'm just turning thirty, and I want everyone drinking gin with little secrets in it.'

She had choppy hair and tattoos and wore overalls and I wanted to go to the party. In the dream she put me in the trolley and brought me out when it was time for cake, and kissed me in front of everyone, saying, 'I'm turning thirty, and she's my gift to myself.'

The Book of Mary 2:1

The soup is fine. Chicken flavour, MSG and shit, but it's fine. Has those little dried peas that don't actually get squishy once the water hits them, so you chew them like old sultanas.

Baby kicks me, as if to say. 'What the fuck girl? This is mud.' I give the rest to Dog, who laps at it.

I see folks I know from other parks, other soup trucks, other tables. They don't look at me. Focus on the food, eyes down. If you don't see anyone, you won't be seen.

I haven't met the man handing out the soup before, but I know he is in charge. He has a big tummy and wears a uniform and has crinkly eyes. Kindness, maybe. *We could eat you,* I think. *And then we wouldn't be hungry anymore.* They said showers, but the showers come with the beds and the beds come with signing up. No-one really wants to sign up. It means you go to church and agree to be clean. That's not always so easy. Not when things hurt. Baby and I are clean as a streetie's finished plate. We couldn't be cleaner. Except the dried piss in my hair, yeah sure. But we have Dog. And we don't do church. Not like this.

I go up to the kind round man and offer my cup again.

'Where did you come from, kid? And how far along?'

'I'm from down south. Got a place to stay here in Brissie, but just have a couple of nights to fill. Baby is six months in, I reckon.'

He notices my stomach, eyes bright.

'Have you seen a doctor yet? We have resources to help. Beds, showers, social workers. We can get you into a good hospital, get baby checked.'

'Baby is fine. I'd like a shower, though.'

He eyes Dog warily.

'Will you join us for the Saturday night service?'

'Not really into the institutional worship myself, Reg.'

He pauses. He doesn't remember telling me his name. I always like this bit.

'I'm here to see Frances Kocsmáros, actually.' I say it as gently as possible.

He pales. 'Frances Harkin?'

'She isn't married anymore.'

'Why do you need Frances?'

I stick out my belly and smile broadly. 'I'm in a unique parenting situation. I reckon she'll be able to help me.'

Reg moves away from the soup truck, ushers me to a nearby tree in the park. There are stars in the black coffee, clouds in the tea, golden coins in the Arnott's assorted creams left on the trestle table. I know it is time to be honest, but no-one ever wants to hear it.

'Frances doesn't work here anymore, love. Let us help you out. Did baby's father abandon you?'

'Baby doesn't have a father.'

'Ah, I see.' He does not see. 'Did you experience something non-consensual?' He pauses, stutters. 'I'll get another woman – I'll get you a woman to talk to . . .'

He ushers over a young blonde thing with perfect orthodontic work. She'll be married by twenty-two, if she isn't already.

'Kayla is studying counselling at university, you can trust her.'

Fuck I need a shower. Need to get it over with.

Dog wags his tail, keen for whatever meal awaits.

'I didn't experience anything.'

Reg nods, eyes soft with practised empathy.

Kayla places a hand on my belly without asking.

'We don't judge if you have sex,' she whispers breathily.

'I've never had sex.'

This is when the left eye of Kayla the twenty-one-year-old virgin starts to twitch involuntarily.

'An angel told me I'd get pregnant. Two weeks later I did.'

Reg and Kayla look at one another. Every other traveller in this corner of the park hears the echo of another place, another sky, another meal – and they look at me, all at once. The silence lasts a lot longer than eternity.

Kayla pipes up, saccharine-sweet. 'If you would like accommodation, you will need to be clean. Our program is faith-based rehabilitation. We also have community mental health services for those in need of psychiatric care. And our patrons come to our Saturday night services.'

Every time. I have to hand it to them: for a bunch of people who believe God gives them the best car parks, they don't really like actual miracles.

'Call Frances, and I'll come to church. But I need a room that allows dogs.'

The Gospel According to Frances 6:1

Neve is raging, body thrown to the ground, fists in little balls. The chocolate sprinkles lie across the kitchen floor like an overturned pot plant.

'YOU DIDN'T DO IT RIGHT.'

'Neve, baby, I *tried.*'

'BAD MUMMY.'

'Stop hitting –'

'BAD BAD BAD BAD BAD.'

I crouch down beside her, attempt to get the little limbs to soften under my touch.

She lashes out, punches and scratches, and I scoot out of range on the kitchen tiles.

'I'm here when you're ready for a cuddle.'

This is what they say to do. Don't lose it. Don't leave. Don't punish the behaviour. *Allow all feelings, remain through all feelings, be the calm in the storm of all feelings.*

Neve screams because the sprinkles were not for dinner. Neve screams because her body hurts, and her meds make it worse. Neve screams because she has *two* homes, her mouth turning down in disdain every time we attempt to explain it with false excitement. Neve screams because her parents are 'high conflict, low communication', according to family lawyers. Because she has seen us fight over her like she is a toy, like we are nothing but kindergarten children ourselves.

Neve screams.

I look at her, hysterical, and I feel like getting down there, too.

I get it, kid. Let's smash the ground with our hands, let's open our lungs into oblivion.

The grief leaves her body in waves, until she is limp on the floor. I lie beside her, in awe of her stillness. Nothing ever leaves my body except Neve.

'Do you want a cup of milk?'

'I want it warm, in the blue cup with the red lid.'

'I can do that.'

'I want a cuddle.'

'I can do that.'

She clambers over me, all limbs. She breathes heavily in my ear and pulls at my hair as I rock her in my arms on the floor. Tear streaks stain her face and her skin looks more mottled today, like someone has painted it in watercolour blotches of pink and purple. Her belly is so distended she looks like she's pushed a balloon under her shirt, pretending to be pregnant. Our breathing syncs slowly. She lets me kiss her eyelids, closed in exhaustion.

It always takes at least two nights to ground her, to help her shed her confusion and anger at me. She feels abandoned, no matter how many times I attempt to explain it isn't my *choice*. She growls at me around the house, withdrawn and cold, then after two nights folds into me, as if finally trusting we are back together. Trusting that I have missed her after all.

After two nights it's often time to leave, and the cycle begins again.

I hate him for this. I can forgive almost all of it, but not this.

Short breaths find a longer rhythm. Her neck goes limp against mine. Neve has fallen asleep in my arms. Fuck. I stand up with her little body, attempting to wiggle her back into the evening.

'Nevie, we have meds before bed.'

She whispers a slurred no.

'Nevie, wake up. Meds and then we go straight to cuddles, and stories, and teeth, and –'

'Please, Mummy.'

And what do I do, with that small will? The one that chose none of this chaos, but right now chooses sleep?

Do I lay her down, the sleeping child, finally breathing so steadily against my breast?

Or do I rip her from peace, throw holy water on the burning body? Maybe gain another hour on the loudly ticking clock of her tiny life?

The meds sit heavy on the kitchen bench. Poison that might mean life. Brutality that might mean kindness.

I wake her, and she screams.

Email correspondence between Kayla Stilwell, Rev. Reg Holland and Tom Singh, 15 August 2022

Dear Pastor Reg,

I was able to place Mary in the rehab unit but they're not happy about the dog. They said they'd be in contact? I contacted Carmen about her too but Carmen's caseload is full apparently. Will you contact Frances?

Not sure what to do here but Mary said she'd come to church on Sunday, praise Jesus.

Kayla Stilwell
Proverbs 31 / † = ♥

–

Dear Kayla,

Thank you for this update. It's a bit of a tricky situation. We often have patrons with animals who are unable to participate in accommodation services but this situation is a little different. Have you suggested the RSPCA? Or finding someone in the congregation to foster? I'm sure someone would take in a dog.

I'll await Tom's update from the rehab unit. Do not contact Frances.

Stay safe, many blessings and see you at church!

Rev. Reg Holland
Senior Minister, Eternal Fire

–

Reg,

I got the new intake – Mary. We've kept an eye on her and I think she's in the wrong place. She definitely doesn't use, for one. Could be psychiatric but none of the detox assistance is applicable and she's taking a bed someone else really needs. The dog is causing upheaval because old Timmy got kicked out only three months ago when he found a kitten and decided to keep it in Greg's sneaker – remember? We've got to work within the standards they hold themselves to.

Anyway I've got to run but let me know ASAP if you can find another place for her. Rehab is no place for a preggo sixteen-year-old if she's clean.

Tom Singh

The Gospel According to Frances 6:2

'Mummy, look – I'm like Elsa.'

Neve practises ballet in puddles, and the summer rain in Brisbane suddenly feels romantic again – like it did when I was young. I remind myself of when I was a student, and rain meant I would routinely have to catch three overcrowded buses to university without an umbrella, soaking my belongings and leaving me shivering. The smell felt hopeful then. A kind of wayward freedom I haven't tasted in a while. That was before Jesus. Before all of it.

I readjust Neve's hat to protect her hearing aids. She had perfect hearing before the chemo, and now her left ear is compromised. Now, now, now. Everything is different *now*.

Now, buses are not a sign of my youthful poverty; buses are special. We catch buses into the museum, and we catch buses into appointments with Dr Simon. Neve doesn't mind it. Dr Simon never uses needles and always gives lollipops. He has an excellent bedside manner and loves making children feel like they've just visited Santa instead of an oncologist. I would like Dr Simon, if I didn't hate every single word that came out of his mouth. If he didn't hand down our sentence each visit. There are so many kinds of judges in this world.

Neve twirls and lands with two feet, water and mud spraying all over her brand new Kmart outfit. She wanted a ballet dress, but her limbs are too shrunken, and her belly too huge. ('One day,' I promised. Maybe I'll learn how to sew?)

Neve holds her landing pose, waits for my validation.

'MUMMY, DID YOU SEE THAT?'

'Nevie, please just jump a little softer. Don't get too wet.'

She looks at me quizzically. 'Why not?'

'Because if you get too wet, I'll need to dry you off. Maybe change your clothes.'

'But *why?*'

'Because we have Dr Simon. And Daddy will be there. And we want to look clean and dry and feel nice and comfy.'

She shrugs. 'Nah, I don't mind.' She jumps back into the puddle.

The bus should have come by now and I can feel the cortisol in my body rising. We cannot be late. Every single time there is the slightest thing out of line, Lucas gets out his phone and notes it, a half-smile on his face, as if this one error is the straw that will break the camel's back. The final piece to his case against me.

My phone dings with a message. My nervous system goes into overdrive; I don't want to read it.

Neve grabs my hands, tugs me away from my brain.

'Why don't you ever jump in puddles, Mummy?'

I pause, my body heavy.

Because I know too much about cold feet.

Text message from Cress Charalambous to Frances Kocsmáros

Babe can you work Friday, 5.30–11 pm? It's the 'Night with the Artists' and we sold out. Sorry for the late notice. (1.50 pm)

Text message from Celine Riot to Frances Kocsmáros

Still on for Friday night, Frankie? (2.15 pm)

The Gospel According to Frances 6:3

Simon's rooms in the children's ward of Brisbane University Hospital are almost vomitous in their serenity and child-focus. They could be a Montessori preschool.

Lucas is early, and I have two missed calls from him. He ignores me, and opens his arms wide for Neve to run into.

'Did you bring her bag?' He still won't make eye contact.

I reach for it on my shoulder, but there is only my own. Her koala backpack isn't there – *it's not there, I forgot it* – it's on the bus – no, it's at the bus stop – *fuck fuck fuck* –

'It's . . . I forgot her bag. I'll drop it over later.'

'Don't.'

He gets out his phone, sighing, and writes hurriedly. The half-smile appears, then vanishes.

We agreed to make this appointment the handover, to save her the confusion. Neve snuggles into him for a bit, then comes back to me, her hand stroking my face.

I pull out of my own backpack a Tupperware container of chopped cucumber and cheese (*I AM A VERY GOOD PARENT, SEE?*) and offer some to the soft animal trying to curl into my lap.

'Dr Simon is going to give us all *lollipops*, Mummy. Don't be sad.'

Yeah, right. It'd be nice if doctors handed out adult-equivalent self-soothing treats to traumatised parents.

You've done so well, guys, it isn't easy – do you want a Valium, a medicinal CBD oil prescription, or just 10 mg of Ritalin to get you through the rest of Tuesday? Here, have two.

Dr Simon comes out, all smiles. Neve lights up and I am fractured by it. That this is joyful for her is such a precious silver lining, I don't know why I want to fight it.

Lucas and I follow the doctor and child into his office, sombre and stiff. Dr Simon is used to us being like this. He doesn't pay it much attention. His focus is her, while she remains in the room.

'All right, my little warrior, let's get you up on the bed and we'll have a poke around your tummy! How have you been feeling?'

'A bit bumpy.'

'A bit bumpy, hey?'

'But on the weekend I watched *Paw Patrol* with Daddy.'

'*Paw Patrol*?! That is *fantastic* news. How do you like the special medication that we sent you home with last time?'

'It's so yucky.'

'Oh is it? Maybe we can find a way to make it yummier for you. Just one more check: I'm going to listen to your heart and then your lungs with the cold stethoscope, then check your ears . . .'

'Do I get a lollipop today?'

'Absolutely you do. How is kindy going, Neve?'

'I am in the big girl class because I'm four turning five.'

'You're FOUR? Wow!'

'Did you know Mummy and Daddy are both here today? My mummy didn't want to love my daddy anymore and so she left and I have two homes now, because –'

'Really? Well that is *very* special.'

She delivers this spiel to everyone, repeatedly. Direct quotes from the Gospel of Lucas.

Dr Simon finishes his checks. Like every specialist he is deft, speedy – you would hardly notice his work at all, if you didn't know what to look for. I wonder what he sees in the silent clues of her body. Are her glands up? Are her kidneys swollen? Her heart rate irregular?

'Neve, you know how we did some special scans the other day?'

'Yes.'

'I want to tell Mummy and Daddy about those scans. Would you like to go and play with the toys in the waiting room with Miss Sarah?'

Neve *loves* this bit. She goes willingly. The lollipop comes straight after.

Lucas and I shift in our chairs.

'How are you both?'

Dr Simon drops the bravado almost immediately. His voice even lowers a register. He suddenly looks old and tired, and I am reminded of seeing before and after photos of people using heroin. It's like he has removed the children's Instagram filter, and the weight of mediating so much agony suddenly lands back upon his body.

'Fine thank you,' says Lucas, stony-faced.

'Frances?'

'I'm worried.'

'Why?'

'She seems exhausted. Restless. In pain but not able to pinpoint it.'

'And she's obviously more jaundiced,' Lucas adds, grimacing. He's right.

Dr Simon nods, pulls out the scans. There is a detailed write-up; he ignores it.

'We are seeing a much larger growth in the liver this time – to the extent that surgery is simply not an option.'

Lucas straightens his back, steeling himself against the hit. 'So we just go back on chemo until it can be operated on, right? We shrink and we resect, like last time.'

'Well, yes. Yes. I would recommend another couple of months of chemo if you felt it was right. But while this kind of cancer generally responds well to treatment, it hasn't in this case. I don't believe resecting will be an option with those metastases, and it is likely that chemotherapy will not cure the cancer, but simply provide you a bit more time with Neve. If the chemotherapy does not eradicate the growths, we will look at palliative care. We will take a curative approach until we simply cannot, but I think we need to look at this honestly, now.'

The room feels strung up in time – like a children's painting hanging by pegs. We are frozen around this news, the three of us retreating from the trauma of it. I am never energised into action by these appointments. They make me want to sleep and never wake up.

'How long is the prognosis if we do not do chemotherapy?' I ask.

'Nothing can be certain, but we would be looking at a couple of months.'

Dr Simon does not break eye contact with me.

'And with chemo?'

'Possibly six months to a year.'

Chemotherapy is torture. This is not a clear choice. Two months of peace, or a year of suffering? I realise I am punctured, bleeding out.

'So she won't make it to her sixth birthday, regardless?'

'Of course she will,' Lucas interjects, furious. 'Don't speak death over this situation, Frances.'

Dr Simon looks at us: aggrieved, human. 'I know you would like to believe the arc of the universe's story bends towards justice. My work tends to offer a different narrative. That narrative is chaos.'

Lucas shakes his head, indignant. 'Our faith contests that.'

'I am not meaning to be cruel. It's simply that things don't follow *right* and *wrong* in a children's hospital. There is no-one who deserves it. Things happen without warning or justification. But that chaos applies to healing, too. Sometimes the impossible happens. Sometimes people have less time, sometimes they have more. It cannot be accurately predicted or replicated. You can only try. So if you'd like to try, I will try with you.'

Where is she? I need to hold her, touch her –

'We reject death as an option.' Lucas is brimming with poison.

'I don't think your faith does that, Lucas.' Dr Simon is calm, lucid. 'I think it embraces death.'

'It might, but I do not. My community will be fighting it. And I will be seeking a second opinion.'

I understand implicitly the battle between the God we want and the God we get, right in that moment. I feel sorry for the broken-hearted pastor sitting next to me, the one I used to nip the ears of when we made love, the one who would feel guilty about lying in the sun listening to Bob Dylan, not realising that that too was worship. The one who hurt me in the name of God time and time again, addicted to orthodoxy and numbed by self-righteousness.

I wouldn't wish this on my worst enemy, and that person is most certainly him.

I reach across to touch his shoulder. 'Lucas, we need to discuss our options with Simon.'

He turns to me, grief crystallising into hatred. 'Options? You don't even remember how to pray.'

He's not wrong.

Dr Simon Yates's notes from the CT scan of Neve Harkin's liver, pancreas and surrounding tissue

> Malignant metastases throughout the liver – inoperable. Seventeen small tumours, 0.1–0.25 cm in diameter. No metastases in pancreas at this stage. No metastases in lungs at this stage. Bile duct still clear.
>
> Seven-week course of chemotherapy again. Public hospital (BUH), private patients. Palliative care within three months if liver does not respond to treatment.

Neve Harkin's drawing in the waiting room

'This is a picture of my insides. This is the scan, and inside my body is my liver. And my liver is beautiful and pink and has sparkles in it. And this is the doctor cutting all the sadness out of my liver. And this is my mummy crying because the doctor gave her all my sadness but now she's better. And this is my daddy praying for Jesus to die for my liver. And here are the fairies that live at the hospital. And see here, they give you lollipops. And that is a rainbow.'

The Gospel According to Frances 6:4

In the playroom that doubles as a waiting room, Neve's little eyes light up in recognition and delight. She's been drawing, crayon in one hand and lollipop in the other. Lucas blocks her body from me with his own, and lifts her away from her elaborate illustrations and into his arms. Neve spins to catch my eye.

'Mummy!' she cries, reaching for me.

'Say goodbye to Mummy.' He holds her back, indignant.

'Lucas, let her hug me –'

He doesn't. He lets her wave, and even blow a kiss, and then they leave through the glass doors. He clutches her body like he owns it. Like he can command it.

But isn't that the point of everything that has happened between us? We command nothing. We control nothing. We receive and receive and receive, and some of it is beautiful and some of it is absolutely fucked. I know I am in shock, and I know the feelings will decide they want to speak at four in the morning or some such hour, but for now I feel nothing but a practical acceptance. Life is fucked. Life is entirely fucked and there is nothing we can do about it. No amount of missions or outreaches or fundraisers or social media campaigns will change it. Our child is dying. We've already lost.

Dr Simon comes out to speak to his receptionist, and sees me standing in the waiting room. Without husband, without child, just a backpack on – like a hitchhiker.

I wonder what he thinks of us, if we're the worst he has had to deal with in terms of parents. If he blames us, or if he feels sorry for us.

He gives nothing away. Just nods, and comes over to me.

He places a hand on my shoulder and squeezes it, firmly. 'It's not over yet, Frances. Even when it ends, it isn't over.'

That's what I'm afraid of, you beautiful fuckwit.

He turns from me and shifts, that filter appearing on his skin, and suddenly he looks *young* and vibrant and hopeful – the perfect doctor for a terminally ill child.

A boy with black hair sits up in the soft play area at the sound of his own name, as Dr Simon greets the harrowed parents, holding their breath for the next dose of devastation.

I leave empty-handed. Invisible once again.

Church staff newsletter: Urgent Update, 16 August 2022

Hi Team,

This is an urgent prayer request for Lucas Harkin's daughter, Neve. After two years of battling liver cancer, she has been given only months to live and has been placed on chemotherapy again.

Obviously we believe in the power of Jesus to heal, to restore, and to ultimately beat death. We will be having a special service on Sunday to pray over Neve and Lucas, and will be taking up an offering for them. Expect miracles! By his stripes we are healed! Please spread the word to your connect groups also.

Make sure you bring your kids into the main auditorium on Sunday – it's powerful when kids pray for other kids.

Please send any queries for Lucas through Pastor Reg, not to Lucas personally.

Blessings,
Kayla

The Gospel According to Frances 6:5

On the bus, I listen to indie music from 2007, interspersed with smatterings of nineties pop.

Here's the weird thing – I stopped listening to normal music after I converted. I only listened to worship. Not hymns or gospel; nothing cultured. Just the Christian equivalent to all the 2007 sad-boy folk I had been consuming. It became an alternative universe to retreat into, a place that my previous life hadn't touched. A place I wouldn't find my old desires or fears within.

Now, I've reverted back to the same songs I ran from, having ingested nothing up to date in the past ten years. Now, I avoid anything my evangelicalism might have reached for. I find myself trapped in time, eternally aged twenty, still dreaming about failed relationships to the soundtrack of my sins.

The music bumps as the bus doors open and a young family get in and park their pram. A young mother, capable, wearing linens. An involved father holding a baby. They go to sit. As the bus lurches, the baby almost falls from the father's arms. I jump, body suddenly white-hot. The mother reaches for the baby, to relieve the father, let him get his balance. He refuses her silently, grips the baby harder, pride and possession suddenly making him his child's captor. The baby cries, blindly searching for its mother. The father forces false comfort. The mother flinches. *I know that flinch.*

Suddenly I am vomiting on the bus.
Suddenly I am on the ground, in my vomit.

The bus does not stop, the people yell, the lights go long and elongated, the inside of me is on the outside and my arms are empty, there is no baby in my arms.

The bus has stopped, someone is yelling, someone touches me. I vomit again.

The woman comes to help me and the man stays in his seat, holding on to the child like it is the steering wheel, and his wife is the bus he has finally decided he will drive off a cliff.

Paramedic's report – Frances Kocsmáros, 16 August 2022

> Patient vomited and fell on bus – symptoms of a delayed shock or possible panic attack.
>
> Insisted on walking home.
>
> We gave her water around 2.11 pm.

Voice messages from Rosemary Kocsmáros to Frances Kocsmáros, 16 August 2022

'Franny, just calling to see how the appointment went. Let me know.' (2.08 pm)

'Frances, I'm calling again, just checking the scans were good. What are you up to today? It's your day off, yes? Are you cleaning?' (3.33 pm)

'Frances, I've been to Kmart and found a really good mop and was thinking I might bring it over. Help you out a bit. Let me know if you're home.' (5.06 pm)

The Gospel According to Frances 7:1

I'm back in my theatre blacks, and Cress's hair is going grey before my very eyes. Subscribers, press and industry are swarming (there's free wine) and I think she considers it *networking*, so she's topping up every glass and barking at us to clear platters before they're even empty.

I've come to work because I do not need to be honest here. I'm fine, in theory.

I signed up for a theatre job, but this has its resonances with the mission's Saturday night shift in many ways: doling out free food and drink to a group of people who have a lot of opinions about it; ensuring nothing is broken or spilled; cleaning up once they are safely in their seats for the *show*. Except, of course, these people aren't here under the duress of empty stomachs and street bench beds, and almost every single one of these people can afford to go to the most overpriced of adult recreational activities – the theatre.

Theatre is a bourgeois pursuit beyond the working-class pleasures of cinema or football games: it requires the kind of money only the middle and upper classes have access to. Unlike TV, its very nature is inaccessible, excluding parents, children, the sick or injured, the elderly, those who do not look the part and those who simply cannot pay. My old patrons would hate the theatre, I suspect. There are very few plays produced for the lived stories or tastes of street folk, and they would heckle the fuck out of anything on this theatre's stage. It's a hobby for the privileged few who can afford to consider life through a reflective lens, not through a survival mechanism.

I am glad there are no children here. I am glad most of the people here are not parents of young children, or spend even more than a moment thinking or speaking about children. I give kohl-black side eyes to the power lesbians, the PR queens and bespectacled male journalists wearing scarves. Offer them Vietnamese spring rolls. The Nuóc Châm sauce makes me think of my feasts with Celine, and I flinch a little at my cancellation. It isn't personal, though; I needed to work. What we have is entirely transactional. I keep imagining her fingers on my back as I spin through the room with plates of food. I encourage the thought. That thought is not Neve.

I turn towards the stage door and see a disembodied hand stretched out from behind it, beckoning me over with fervour.

I hesitate.

It points at me and beckons again.

The grinning head of Ruairí pokes out, brightly painted eyes on the food. They're luminous, camp and intoxicating.

I walk over, caught in their headlights.

'We're starving. Can you spare just one tiny little spring roll, *please?*'

After my permissive smirk they snaffle a bunch into a serviette before placing a hand on my shoulder.

'Frances, when are we getting a drink? It has been so many years.'

'We should. Soon.' I quiver a little, so full of shredded secrets.

'Are you here every night? Are you studying or something, or is this your main world?' They are so eager, and – I realise with a jolt – so oblivious.

'I've got some other stuff on the side, so here three nights a week,' I answer with as much confidence as I can muster. 'I'm watching the show next Friday night, as an usher.'

'Next Friday night it is then.'

They grab another two spring rolls, and their fingers brush my arm. Different from Celine's, but it produces the same shiver in my body. I note that. Maybe Celine will have a late vacancy.

I walk back into the crowd, crashing and soaring simultaneously. My arms are full. Full of platters. Full of alternate realities. Full of every distraction possible.

Facebook Messenger exchanges between Ruairí Hickson and Frances Kocsmáros, 4 June 2007

2.05 am
Frances: *heyyyyyy, where did u go? I waited by the toilets*
Ruairí: *Oh my god I lost you. i'm so drunk.*
Frances: *You're such a good kisser.*
Ruairí: *Come to my place*
Frances: *arghhhhh okay*

7.14 am
Ruairí: *hey have you left? are you okay?*
Frances: *yes sorry I had to get my flight*
Ruairí: *when do you fly?*
Frances: *in like 2 hours*
Ruairí: *come back soon little bird*

Celine's iPhone notes: last updated 19 August 2022

This Week's Schedule

<u>Monday</u> ($628)
Tom (🎲)
KK (🍑)
Harrison (🙊)

<u>Tuesday</u> ($450)
Lionel (👀)
Jim (🍑)

<u>Wednesday</u> ($500)
Reg (👋)
Sean (👽)

<u>Thursday</u> ($1000)
Sarah and Jonathan (👯)
Carl (✊)
Tom (with Bree 👯 ♀)

<u>Friday</u>
Samuel (💦)
~~Frankie~~ (🌹)
Frankie (🌹)

<u>Saturday</u>
N/A

<u>Sunday</u> (TBC)
Reg (🍍)
Tim (💦)
Eugene (🖤)
Kane (🧝 ♀)

The Gospel According to Frances 7:2

Waiting Room 2 tonight. I see a girl rush past in a towel as I go in. She rolls her eyes, grins at me. I never see the men, except in the car park. Celine tells me they are almost always men, many of them married. A lot of utes, family SUVs. They park behind high walls, hiding from the street. We have enough discretion to wait for one another to enter, so as not to cross paths, like clients in a psychologist's office. Same price per hour, but this feels more authentic. We admit something here that we cannot admit in any other room. A base truth, brought to a dimmed light.

I want something I believe I am too broken to find for free.

The plod of Docs on tile. Celine comes through the door, eyes alight at my presence. She takes my hand. I wonder if she takes every person's hand like that, fingers interlaced. Intimate, like we might know one another. It stings a little that we don't.

She closes the door of Room 5 then eyes me.

'I feel like you want a service tonight.' She grins. 'I think you *need* one.'

I nod, a bit frozen and awkward. It never gets easier.

'I'm outworking something.'

'Get on the bed then – let's check you.'

She gives me my medical, which is always surprisingly simple – exactly like a gynaecologist appointment. I've given birth, I have no qualms about asexually spreading my legs anymore. I shower, and she watches from the bed, slowly beginning to masturbate, shifting the clinical energy in the room. It's arousing, but also a little intimidating. I can never know my way around another woman's body better than she does.

When I've dried off she beckons me over, a slick plastic glove on her left hand. The gift and curse of brothels: the sex is as safe as it can get.

'What is happening for you tonight?'

I sit on the bed, exhale. Clitoral orgasms are basically bodywork. They don't happen unless you surrender to the emotions they want to illuminate.

'I need grounding. I need to concentrate. No distractions. I have had a shock. And there are distractions brewing.'

Celine nods, runs an ungloved hand down my naked torso.

'Correct me if I'm wrong, but it sounds like you're choosing to be closed, when the invitation is to be open.'

I flinch. 'Open to *what,* though? That's the risk.'

'I don't know, kid.' She pauses. 'Why don't you try dating a woman?'

I go electric, slapped hard by the question. Celine questions me, incessantly, but never about *that.*

'I don't have room for that right now.'

'Do you think it's wrong, Frank?'

Yes. No. I don't know.

'I don't think it's wrong. I had a girlfriend a long time ago. It was intense. I had my heart broken, hurt her, did everything wrong. And I think I would do it wrong again.'

'Do you date men?'

'Not anymore, no.'

'But you're attracted to them?'

'I'm attracted to people – sometimes men and sometimes women, yeah. Sometimes I'm attracted to nothing, no-one. But when I feel that kind of connection I make mistakes. I fall in. And for some reason it feels like falling into a woman's life isn't fair. Men can be neglected, but women can't. I'm not good enough for that. I would fail.'

Celine nods.

A bit pissed off at the Spanish Inquisition, I turn it on her. 'Why don't *you* try dating?'

'What makes you think I don't?' She frowns, bemused. 'Do you think I have sex with clients because I can't have sex with anyone else?'

I shrug, feeling stupid. The mood is sufficiently ruined. I should go. Celine lies back, suddenly showing her own exhaustion.

'If you're asking, I do have a partner, Frank. We've been together a long time.'

'Do they know what you do?'

She grimaces. 'Why is that always the first question?'

'Because it would be the scariest part, to me.'

She shakes her head. 'It isn't. The scariest part is loving someone so wholly that losing them is kind of like losing yourself.' She meets my eyes. 'Love is not the same as transparency. Honesty and secrets are just tools we use to communicate. Love goes beyond that. There are a lot of reasons I cannot be transparent. I live to love my partner. And I work in order to stay alive.'

'Financially?'

'Financially, sure. But spiritually, too.'

She comes back to me, noticing my breathing, my nervous system on high alert.

'Have you ever cared about someone that much, Frank?'

I begin to shake a little.

She puts her hand on my waist, gentle and leading.

I kiss her in answer. Let her limbs grab me, pull me in.

We are strangers, masked in our nudity, honest in the lie. Bodies embracing in their own lonely longing, trying to stay alive for the ones we love.

Bank statement of Frances Harkin *née* Kocsmáros, 19 August 2022

— Uber: $16.70 – 10.45 pm
— Celine Riot, Expert Consultancy Services: $270 – 11.03 pm
— Uber: $11.40 – 12.08 am

Text messages between Frances Kocsmáros and Kelly Linden, 4 February 2012

Kelly: *Hey, it's been a long time. I just saw on insta that you got married, to a guy . . . I don't really know what I wanted to say. Congratulations, maybe. I hope you're really happy. I hope you found what you were looking for in all that churchy stuff. I miss you sometimes. Just remember, if there is a God, She loves you exactly as you are.*

Frances: *Kelly, hi. Thanks. This is very kind. I have found what I'm looking for in God. He's given me a lot of clarity and a lot of freedom. If you are ever curious, I'd love to talk to you about it all. It's really changed the way I see my own sexuality, our relationship, and the pain that we went through. I have a lot of regrets. I'm really thrilled to be married – Lucas is incredible. Is there anything I can pray for in your life?*

Kelly: *I'm glad Lucas is incredible. You deserve that. I don't really see our relationship as something I regret, so I'm not sure what you mean by your perspective shifting, but I hope it's in a good way. I don't really want prayer, either. I just wanted to make sure you were okay.*

Frances: God loves you, Kelly.

Kelly: *Frances, I don't care. I just hope you have made the best decision for your own heart.*

Voice messages from Rosemary Kocsmáros to Frances Kocsmáros, 20 August 2022

'Frances, you can't just send me a text message with that kind of information. We need to discuss your options.' (8.04 am)

'Frances, I've done some research into outcomes and I'm very concerned. I think you should get a second opinion, just in case. Maybe we can find some clinical trials. I found one in Sweden. Has Lucas got Neve? Call me back.' (9.04 am)

'Frances, I know you like to pretend things aren't happening, but you need to pull yourself together. You are hurting us.' (2.03 pm)

The Book of Mary 3:1

Dog shat on the carpet under the pulpit. Which they really should have found exciting, in my opinion. They kind of invited it. Said he couldn't sleep in the room with me and baby anymore. Said I needed to find alternative housing for him. And the only free room was the chapel. I couldn't exactly tie him up in the park.

We slept on the pews together. But then the chapel got locked and we couldn't get out and he needed somewhere soft and previously soiled to do his stuff. Go figure. Poor sod.

Rehab don't want me anymore because I'm not a junkie. What a catch. But we already knew that, didn't we? It's only a couple of more really rough nights.

I haven't gone back to the Inn for a while, because I don't want to go without Frances. That's the thing, see. I have a job to do. And I take this job pretty fucking seriously.

Baby has the hiccups as we sit on the brick wall outside the mission. She'll come find me soon. It's Sunday, after all. And this is the only way. Sorry, Frances. But it's the only way.

The Gospel According to Frances 8:1

I wake in Neve's bed yet again. The Sunday creeps up on me like a ghost. An internal, abandoned alarm that keeps going off. *You used to wake now, you used to get up and rush and park and take a seat right at the front. You used to be early.* And now Sundays without her are empty. I lie in bed. I make a tea. I scroll and scroll and scroll my phone, looking at the lives of other people and wondering how happy they really are.

I scroll past the strange melting pot of posts from different people in my life. People from my youth. People from the church world. People from the theatre. There's Ruairí, posting a still shot from the play. There's a post from a Christian mothers' group, questioning vaccines. Shots of young people getting engaged or having babies. Shots of holidays, home-cooked meals, of children glowing beneath the life-giving sun of their perfect nuclear families.

I scroll again, and there is a post from Eternal Fire. I read it once, then I read it again.

I am paralysed with anger, until suddenly I realise I am not paralysed at all.

I am moving. I am unstoppable.

I get out of Neve's bed, and I rush, rush, rush.

Instagram feed of @fransal90

@ruairihicks
Description: A performance shot of Ruairí in profile wearing a pinstripe suit and novelty sunglasses, mid-outburst.

Caption: *Only two weeks left of this beautiful, provocative play. I feel so privileged to be able to play over fifteen characters every night of this run. Never going back to Ray-Bans, tbh.*

—

@livelovenurtureinhim
Description: A softly lit photograph of a Caucasian mother embracing her two fair-haired children.

Caption: *Christ bought us freedom, and in Him we are free indeed. We must fight for that freedom for our children. We must fight for our God-given autonomy to parent with safety and independence from Caesar and his empire. Generation after generation, let us remember the blessings.*

For those asking, we are PRO-CHOICE for vaccines, PRO-LIFE for the unborn. We will not poison or kill the bodies of our children. Seek God in all things, and know He will fight for you and your family when you embrace His path.

—

@eternal_fire_qld
Description: A picture of Neve Harkin and her father, Lucas Harkin, smiling joyfully at the camera.

Caption: *Please join us at the 9 am service as we pray for the beautiful Harkin family and a miracle in the body of young Neve. We are going to lay hands and petition the Lord! We expect full healing, in Jesus' name! We will be accepting an offering for Lucas to support her medical expenses as well.*

The Book of Mary 3:2

I sit up the back and Dog sits under my feet. Every now and then he sniffs a bag or a shoe and people lose their shit about it. Good thing they don't know about the pulpit. This place is full – like three hundred people. Big place. The streeties linger near the tea station. Good to look busy. The ones who want to worship will do it up the back, too. The rich folks all have special places where they sit with friends, and all the leaders are up the front, name tags on. Purposeful.

Neve Harkin sits on a chair by herself in the front row while Lucas chats with Reg to the side of the raised stage bit. She plays with a plush bunny, kind of worn and raggedy. Makes a little voice for it, invites it to have some milk and a nap. Dog would love to rip that thing up. Need to make sure he doesn't.

I walk up the aisle to the kid. Everyone is so busy chatting pre-service they don't notice.

'Hey. Nice bunny.'

'Thanks. Her name is Peach.'

'Cool. This is Dog.'

She looks at Dog in surprise and delight.

'You can pat him, but don't give him Peach.'

She strokes his nose. Such a gentle child.

I lean closer, bring my voice to a whisper. 'Some weird things are gonna happen today, kiddo. And when they do, I want you to turn around and look at Dog. We'll be in the back row. We're gonna have fun, okay?'

She looks confused. 'Weird things? I go to kids' church and we do colouring-in.'

'No matter what happens, you hold on to Peach and look for the silly little dog.'

Lucas turns and notices me. He grabs Reg by the shoulder, but I'm already gone. An invisible guest at Jesus' weekly funeral.

The lights of the chapel dim: the show is about to commence.

Lucas lifts up the body of the tiny child like a sacrifice as the music rolls in.

Automated transcript of the Sunday 9 am service from the Livestream, 21 August 2022

Reg: *Okay, thank you, creative team, that worship was so anointed. I can feel the presence of the Lord in the room. I know we've all come this morning expectant, ready to see a miracle, ready to see the goodness of the Lord in the land of the living – AMEN?*

[cheers from the crowd]
YES, JESUS!
WE DECLARE HEALING!

Reg: *Lucas come up here with little Neve. The presence of God is so strong. Let's lay hands now; let's do it before the sermon. I want you all to pray, and as you all pray, consider what you feel led to give financially to their situation.*

Okay, okay. Hello, Neve. How are you feeling?

[Lucas off-microphone: *Neve, answer Pastor Reg*]
[silence from Neve]

Reg: *Don't be afraid, little one. I know there are a lot of people, but God is going to heal you today. Isn't he, church? We're here to pray the cancer OUT of Neve's body. Whatever hold the devil has on this child, we ask for a flooding of the Holy Spirit. Lucas, will you lead us? Marie, come up – I'm going to ask you to prophesy.*

Lucas: *Heavenly Father, we know you are good, beyond all our experiences, beyond our suffering. It is not your will that we should be afflicted, but that we access healing. I pray for healing for my daughter, Neve, in agreement with all the people in this room. Where two or more are gathered, you say you are, and here we petition you.*

No more cancer. A new liver. A restored liver, a full life for this child. We cast out any spirit that is not of God. In Jesus' name, Amen.

Reg: *All right, Marie . . .*

Marie: *I just see a picture of a table, and you're eating food at the table, Neve, and God says, 'Get up, little girl' – that Aramaic phrase the Bible uses:* Talitha koum. *I just feel so deeply that he wants to heal your body, that you will be healed. That the spirit of death on this family must be released in the name of Jesus . . . Neve, it's your turn. Say into the microphone: 'God, I repent of any sin that may have allowed Satan access to my body –'*

[off-microphone: *DON'T YOU DARE!*]

Marie: *Someone's up the back –*

[Lucas yelling: *It's Frances –*]

Reg: *Wait, it's Frances –*

[off-microphone: *GET MY CHILD OFF THAT STAGE! THIS IS ABUSE!*]

[Yelling from the crowd: *GET HER OUT/oh my God/JESUS, DELIVER THE DEMONIC HOLD ON THIS WOMAN*]

[a dog begins to bark]

[*NEVE, IT'S OKAY, COME TO MUMMY*]

Lucas: *Don't touch her, Frances.*

[a dog barks and barks]

Lucas: *Frances, you have been asked to leave. We will call the police if you do not leave.*

[*She is CRYING, let me hold her, you have scared her –*]

Reg: *Frances, we have warned you.*

[*How DARE you. How dare you. Give her back to me, give me my child –*]

Lucas: *Reg, call the police – now.*

[*THIS IS A CHARADE – YOU SHOULD ALL BE ASHAMED OF YOURSELVES*]

Marie: *Can someone please turn the microphones and livestream off?*

The Gospel According to Frances 8:2

They hold my elbows.

I kick and I twist because I finally have something tangible to fight against. I have something to blame. I have something to hate. I have something to *hurt*. Even if that something is myself.

On the stage, Neve is shaking in the arms of her father, clutching her bunny. Her eyes are fixed on the back of the room, where there is, inexplicably, a *dog*.

I beg to any fucking god that she does not see me as they bend each of my arms behind my back, dragging my legs behind me.

I turn from my frantic violence to make sure, to calm her, to whisper that I love her, but Neve does not take her eyes off the dog. It prances around with a Bible in its mouth, gleefully ripping out pages one by one.

The Book of Mary 3:3

They run around the building in a frenzy. Reminds me of that time I kicked an ants' nest. I pick up a half-chewed page.

> Even though I walk
> through the darkest valley,
> I will fear no evil,
> for you are with me;
> your rod and your staff,
> they comfort me.
>
> You prepare a table before me
> in the presence of my enemies.
> You anoint my head with oil;
> my cup overflows.
>
> Surely your goodness and love will follow me
> all the days of my life,
> and I will dwell in the house of the Lord
> forever.

If I could read, maybe I could try to rewrite it.
Dog was hungry, so he ate it.

If only they knew: there is no such thing as the right words.

Police notes by Senior Constable Madonna McKenzie, Monday 22 August 2022

33yo female Frances Kocsmáros entered the church Eternal Fire at 9.21 am on 21/08/2022 and disturbed the service. She attempted to forcibly take her biological child, Neve Harkin, from the child's biological father, Lucas Harkin, as the service was proceeding. Police were called and the mother physically restrained and removed from the premises in a heightened emotional state.

Ms Kocsmáros is accusing Mr Harkin of spiritual abuse. Mr Harkin is accusing Ms Kocsmáros of stalking and attempted abduction. As it was not private property, no charges have been laid. No DVOs have yet been requested by either party or police.

Phone calls were made to both parties the following day. They claim to have already been through an unsuccessful mediation process as part of a high-conflict separation. They have a 50/50 care arrangement that is not in a court order or a parenting agreement. Mr Harkin is considering legal action to increase his care of the child.

We gave both parties instructions to seek a written agreement, and to re-enter mediation regarding the spiritual upbringing of the child. It is also understood the child has a terminal illness, and this motivated the complex circumstances. We informally advised Ms Kocsmáros not to set foot in the church again, warning that if the situation was to have escalated, charges could have been laid against her.

Instagram post, 22 August 2022

@kegstar_perfume
Description: A fifteen-second video of Frances Kocsmáros being removed from Eternal Fire Church by two police officers.

Caption: *This photograph was taken by a friend of mine who attended a service at Eternal Fire on Sunday. A woman came in visibly distressed and was forcibly removed by police. This is the 'charity' taking thousands of dollars from both the government and unsuspecting givers every year to apparently feed and house the poor. They preach light and love and treat the disenfranchised of society like absolute shit. They won't comment on their LGBTQI+ policies, won't denounce conversion therapy, and make the people they help attend church in order to have their basic needs met. This is footage of a church kicking a woman in need out onto the street.*

This place is POISON.
BOYCOTT.
DO NOT DONATE TO THEM.

15,349 views. 2456 likes. 578 comments.

Top comments:

@samantha.gold *They're all the same. Charlatans. Absolutely disgusting.*

@richardthethird *I had a monthly donation set up before seeing this footage. Heartbreaking. My money is going elsewhere.*

@soapbox76 *Is someone trying to cast a demon out of her in the background?*

Reply: @kegstar_perfume *Yep. Classic Pentecostals.*

@grahamandtina *Pray for this woman, pray for this church. They have left The Way.*

The Book of Mary 4:1

In the rehab hostel there is a single mattress and a sheet. I have folded the sheet like they asked me, because I'm not a grub. Even if they are being fuckheads. My bag is packed. Dog lies at my feet, a bit of drool dripping onto the linoleum.

Next door, Gregory is laughing uncontrollably at something. As if he's clean. It doesn't matter, really. They'll work it out soon enough.

Captain Tom comes up to my door. I don't know how he can keep a straight face. Dog won't look at him. He doesn't like authority.

'You ready, kid?'

'Yeah, obviously.'

He leads me downstairs and I nod to Dog, who follows quickly.

In the foyer, a young dude with dark circles under his eyes vomits into a bucket. He'll be having my room, then.

'What's your plan for tonight?' Tom asks, without making eye contact.

'I dunno. Park?'

'Kayla is going to call the women's shelter the Catholics run, just to check for you. You know where the soup truck stops, yeah?'

Kayla sits behind a desk, bright-eyed and bushy-tailed. She picks up the phone, about to call, when Reg walks into the foyer. He's puffing. I had wondered when he'd get here.

Tom is clearly a bit pissed. 'What are you doing here, Reg?'

'Are you releasing Mary?'

'We've discussed this. She refuses to be parted from the dog. Sunday confirmed that it was the best choice for all the patrons.'

Reg wipes his hands on his pants. Sweaty bastard. He ushers Tom over to the office.

Their voices get loud. Words like *funding . . . safety . . . public.*

They come out red-faced. Stupid old men and their hot air.

Reg smiles at me, strangely.

'Just . . . give me a few hours, Mary. Wait here, yeah?'

He looks at the plastic seat next to the withdrawing junkie.

I shrug.

The Gospel According to Frances 9:1

Mum is mopping, again.

You can't scrub it off me, Mum. I've already tried.

She cleans with an extra clatter and bang when I'm in bed. I think she considers it a helpful reminder that THE DAY HAS BEGUN. That she's there, and she's cleaning, and I could be productive if I wanted. I do not want. But the slamming of cutlery into a drawer makes me want to get up and run across Australia in bare feet, simply to get away from it.

I called her from the church car park, hysterical. At first she thought Neve had died.

Later, when I explained the service, the *crime* of it, she refused to make eye contact with me.

'They were praying for her healing, Frances. I suppose people express their faiths in different ways. You've certainly done that kind of thing with great enthusiasm before.'

I shook my head, enraged, but knew better than to continue to explain.

My parents attempt a passive-aggressive approach to me, diplomatic for no-one's preservation but their own. I get it. My Messianic-Jewish grandmother beat religion into my mother's bones, and Mum in turn grew up with fear and loathing for all orthodoxy. Nana defended the Torah until the day she was apparently Promoted to Glory. She understood it as her responsibility to advocate for the body of Christ, no matter how many times it enacted violence on itself and others. My mother, formed by years of compliance, will not fight religion openly but smiles sweetly as she declines it. Dad, the consummate atheist and pacifist, will just raise an eyebrow and mutter, *I told you so.*

Dad had pushed back when I converted. Mum had pushed back when I married young. But the church had given me purpose, and friends, and a family, and a job. It had taken care of those questions of belonging. It had been an outlet for every bit of energetic zeal and wonder that I could have been directing at sex or drugs or dance floors or international travel or fine arts degrees. My rebellion into Christianity made me into a perfectly obedient daughter, and I think for that they just accepted the benefits of my good behaviour and tried to ignore the weird shit. It was innocuous, for a time.

Now, they have to go through parenting a teenager all over again, but with a thirty-something divorcee who is about to lose her kid to custody battles, cancer, or both.

I hear Mum's heavy footsteps loudly on the tiles, like she's making a *point*. The build-up of sounds before she chooses to speak are painfully predictable.

My mother is at her wit's end with my grief, and she comes into Neve's bedroom to remind me.

'You haven't cleaned out your fridge in weeks. You're going to have child services in here, and they'll give Neve to Lucas, and then I'll never see my granddaughter again –'

'Mum. Stop.'

Lucas has 'held off pressing charges'. He told the police I was mentally unstable and abusive. In the moment, on the phone to a brittle policewoman without an ounce of empathy in her body, all I could do was cry. The lies sat like lead, so heavy I could barely rebut them.

What about every time I sobbed in the shower? What about the times I called the hotlines? What about the help I received in order to leave?

The church has informed me that I have two weeks until I am evicted from my home. It was a property provided for when I was an employee, and it belongs to them. They allowed me to stay on for the sake of Lucas and Neve. For *stability*. They know I do not have a hope in hell of getting a lease independently. They know I will have to move in with my mother and father, or seek out services like the ones I used to provide. They know what this will look like in the family court.

I will lose her. I will see her once a fortnight, and there may only be six to twelve fortnights left.

Mum's footsteps intensify again. Fuck.

'Frances?'

I nestle deeper into Neve's pillow.

No. I am not present for you yet. I am not present for anyone or anything but my child. And she is not here right now.

'Frances.'

'WHAT?'

'There is someone at the door.'

Text messages between Rosemary Kocsmáros and Ted Kocsmáros, 24 August 2022, 9.03 am

Ted: *How is she going?*
Rosemary: *I've cleaned and have some ingredients to make some broth.*
Ted: *No, how is Fran?*
Rosemary: *She's still in bed. Being difficult, as per usual.*
Ted: *I contacted that lawyer friend of Lewis's, Fiona Ramke. She said she would take a look at it all for us for a fixed fee.*
Rosemary: *That's good. We should do that. I'm worried they'll press charges.*
Ted: *I think we need to stick with what we discussed.*
Rosemary: *She doesn't have the money.*
Ted: *There just needs to be a limit. She needs to be able to do this herself.*
Rosemary: *What about Neve?*
Ted: *We already cover her half of the medical expenses.*
Rosemary: *Let's see if she can get out of bed.*

The Gospel According to Frances 9:2

I stumble through the house, pulling on tracksuit pants as I head for the door. Mum looks at me, eyebrows raised, keeping her opinions to herself for now.

The air is colder, sharper somehow, despite it being almost spring.

Reg stands on my front porch, his uniform on and face impassive. 'Good morning, Frances.'

I cross my arms reflexively so he doesn't notice I'm not wearing a bra. Too many years of being told to hide any indication that I am, in fact, a woman.

Reg only became the pastor of the church five years ago. His duties previously were purely in street outreach, until the leaving leaders realised he could speak publicly with an appropriate smattering of dad humour, voted for the LNP, and had trouble saying no – essential qualities for the senior pastor starter pack. Being good with people isn't a prerequisite it seems.

'Can I help you, Reg?'
'Actually I am hoping so, yes.'

He shifts on the porch, uncomfortable.
I don't move. He cannot come in.

'I understand you have had a traumatic few weeks. I'm very sorry for the events on Sunday. It grieves me to see such conflict between two people who were such prominent leaders in our congregation. It grieves me that Neve is in the middle of that. It grieves me that you have had to go through such hardship.'

'Right.'

'I hope you can see that God is still good.'

Don't answer him. Don't answer him, Frances. Don't –

'No, I do not see that at all, Reg.'

'Remember "His love endures forever". Even when your circumstances become difficult, God remains faithful. We just can't see yet how He will use this situation for good. What is yet to be *restored*. He can restore anything, Frances. Even you and Lucas, if you let Him.'

The gall. The audacity. I can feel the self-control unravel like a pulled thread.

'You think God could restore me and Lucas?'

He nods fervently. 'Absolutely. If you are surrendered to Him.'

'God can restore my marriage?' I whisper. 'My marriage, in which I was worn down, attacked, coerced and controlled? My toxic, loveless marriage? God loves me so much, He would throw me right back in the ring? God loves me so much, He would give my child a death sentence and ask me to spend half of her life away from her? God sounds so fucking good. What a kind, generous guy. Sign me right back up, Reg. What do I need to do? You want my money, my time, my home, my future? What else?'

'You used to understand the paradoxes of faith –'

'I used to bandaid life with faith. I used to numb it with God's apparent goodness. But it doesn't stop life from bleeding out, and you already know it. Thanks for your visit, Reg.'

I go to move back inside but Reg's quivering lip stops me. Something else is going on.

'What?' I ask him.

I have tears building, pushing, jostling like a crowd at a train station. He needs to hurry.

'I have a proposition. For you.'

I don't want to know. He continues, taking my silence as openness.

'We have a situation in the rehab centre. A circumstance in which we need extra resources and support.'

'You have a congregation of eight hundred people who actually give a fuck, Reg. Ask them.'

'This situation is unique. The person in question is clean, but vulnerable. She requires church accommodation that has . . . alternative needs. She requires residential supervision.'

'I do not work for you anymore. What's more, I am not allowed to step inside Eternal Fire. Your teaching pastor is about to take legal action against me for custody of our child. This doesn't make any sense.'

Reg looks visibly sick. I realise he knows all this already. I realise he does not actually want to be here.

'What happened last Sunday has had an impact on the public appeal of our ministry. We cannot let certain needs fall through the cracks. This person needs help, and she is only willing to receive help from one person. You.'

I haven't worked there for over two years. There's no patron who comes to mind, none that ever attached to me specifically.

He continues. 'I would never – it isn't appropriate for you to participate in our ministry. It's against our code of conduct. Except, you still live in church accommodation. Church accommodation with spare rooms. And if it was on a voluntary basis, if you were to cover this base for a few weeks or so, until child services could get involved –'

'Child services?'

'You could stay here, Frances. Long enough to get yourself together. To provide a home for Neve.'

'You want me to let a patron move in?'

'Only for a few weeks.'

'A judge would laugh in my face.'

'They wouldn't if I provided you with support documents. If I provided letters in your favour. If it proved your character and your stability.'

The sun shifts itself into position over my porch, drowning the garden in light.

Reg stands stiff in his uniform, the question pressing in around us.

'Why would you help me?'

'I do as Christ would do.'

'Bullshit.'

'I need this. And you need this, too.'

I am beholden. Even after everything. No matter where I turn, the church finds me, corners me.

'Lucas would agree to this?'

'Lucas does not formally need to know who volunteers in outreach ministries.'

I feel the radiation on my skin, my body so thirsty for the vitamin D I want to throw myself into it like a pool.

'Will you take her?' he asks, sweat beading on his brow.

I can hear Mum clattering cutlery in the kitchen and imagine what it would be like to move back in with my parents. I breathe in the house, the rooms Neve knows as home. I breathe in every memory of my child. Everything I am set to lose. Everything, everything, everything.

I breathe in, and I nod.

The Book of Mary 4:2

We don't talk in the car. Dog tumbles around in the back seat as Reg takes turns too quick. I hold on to my big old belly. Baby is asleep.

'This is a home, Mary. It isn't a hostel, or a boarding house. It's not your space, you're a guest. It means being respectful and tidy. Dog sleeps outside.'

'Dog doesn't like sleeping outside.'

'You'll have to bring it up with Frances. She has a daughter who also lives in the property.'

'Neve.'

'Yes, Neve.'

He bites his lip and looks down at my belly. I wonder if he'll say anything.

'Mary, your baby . . . what's the plan?'

We've pulled up at her house. It looks okay. Kind of cold. We will work on that.

'I'm going to have a hypno-water-birth and raise the kid on Baby Einstein videos.'

'Sorry?' He doesn't get it.

I grab my bag and the scruff of Dog's neck. 'Shall we?'

I can feel the edges of the worlds as they begin to overlap. I can feel the rain in my throat. I can feel the honey in my hair. It's almost time, Frances. The table is set.

Reg knocks on her front door, and when she opens it, the universe turns in on itself. No-one notices.

Part Two

The Gospel According to Frances 10:1

The girl can't be a day over fifteen. Maybe sixteen. She's got cheap sneakers on, no socks. A floral dress, buttons bursting around a pregnant belly. A nose piercing. Hair cropped short, like it was shaved only a couple of months ago. She grins giddily, a feral-looking animal in her arms. Reg did not mention the animal.

Reg looks at me like fire, eyes pleading.

I hate him, I hate them all, but God it feels good for him to *need* me.

'Frances, this is Mary. And . . . Dog.'

I can't shake her hand; her arms are full. I hover, gesturing to the door, when suddenly a ball of floral baby bump, backpack and mongrel barrel me into an embrace.

She smells like the street – sweat and garbage bins – but I know that smell to be an old friend. It doesn't repulse me, not like it used to at the start. The dog, inexplicably, smells . . . good. I lean further into his fur for a second whiff, aware that the arms of the waif remain tightly around my waist. God, he smells like –

'Herbal Essences, Coconut Water and Jasmine,' she gushes into my shoulder. 'Lucky little fucker got his first shampoo at rehab.'

I detangle myself and try to catch Reg's eye, but he is buried in his phone, his priorities already elsewhere.

This is how I remember it. They wash their hands of the blood, and they move on to the next 'miracle'.

'A few weeks, Reg? You mean until the birth?'

He looks up from his phone, startled.

Mary rubs her protruding bump, seemingly oblivious.
'I'll send you the paperwork, Frances.'

The pastor pats the girl on the shoulder like an estranged uncle and I have an involuntary urge to slap him.
Mary just smiles and puts the dog down on the doormat.
'Goodbye, Reg. Thanks for the lift.'

She looks to me, all eyes and belly.
I let her in. And I know, as she crosses the threshold, that the air has changed. The senses prick, darting like fish, careening down walls like scared spiders. Something is wrong and altogether right, and I have just let that something all the way in, to the only home I have.

Woolworths online order: Shopping List 1, 24 August 2022

Farmer's Choice full-cream milk
Oat milk
Arnott's Shapes – mixed lunchbox packs
Mandarins x 7
Veggie Sticks
Kids' Bliss Balls
Apples x 7
Rye bread
Tofu 200 grams
Free-range eggs x 12
Grass-fed beef mince 500 g
Spaghetti
Zucchini x 2
Tinned tomatoes 400 g
Carrot x 2
Onion x 1
Garlic – crushed
Night-Time Pull-ups, Junior, 3–4 years
Face masks – 10-pack

Woolworths online order: Shopping List 2

Sour Worms
Dog food
Pringles – salt and vinegar
Pepsi Max
Connoisseur ice cream – cookies and cream
Chocolate milk
Anchovies

The Gospel According to Frances 10:2

She sits at the kitchen bench in the last sliver of sun, legs crossed on the stool as if she might be levitating. The dog is curled up asleep beneath her. I've discussed the boundaries: he isn't allowed on carpet or in bedrooms. I feel deeply uncomfortable about the whole thing. There will be dog hair everywhere. My Dyson will probably cark it.

I prepare the bolognaise, the mince frying and curling tastelessly.

'Can we put anchovies in it?' she asks innocently. 'Cravings.'

I pause. There is a pregnant teenager in my home. I hate anchovies. What is happening?

'Let's add them to yours later.'

'Fine.'

It's been a while since I've sat with patrons and made small talk. I used to speak with the smooth confidence of someone who had answers. I used to offer services with authority, demonstrate love out of obligation. It feels strange to not be 'called to serve' anymore. There's nothing to punish me for being selfish or resentful. I realise too late that I am probably too selfish to be doing this. I wanted to think I might be the same generous person without Jesus telling me to do it. But I'm not. I don't want a homeless kid in my house. I want my space back, and it has only been an hour.

I stare at Mary's tiny frame, so weirdly similar to Neve's – that same basketball poking out from beneath her clothes.

'So what's your story, Mary? What brings you to Brisbane?'

'You, Frances.'

Her face remains impassive.

'Oh really?'

'I've been moving around the east coast for the last eight months or so. Kind of go where I feel, finding the right place to land. The bump showed up seven, eight months ago. Wasn't in the plan. Got sent to Brissie to speak with you, and just happens you were harder to get to than they let on.'

'Who sent you?' I ask, trying to sound casual. 'Tara Westbrook?'

I think about the church plant in Melbourne. Tara probably gave Mary my name, knowing she was travelling north. I make a mental note to tell Tara I am no longer working for Eternal Fire. She can't send patrons personally into my care; it just doesn't work that way.

'Who's Tara?'

'An old colleague of mine in Melbourne.'

'I haven't been to Melbourne.'

Right then.

I try again, turning to meet her eyes. 'What has it been like, dealing with the pregnancy?'

'Fucking awful. So uncomfortable. I vomited the first ten weeks. I like it better now he is kicking and stuff.'

'Oh, have you had an ultrasound? You know the sex?'

'Nah, they told me.'

'The doctors?'

'No, I haven't seen doctors. I don't have Medicare – it's all a bit of a mess. I know it's a boy because the Innkeepers told me.'

Huh?

'So you've lived in hostels, up until now?'

'No.'

'So the innkeepers . . .'

'Are not like *that*, Frances.'

Mary sighs like I'm the biggest idiot she's ever come across.

I feel like I can't put a single foot right in this conversation, and there is an ache in my neck that is increasing by the minute. I wonder if I can get her into a better program. A school, even. This was never going to work.

'Mary, would you prefer we not discuss the pregnancy today?'

Mary shrugs. 'The Innkeepers told me you knew them. That we could help each other. That you would understand what happened with the baby.'

Ah, that makes sense. These kids get into crisis pregnancies and don't have clear access to abortions or to support as parents. It's lose-lose, and when they realise it's too late they panic. It's sometimes rape, statutory or otherwise. Other times it is a result of street sex work.

'And what happened with the baby?'

'He is a miracle.'

'I mean, yeah. Babies are . . . good.'

'No, I mean immaculate. He just . . . appeared.'

We hear this one sometimes. Classic junkie move.

But I've never touched drugs ever. I've never ever had sex.

'He was a surprise?'

'Frances, he was given to me. *Behold, the virgin will conceive and bear a son.*'

Fuck this. Reg has set me up with a psychosis case. This also happens a lot. It's not unexpected, but it is not what I signed up for. Behavioural problems maybe, but not delusions and hallucinations. I can't be responsible for that. I have a child in the house.

She is watching me closely.

'Do you think I'm being crazy?'

I try to be gentle. Diplomatic. Calming. Like I was trained to be.

'I think you're possibly confused, Mary. I think it is unlikely you are giving birth to an immaculate conception. Every child is a child of God, however.'

Reg and Lucas would have *loved* that last touch.

'I know you don't believe that child-of-God shit.'

I'm surprised. 'What do you mean?'

'Why are you being so fucking condescending? I came here for *you*. To help you.'

She watches me cook in silence, the sounds of oil and heat and shrivelling grey meat speaking out the discomfort for us.

I feel exposed. Little children – especially your own children – can scream their hate, disgust and rage, then turn around and whisper their secure affection. They're forgiving. They turn back to the source of comfort. Teenagers watch, judge, form strategic positions and then attack. They blame, recklessly. They believe they can do it better on their own. They have no concept of safety or responsibility or mortality. I have always been intimidated by teenagers. Even slightly afraid of Neve becoming one.

Perhaps it is only right, that she won't become one? Fitting that she will be preserved in an eternal state of infancy? You would never have handled it anyway.

I am so repulsed by my own thoughts that I jerk forward to escape them, my hand hitting the gas stove, the side of my left palm immediately burning.

'FUCK.' The rage and shame rear up.

I run lukewarm water over my hand.

Mary watches. 'What? Did you burn yourself?' She offers a hand, quivering a little. 'Let me touch it, I can heal –'

'SHUT THE FUCK UP.'

I stare at the running tap water, eyes pricking with tears in response to the excess of it all – the freedom with which that water is allowed to express and unleash and run run run run run run. My body seizes with the permitted pain. I cannot cry for my own pitiful life, or even for Mary's terrible circumstances, but by God I can cry over a burn, and now I am the tap, and the water is running over the wound, and I am rushing, heaving over the sink.

The meat cools, and the teenager watches, and I know that it is over. I will send her back to them. I will lose the house, and I will lose Neve, but I will not have to hear about healing ever again.

The Book of Mary 5:1

You learn that it's all temporary. A bed is just a bed for a night. Not even.

A home is just a home for a few weeks. Until they realise.

The earth is dying, they're all dying, and they still don't want to admit it's all temporary.

The stupid baby thinks that the inside of my belly is the whole universe, and I wish it was.

A draft email from Frances Kocsmáros to Reg Holland, 24 August 2022

Reg,

Just informing you that the arrangement with Mary proved not to be tenable.

I have referred her to various alternative services and provided her with $100 cash to assist in the interim. Please do not engage me in volunteer services for Eternal Fire again.

My lawyer shall be in touch with your lawyer regarding the circumstances of my living arrangements.

Frances Kocsmáros

Text messages between Frances Kocsmáros and Lucas Harkin, 24 August 2022

Lucas: *I would like us to do drop-off at the McDonald's playground tomorrow morning.*

Frances: *Why?*

Lucas: *Please no longer come to my place of residence, and I will no longer come to yours.*

Frances: *Which McDonald's?*

Lucas: *The Annerley one.*

Frances: *That's fine.*

Lucas: *I would like to attend her first chemo session also.*

Frances: *I don't think the added stress of both of us is necessary.*

Lucas: *It's my right. Since you'll be with her until the general for the portacath insertion, I would like to stay the night so she can wake up and see me.*

Frances: *But it's my day with her? There will be more chemo, Lucas.*

Lucas: *I'll speak to my lawyer.*

The Gospel According to Frances 10:3

She asked to be dropped in New Farm Park. I get it. The soup truck stops there morning and evening.

New Farm is an old suburb, crisp, white and affluent, but the land is Native Title of the Turrbal tribe, and traditionally called Binkinba – place of the land tortoises. It seems fitting: the streets are ruled by rough sleepers, homes carried on their backs. Residential hostels stretch defiantly along Merthyr Road to shelter society's undesirables, or for those without beds the park has benches to sleep on, toilets and soft grass. At night, there is enough light to see by, but enough darkness if you need its cover.

The park itself is expansive, stretching across playing fields and rose gardens before tumbling into the river. The grass is dotted with jacarandas, coral trees, poincianas and fig trees, which frame an idyllic view of the city.

The playground is Neve's favourite and is disarming in its wildness: a hidden mass of banyan trees, with a wooden castle built into the exposed roots. The banyan trees arch around one another, heaving with their own weight. Their roots cascade from high up in their branches, twisted and knotted like locks of salty hair, reaching down to the ground. Living stalactites, breathing with memory, patiently allowing the children to tug and scramble and swing on fistfuls, as they continue their ancient sleep. I played there as a child, and now Neve plays there too, both of us adopted children of the perpetually exhausted banyan mother.

As I turn into the park's gate in the afternoon magic hour, I see the shapes of healthy, spritely children clambering over the treehouse playground, roots veiling bridges and slides. The shapes of dragons and ladybirds peer out from the branches, and the streeties steer a wide-enough berth around it during daylight hours to obscure the knowledge of good and evil. Children don't need to see how awful life can be – not yet.

I follow the familiar circular road around its jungled depths, until Mary tells me to pull over.

'I'll get out here.'

She clambers over the seats, her belly suddenly so much bigger to me. Dog follows loyally.

I don't know what to say, so I say nothing.

Mary smiles, as if this is fine – as if I didn't just announce over a bowl of pasta that *this isn't working out.*

'Thanks for buying me groceries, Frances. And for the money. I'll buy something for the baby, I swear.'

I nod, and squeeze her shoulder like a bloody missionary would. I don't know how to explain it. I don't have an excuse. What could possibly justify it?

My baby is dying. I don't have anything left to give. I am afraid of your mind. I'm afraid of your beliefs. I judge them, and I reject them, and for that reason I do not have compassion enough for you.

Mary looks at me, suddenly so lucid and piercing my foot slips off the brake for a second.

'You do have compassion,' she says, scratching a pimple on her chin. 'But you're real fucking tired.'

She runs a hand down my arm, my skin prickling in disbelief.

Then she walks into the trees, the animal trotting behind, and she does not look back.

Text messages from Celine Riot to Frances Kocsmáros, 24 August 2022

Frank, are we on for Tuesday? What are your thoughts? I miss you bb. 🍑 (4.08 pm)

I also have something cheeky for you. 🍀 (4.09 pm)

The Book of Mary 5:2

I've never seen Dog piss on so much. Then roll in so much. He doesn't smell like shampoo anymore.

Close, now.
 I buried the money like a seed, so it grows.

Hey, do you have a spare five dollars? (No, sorry.)

Never ask the mothers; they all say no. You'd think they'd look at the belly and remember their own swollen feet, and the tiny fists punching up against their ribs. You'd think they'd feel those pangs of fury and hot love and just get it. But they all forget, to self-protect. They learn to suffer and survive and starve out the competition. There is no-one here to take care of the mothers properly, so they harden like everyone and everything else.

The only ones who really want to give anything are the pilgrims and the children. The pilgrims give enough to make their religion look real, trying to drown their own doubts in uncomfortable generosity. The children have nothing to give but flowers and twigs; want nothing in return but a behind-the-eyes smile.

The only honest charity is from children, and only the children know that that's the only gift truly worth getting.

The Gospel According to Frances 11:1

I drove straight to work after delivering Mary to the park, and now I'm back in the foyer. Back in my blacks. It is good. I can work without worrying if some homeless kid is burning my house down or stealing my laptop. I can be present, listen to Cress's endless demands, watch this play, assist the audience members. I'm still shaking a little, but it's nothing a cup of tea won't fix. And, later, a drink. With *Ruairí*.

Wow. Fuck. It's been a very long time and many, many haircuts. Ruairí still thought they might be a woman when we met. It's been fifteen years since we took that first-year psychology subject at the sandstone university and swirled drunkenly in the Red Room together after Kevin Rudd won the election. I remember them aged eighteen, red curls and tight flared jeans and embroidered velvet vests. One of those chai-drinking festival lesbians, at a time when I wore toe rings and stick-on bindis and dreamed of getting dreadlocks. We bonded over vegetarianism and folk bands. That was before anything else happened, of course. Now they act in main-stage plays and I turf homeless children in need onto the street, and vomit every time I get an email from a lawyer.

I help the elderly patrons into the front row, like I'm the footman to a procession of thespian queens.

'Don't know if this is going to be my cup of tea,' mutters an old dear with a walker. 'Never usually like the new writing. Always a lot of yelling and nudity. Very dull.'

'This one is a verbatim piece, it says.' Her friend is reading a program beside her. 'So they collected interviews from all these people who have experienced profound grief and suffering, and put them into a piece of theatre. All their real words!'

'Lordy. Sounds . . . uplifting. Might need a gin.'

I stifle a laugh as I park the walker, and set about finding my own seat in the aisle.

The audience's chatter increases, almost in anticipation, until the lights dim and they collectively hush in relief. It is its own theatre, really. I'm tucked away, tasked with eyeing off patrons who pull out their phones or crinkle lolly packets, and watching the traffic of the stage.

Ruairí walks on as a single light begins to glow. They are wearing a short dress, with a backpack on their back. They hold something small and soft. A sharp inhale, and their voice echoes out into the hungry theatre.

'You wouldn't believe me, if I told you. That in all of it, there are places you still feel like you belong. I don't have a home, here. I'm not welcome anywhere. But after I saw the truth, I started to see every bit of the world as mine, instead of none of it. There is the dangerous stuff, the people who want to hurt you. There's the awkward begging or asking for help from people who don't want to stop looking at their phones long enough to look at someone worse off than them. Nobody wants me to exist. There's the pity and the abuse and the embarrassment of all of that – yeah, sure. There's the cold, and the hardness of the ground, which is a fucked part because I have a puppy, you see, and I don't like seeing him shiver or anything like that. I feel protective. But there's this place you get to, when you've gone lower than low. When you have nothing and nobody, or when the pain is too much to actually cope with. There's a secret place that opens up and lets you in. A place of real beauty and real rest. Only people who have really been hurt, really been broken, get to see beauty like that. It's the paradox of all the pain. It grants me access to the kindest thing, the brightest thing. And I don't think I would trade that for any bed.'

Ruairí stands a little taller, shifting out of the familiar hunch of the character they have just been playing.

I am frozen to my seat, heart trying to climb out of my ears.

'Mary, fifteen years old. Kings Cross.' They lift up the pile of fluff in their arms, chuckling. 'Oh, and this is Dog.'

The audience laughs along.

A new character enters, the lighting state shifts. The story moves on, the actors move on, the audience moves on, and I stay exactly where the feeling found me.

State Theatre FOH shift notes, Cressida Charalambous, 24 August 2022

> Full house. 214 drinks sold – $3140 in sales.
>
> One elderly woman in a walker left at interval, asked for a gin and a refund.
>
> Staff member Frances Kocsmáros (on usher duty) left in the first ten minutes of the play, stating a family emergency.

The Book of Mary 6:1

(Move along, kid, this park isn't safe at night.)

I'm fine, mate.

(There are a bunch of people who will make a claim on that bench tonight, and won't be polite about it. Find a shelter, yeah?)

I'm fine.

(A girl your age got stalked here three nights back.)

Is she okay?

(I don't want to tell you again. The wrong sort of people come here.)

I have a right to sleep wherever I find.

(And I have a responsibility to inform you about what is safe. If you ignore that, it reflects on you.)

I'm taking it on board.

(Are you soliciting?)

With this belly?

(What's your name?)

Penelope.

(Well, Penelope, let me remind you that we patrol this area and enforce the law.)

Then I don't have anything to worry about, do I? You'll protect me from the baddies.

(Move along, or you'll regret it. We will take you in to the watch house if necessary.)

Fuck off, you pig.

The Gospel According to Frances 11:2

I have been home for three hours. I had a cold shower, then sculled a glass of sauvignon blanc. Nothing touched it so I took a few tokes of a joint Celine got for me weeks ago. I'm still shaking. Still sober.

My house has three bedrooms and I walk through each of them in a repetitive circle, like a meditative labyrinth. Neve's room, where I'll eventually pass out. The 'office', which has boxes of old superannuation paperwork and orphaned USB and HDMI cords, in which I have set up a permanent futon for my own sorry arse when Neve is actually here. Then the main bedroom – untouched since Lucas's departure. With a towel and a mini shampoo and conditioner on the pillow, intended for the waif.

It had seemed overkill to offer her the king-size bed, but I certainly had no interest in sleeping in it myself. The place still stinks of marital dis-ease. Of passive aggression, turned backs and slammed doors. No-one else notices. It is a spacious, beautiful room, and perfect for a pregnant guest.

Except I have no pregnant guest. She is out in the shadows of New Farm Park, where the junkies and gang members open tightly closed fists behind trees, and the discarded bodies of streeties are found beside well-worn footpaths.

Mary, who has chased me from God-knows-where to here, who has chased me in my dreams, chased me to the *theatre* – the very furthest place from her life, her world – is sleeping rough tonight. At least she has Dog.

I reel through the rooms again, trying to justify it. There is no world in which it would work, even for a few weeks. Lucas would eat me alive, and he would find out immediately because children do not lie. Neve is about to go back into chemo. She'll be immunocompromised. Possibly having a transplant soon. Possibly in palliative care. She may die, while some stranger is taking up space and time and asking me to pick up more anchovies. A stranger going through the final heavy trimester, then going into labour in my home, then requiring intense postpartum care, all while my child needs me.

And after she gives birth?

I resist that thought, because I know what happens. I know the social work girls in child protection. I know the brutality of their job, and the children they've saved from certain hell. I also know some of the mothers who do not have their children anymore, who spiral in their grief to further depths of unsuitability as parents. I can finally conceive to the smallest degree that ache of incompletion.

I know Mary cannot stay here. I know the next three months will be the hardest of my short and pointless little life. I know I do not have capacity. But all I see in my mind as I walk the labyrinth is Ruairí, hunched exactly like her, using the same inflections, as if they've spent weeks studying her form. As if they know her. As if she might have found her way under their skin, too.

I think about the house.
About Neve. About the future.
It can't work. It doesn't work.
None of it.

Facebook messages from Ruairí Hickson to Frances Kocsmáros, 24 August 2022

Hey, was I wrong in thinking you were working tonight? We're all going for a drink at Stage Name if you want to join? What did you think of the show? (9.45 pm)

We're leaving Stage Name so don't stress. Let me know if you're around next week. (11.13 pm)

The Book of Mary 6:2

I'm on a bench and no-one has kicked me off it yet. The pig hasn't come back. Dog is curled up on the concrete below, already asleep. It's colder tonight. Good. Less people out.

There's a sound of a twig breaking behind me. I'm on the bench in front of the playground, under a streetlight. It suddenly feels a bit exposed.

A broad shape moves through the swing set, heavy-set but soft-footed. It pauses, as it notices me. Slowly moves closer.

Dog wakes, smells the danger just as I do.

I hunch down into the bench. Play small, play dead.

Please don't growl, Dog. Don't – don't – ah, fuck.

The shape tenses.

Whatever happens, it will all be over soon enough.

The Gospel According to Frances 13:3

It's 2 am and I'm driving along the road ringing the park, high beams on. There is a fog descending, and curlews crying out. I'm fucking terrified. The long-legged birds lay their eggs haphazardly in open grass and expect to defend them into survival on a busy thoroughfare. They stand guard in the face of cars, children and recreational sports. It's almost comical – they place their incubating children directly in harm's way, then respond in surprise when confronted with loss. At night, they haunt the park with ghost songs to ward off the threats of day.

I get it, I get it – even now I don't know where I have put down the child in my care, or what I have placed her into. How reckless my entire experience of parenthood must seem to everyone looking on. I don't know what defective instinct I acted on in order to give life, to lay an egg in such a cruel world. Mary and Neve have merged into a symbol of my failing motherhood tonight; a single daughter lost to an encroaching darkness. I don't know where to find her, I just know the sound of my own curlew-cry echoing back against the earth as I scramble to stay close to the last place I saw her.

But where is she now?

I pass the playground, with its twisted banyan roots. There is a wooden bench in front of it, under a streetlight. It's empty, except for a backpack I recognise – lolly wrappers spilling onto the ground from an open zip.

I stop the car and rush over to search through it.

The little ziplock purse I gave her – with the money in it – is gone.

I scan the playground – stillness. I scan the broader park; there is nothing but fog.

Maybe she's gone to the toilet? Maybe she's walking Dog?

I know how it sounds, but I don't want to consider my responsibility in this. I don't want to be held accountable by the church. I don't want to have to pass this park every day and wonder what happened to her body. I want this terrible feeling of foreboding to stop.

I sit on the bench. I'll just wait for her. I'll wait, and when she comes back we'll start this whole thing over again. I won't leave. I'll fix this.

The fog washes in like the tide, and takes me under.

Radio exchange between police patrols 1KCD4 and 4RFG7

1KCD4: *Constable Jacobs, there's been reports of suspicious activity in New Farm Park. Are you currently patrolling?*

4RFG7: . . .

1KCD4: *Paul, are you there, mate? Can you confirm you're in the area?*

4RFG7: . . .

1KCD4: *Constable Jacobs, do you copy?*

4RFG7: [A recording of Vivaldi's *Four Seasons*: 'Spring 1' plays.]

1KCD4: *Paul? . . . Paul?*

The Gospel According to Frances 12:1

I wake up, which is the first shock. I don't remember having fallen asleep. The fog has lifted, and the air feels warmer. The bench feels soft . . . but I'm not on the bench anymore. I jump up as if on fire. The bench is now a *bed*. A squashy double bed, with soft cotton sheets the colour of red wine, and a duvet in jewel-like colours. I'm on a bed. *A bed* in the middle of a park. A bed where a park bench used to be.

It's a prank, surely? I search the circle of light around me, stumbling – the streetlight remains the same. The park, in the darkness, still looks like the overgrown jungle it always is. Except there's a brightness now, through the trees. A perceptibly warm hum of light. I move towards it like a moth.

I climb through the draped branches and run my hands along fig trunks. I can just make out a soft green grove beyond them. My bare feet find their grip on exposed roots easily – where are my shoes? The way the leaves close behind me seems intentional. I already feel disoriented, and turn back for a moment to check the position of the playground. Except of course – *of course, you fucking lunatic* – there is no playground at all, but a soaring treehouse, built into the full height of the banyan trees. It glows from within, revealing multiple rooms, and the silhouettes of people. The front door is ajar.

A curlew calls, close by.

I stand before it all, agog, unsure which invitation to accept. The insistent radiance through the trees whispers to me, beckons me – but the house . . .

'We can visit the Inn later – we're late for dinner.'

Mary is sitting on the edge of the park bench bed. She looks entirely different, and entirely herself. She has hair, for one: dark brown curls like a halo around an impish grin. She isn't pregnant, which in this heavy trip, or whatever it is, doesn't seem to bother me. Like, why should she be pregnant? She's sixteen? This makes way more sense.

She clambers off the bed and bounces over.

'There are a few first-timers tonight. It'll be a bit slow off the mark, but I hope you're hungry.'

She takes my hand and I follow her helplessly towards the grove.

I look down at my own body and realise I am no longer in my work blacks. I'm wearing a dress – one I own, but not one I would ever wear. It's Neve's favourite. A pale blue silk ballgown. Outrageous. A stupid purchase from a vintage store. I marvel at my own mind's ability to invent. If this is what crazy means, I'm glad I've finally succumbed.

'It's kind of whacked at first,' whispers Mary, as if reading my mind again. 'But it's special, Frances.'

The grove opens before us. There is a long table laid out upon the grass. A selection of twelve pillows are placed as seats upon the ground. Lanterns hang from the trees, as if we were attending a wedding in the middle of a forest. The table is set with golden knives, forks, spoons and chopsticks. The placemats are a soft paper – a kind of papyrus dyed an ocean green – and golden plates sit atop them, adorned with sprigs of jasmine and basil flowers. In the centre is a banquet, the dishes so lavishly prepared I can hardly recognise what each might be. Five other people are seated around the table. They do not speak, and are not sitting close to one another. They either look down at their hands, or stare at the untouched food as if it might be poisoned.

Mary beams. She's wearing a dress covered in sunflowers; I hadn't noticed it until now.

'Welcome to dinner, everybody.'

They peer up at the tiny teenager, entirely perturbed. I'm confused by their distrust. *Surely we're all on some outrageous bender together. You might as well lean into it.*

Mary raises an eyebrow at me, as if to take my thoughts captive. 'You're all here because you were invited. Not by me.'

She gestures to the table. On each of the plates is a piece of silk with a name written on it in a child's scrawled hand.

Mary breathes out, and turns back to the five other guests. 'Don't wait for any special words. Just eat.'

She leads me to a cushion, and I sit. The name on my golden plate reads *Frances.*

To my left is a brown-skinned woman in her fifties, lithe and regal, dressed in a beautifully tailored green suit. She looks like she could run a country, and that this place is a country she definitely does not approve of. The name on her plate is *Glenda.*

On my right is a younger woman, barely in her twenties, trussed up in what could only be described as a wedding dress. She has long, pearly blonde hair, high cheekbones, and a series of ornate piercings arching up her left ear. She reaches for meat with her bare hands, unabashed and hungry. On the piece of silk is written *Sylvie.*

Across from me, a Caucasian man in his forties, wearing a tracksuit, has his arms defiantly folded, chair pushed back. He is muscled, balding, clean-shaven.

'Paul,' calls Mary, as if on cue, 'you are welcome to eat.'

He scowls at her.

Mary sits herself happily at the head of the table, cross-legged, and grabs a chunk of bread from a platter. She chews with her mouth open, and Glenda flinches.

'This is it for tonight,' mutters Mary through her mouthful of bread. 'Pretty quiet in the park.'

Further down the table is a young man in his teens, heavily tattooed and wearing a hoodie and fancy sneakers. He looks like he might be about to make a run for it. A few seats down from him is a person in their sixties, wearing a traditional *chut* Thai. Their hair is long, grey and plaited. They sip from a cup nonchalantly, and stare off into the trees.

The hoodie kid suddenly sits up straight, anxious. 'Can we just leave when we want to? Is this like a cult where you make us stay?'

'Yeah, we make you stay and then we harvest your organs, Jasper.' Mary keeps a poker face, still chewing bread. There's tension here.

'Who set this shit up?'

'The organ fairies, dumbass,' Mary spits back, but I see her eyes dart back towards the architectural wonder that has replaced the playground.

'The Innkeepers invited you,' whispers a small, accented voice. The person with the grey plait – not of any gender recognisable to me – nods gently at Jasper, the little gangster. They hold up their own name, written on a tiny piece of silk. *Achara*.

'This meal is a profound honour. You can leave at your leisure, by returning to the bed you arrived in.' They sip their tea with a practised patience, and reach for a bowl of noodles. 'But I would stay for some food, if I were you. Food can do a lot to ease the mind.'

The rest of us watch Achara, who commands reverence. They don't make eye contact, but continue to eat.

Glenda shifts uncomfortably in her pressed suit.

'I would like some more answers, if possible. Because this is not my, ah . . . my usual situation. The circumstances that led me to the park –'

'Are precisely the circumstances that qualify you to eat at this table,' says Achara.

Sylvie nods enthusiastically. 'This is my third table. There's one at the public hospital, one at the watch house, probably other places too, if you end up there at the right time. If you're invited, of course.' She dips bread in sauce casually.

'There is nothing like this at the watch house,' spits Paul, who has remained silent until now, and leans forward with menace, as if to force Sylvie to correct herself.

She is oblivious. 'Oh, trust me, there is – it's amazing. Like a ball, in a ballroom, with a three-course meal, and we wear costumes and we even dance. And the hospital one has the best beds, and a tiny beach tucked inside of it, and this dining terrace on the roof. This one is still my favourite, though. Because of the gifts.' She smiles to herself, and smooths out her fluffy wedding dress, complete with its veil.

'They don't know about the gifts!' Mary exclaims, clapping like the child I have to remind myself she is.

The two girls giggle excitedly, Achara smiles knowingly, and the rest of us stare at the food in utter confusion.

We're at some Mad Hatter's dinner party. A surrealist joke. An immersive theatre piece. Anything but what they're claiming it might be.

Achara stretches their neck and reaches for more noodles. 'Go back if you want to, friends. But if you're hungry? Eat.'

I look at the dish in front of me. It's a dhal of some kind, topped with yoghurt, pickles and chutney, and sprinkled with herbs. I spoon some onto my golden plate, desperate not to spill anything on the immaculate papyrus. Dream or acid trip or psychotic hallucination, I want to conduct myself with *dignity*. I lift the spoon to my mouth, and let myself taste it.

As the food hits my palate, the lights flicker in the trees, the eyes of my heart open before the truth, and for the first time in this cruel little life I can *see*.

The Book of Mary 7:1

You never get all of them eating. And it's not like it's a trap or anything. It's just the only way to say the things that need to be said. Because before you eat, it isn't in your body.

Paul didn't eat, but Jasper did eventually. I noticed that. His beady eyes went so blue for a second there. If I didn't want to punch him in the face, I might be happy for him. It's a good thing, to know that you belong somewhere better than the hell you live within.

I hadn't known Jasper was invited. All the beds look a bit different on the other side. He was in the toilet block, curled up in a stall – trying to hide from someone he owed money to, probably. Fucking dealers. He woke up in a *suite*.

The others found their way naturally – Sylvie was in the dugout next to the playing fields, Achara in the rose garden. Frances on the bench in the playground, just as she was supposed to be. Glenda at the park's bus stop. Paul . . . well. That was a rude shock, wasn't it?

He doesn't think he should be here. And that's the first hurdle.

They're drinking tea now, while I listen out for dawn. Soon we will go back to our other selves, like forgotten Cinderellas, but the birds are still quiet. All except the curlews. It's close, but not too close. There is time enough for presents. And though presents are not my job, they are my favourite part. So I will help, tonight.

I watch Frances spill tea on the papyrus.

I wonder if she will remember this.

It's real as real as real as real as real. I believe, but it makes no sense. It isn't whole, it isn't exclusive, it's not a worldview. It's just a *place*. A place I never knew existed. I block out all the other questions it raises: of what else might exist, if this can exist. That doesn't really matter right now. Right now, all that matters is chocolate mousse and candied elderflower.

Glenda caved eventually. When she tasted the chicken she began to cry thunderstorm rain tears. I would have touched her to offer comfort, except she seemed relieved; was quietly complete, from that point. After a few more bites, she began to speak to me. I heard about her brilliant children, their father the artist, her partner Anouk (a poet!), and her beloved dogs Ari and Rufus. I heard about her anthropological research at the university 'back when she was still an academic', about how she became a writer afterwards, about how her PhD shifted how disenfranchised communities were engaged with internationally. I heard about the piece of art she had purchased Anouk for their ten-year anniversary, and how Anouk had unknowingly tried to buy the same painting for her. How Anouk did disability support work at night, so they could both be artists. How they might travel to Antarctica one day.

She poured herself out with such extraordinary detail, glowing with every word. It was such a relief not to be asked any questions about my own life. To receive the story of someone so extraordinary, so *happy*, so lucky. It seemed everything had gone right for Glenda. And in that hazy little grove, under the floating lights and weeping fig trees, I wasn't even jealous.

The dinner party ebbs and flows with conversations opening and closing. I speak briefly with an effervescent Sylvie, who tells me nothing of her own life but snippets of information about the transformed park.

'But it's not as simple as heaven or earth, of course. And most people don't meet the Innkeepers; we just know they set the table. It only opens when you need it . . . like, you can't just turn up for a snack and a rest like at the mission. You have to be invited. And you're only invited at certain . . . low points.' She clears her throat. 'But you know that already, I guess.'

Sylvie doesn't seem like someone who needs a mission. I can't help but wonder why Glenda is here, too. Paul makes the most sense to me. The man clearly hates his life. He just sits there, trying to make his phone work (none of our phones do). I wonder why he doesn't get up and leave. Probably doesn't want to submit himself to an enchanted bed again.

The conversation dims for a bit while we drink tea, and Mary taps on a crystal glass with a teaspoon.

'It's time. Follow me.'

We stand, somewhat abruptly, as Mary scampers into the dense trees. The curlew cries again, and for the first time since waking, I wonder where the fuck Dog is.

The Book of Mary 7:2

The Inn shines in the darkness. Home, if ever there was one.

The guests don't know where to look, and I get it. They take off their shoes at the door.

The Inn is what they need it to be, tonight and every night.

Achara walks with Sylvie. They hold hands, old friends of the Table.

Jasper avoids Paul.

Paul avoids me.

Frances follows Glenda, in awe.

All here. All ready.

Dog is inside. They won't see him in his usual form, which is understandable. I miss his raggedy fur, though.

I knock on the door, and I wait.

The Gospel According to Frances 14:3

The entrance hall of the Inn is like a rainforest lodge. Expansive, with deep carpets, high timber ceilings and soft couches. There are strange references to the playground it masquerades as – a ladder to the second floor, a bridge above our heads. An enclosed slide emerges from the wall in the spot a fireplace might have been. Banyan roots tangle in the walls. A tree trunk towers in the centre of the room. There are four doors on this level, built between grounded banyan roots, and all seem inviting, unlocked. *How Enid Blyton,* I think, remembering how I had read those books to Neve. Oh, how Neve would love this.

Mary directs us to sit, then disappears through one of the four doors with a tentative politeness I've never seen from her before. The ratbag is humbled here. That in itself is a miracle.

It's only as I sink into a velvet armchair that I realise I am tired. This place compels rest. *Be still now, play tomorrow. There will be all the time in the world tomorrow.*

The others seem to be tiring, too. Jasper is yawning. Gosh, he really is just a kid. I wonder where everyone is supposed to be tonight. I wonder if we're missed. If people have found our beds empty. I wonder, I wonder. What possibly brought these people to a park at 2 am?

Mary emerges. 'Sylvie – you first.'

Sylvie jumps up, the white ruffles shimmying on the floor as she runs over and follows Mary through the door.

We sit in silence while she's gone. This doesn't feel like the place to make small talk.

After a few minutes she emerges, beaming. I see nothing in her hands. She resumes her seat silently, happy tears in the corners of her eyes.

'Glenda.'

Glenda enters, then exits again very quickly. She's solemn, but sure.

'Jasper.'

Jasper dawdles in, and is gone quite a long time.

When he emerges, he is softer. He walks back to his seat, deep in thought.

'Achara.'

Achara glides in, and they too are gone a long time.

When they come back to us, they are unreadable.

Achara sits beside Sylvie, and they embrace. I wonder what their history is.

'Paul.'

Paul might be resistant, but he's still participating. He stands, arms crossed, as if he might go in there and beat someone up for wasting his time. I find the bravado comical. We're at the mercy of a world with entirely foreign rules of nature.

Paul is in there only momentarily. As he exits, he pauses in front of us and mutters, 'Absolute bullshit.'

Mary comes out again, smiling at me pointedly, and I am reminded of doctors' appointments with Neve. My gut suddenly wants to retch up the dhal.

Mary sees it. 'You okay, Frances?'

I nod, wondering if the others have noticed. But they're all deep in thought, presumably considering their gifts, whatever they might be.

I follow Mary to the door. We enter into a low-lit garden. In the centre of the room is a patch of soft grass, small jasmine vines growing around it like a lattice of protection. Upon the grass stands a single curlew, and upon a rough nest of leaves a single speckled egg. The curlew stares at me, silent.

Mary points to a pond, hardly more than a puddle, filled with clear water. It's all deeply weird.

'What do you see in the water?' Mary asks.

As the curlew watches me carefully, I peer into the dimly lit pool. A series of objects are submerged before me, nestled on stones.

A two-dollar coin.

A tiny sewing thimble.

And a rose-gold ring in the shape of a crown of thorns.

What the fuck?

'I see three objects.'

'You can choose one of them.'

I gaze at the selection, suddenly feeling an unbearable pressure to make the *right* choice. The ring sits there, throbbing like a wound. Am I a coward for not wanting it? I don't understand its presence. I lost that ring. I did not want that ring, and I do not want that marriage back. Is this where the religiosity activates in this absurd alternate universe? Love and generosity, always with an agenda . . .

I consider the thimble. I was never one for sewing. The coin sits like coins do – heavy, dirty, almost worthless. It's only as I look closer that I begin to realise each object has tiny words engraved upon it. I put my hand in the water. It's warm.

I pull out the thimble. Repeated infinitely in minuscule writing around its circular base are the words: *to mend is to tear is to mend.*

Huh. Weird.

I put it back and pick up the coin, on the rim of which is written: *to cure is to kill is to cure.*

Finally, the ring. I know I never engraved it myself, but there, in tiny writing: *to hold is to let go is to hold.* In my hand, the ring feels exactly as I remember it: too heavy.

I look at Mary, fractured. None of these is a gift I want or understand.

'I know,' she says simply. 'Just take the thing you need.'

Only one word reaches out of that pool of water to grab me by the throat. It doesn't matter that its opposite is my consummate enemy. I need it. Neve needs it.

So I take the coin.

The Book of Mary 7:3

I lead them back to their beds.
Achara to the four-poster bed in the roses.
Sylvie to her vintage caravan with the white linen sheets.
Jasper to his own bedroom with a television.
Frances to her soft, colourful duvet under the streetlight.
Paul up the ladder, to the guest room tucked inside the Inn.

They don't tell me why. They don't owe me any explanation. But I wonder.

The Gospel According to Frances 12:4

This bed is the softest bed I have ever –

I am so tired, I could just –

The jasmine is in my hair, I am dreaming of jasmine. I am dreaming of rings, of thimbles, of coins. Of curlews hatching, and tree trunks growing through the middle of my chest –

The Book of Mary 7:4

While the garden of unearthly delights remains awake, I go back to the Inn's garden bed, where I buried the cash.

Nothing yet. Not for me.

I water it, I wait.

Light sleeps, letting the demons play.

The Word of Dog (Lamentations)

I would have done anything. Anything. Anything.

The shell is cracked around my feet, feathers spread, blood and beak spread further, and further –

You still smell like mine, even in death.

I spread my wings, but I do not fly.

I scream.

The Gospel According to Frances 13:1

I wake in a sun-induced sweat. There's a siren in the distance, and something close to my face – *argh* – fleshy, invasive. I bat it away, and swivel my body up to sitting. I'm still squinting, and my back spasms in pain from the park bench. Everything aches and drips and reeks and, oh God, how I want a shower. I open my eyes, and *fuck above all fucks*, the thing it looks like I back-handed with full force is the face of Lucas Harkin.

I'm in New Farm Park, and there is the soup truck, with Lucas on shift. There are all the patrons I used to serve soup to at 6 am on a weekday morning.

'Frances, you *hit* me!' He hisses it, devoid of any empathy. 'What are you doing here?!'

I don't know what to say. I have nothing, no excuse –

'I went for an early run, and I got a bit light-headed.' I try to pull myself together. 'You scared me. I didn't know it was you.'

His eyes narrow at my work clothes and shoes. I have never run in my life, and he knows it. He gets out his phone and begins to type notes. He then goes to take a photo of me. I'm lucid enough to call bullshit, and place a hand over the lens.

'Where is Neve?'

'With my mum.'

I seethe internally. He has half a week with his child, a child for whom every second is more precious than the next, he pushes insistently for *more* time, and still manages to handball the parenting of her to other people. There are plenty of vollies who would do the soup run. Why is he even here?

I don't ask. I look to the patrons, who are staring at me with their soup in hand, nosy. There is no-one I recognise. Turnover is often high as the weather warms up. I give a little wave, and feel for my keys. Back pocket, thank fuck.

'I'll see you at McDonald's in a few hours, Lucas.'

I walk to my parked car and finally take in my surroundings. The park is its flowering, ramshackle self again. The playground in the banyan trees is simply that – a wooden structure. The park bench I slept on is covered in graffiti. There is dew on the grass, and a chill in the air. I reach for my memories of the night before. They don't feel like a dream, but it all seems very . . . distant. I'm in so much damn pain.

I dig around for the coin, which I had slipped into my pocket alongside my keys, but it's not there. *Hmm.*

I drive slowly around the park, getting my bearings. I don't feel hungover, just shrivelled and depleted – like a used-up tube of toothpaste. As I drive, I notice a woman wrapped in a knitted hospital blanket sleeping at the park's main bus stop. Beneath the blanket she looks bare, almost naked. Her smooth skin and sharp grey haircut make me pause. This isn't a typical streetie. I slow the car, realising with a start that I know that haircut and that severe, handsome face.

I wind down the window. 'Glenda!' I call out, disturbed to be seeing her in such a state.

She looks up, dazed. There is a flash of recognition, then a squint – as if the memory might be a dream.

It is Glenda, but it is also definitively *not* Glenda, not in any way at all. Her eyes are vacant, watery. She is confused and vulnerable. She looks both older and younger than the woman I met last night.

At the sound of my voice, two people – one in uniform and the other in a dressing-gown – run over from a few hundred metres away. They're shouting Glenda's name. The woman in the dressing-gown is almost hysterical. The man in uniform looks like a nurse or care worker. As they near Glenda, they advance more cautiously, as if she might make a sudden, violent movement.

'You must be cold, Glenda,' says the nurse gently. 'You've had a little adventure away from home.'

As the woman in the dressing-gown gets closer, I begin to feel strange. She has cropped black hair, a septum piercing and a tattoo creeping around her collarbones like a vine. She is still wearing bed socks. Bed socks I have learned to love when she pulls off her Docs.

Celine notices me in my idling car, the way I am staring at them all like they are a street parade. Her eyes narrow in disbelief.

'Did you just call her name?'

I shake my head, unsure how to explain it, unwilling to implicate myself.

Glenda looks at Celine, then the nurse. 'Who are you? Where are you taking me?'

Celine tears her eyes from mine to meet Glenda's. She too is entirely different in the light of day, soft and broken.

'It's Anouk, darling. And Peter. We're taking you home.'

'Home? I'm going to work. I'm minding my own business. Please leave me alone.'

Peter moves closer, his arms spread wide, attempting to touch her. 'No, Glenda, it's breakfast time, you aren't going to work today. Your children are coming to visit you, before they go and see the show.'

'I don't *know* you. Get the fuck off me. Get the *fuck* off me!'

She lashes out powerfully, intent on escape. She looks over at me in the car, suddenly cognisant of who I am.

'Frances, help me. *Please help me.*'

Celine, who is actually Anouk, who is actually a sex worker and a poet, stares at me with bewilderment before diving with the nurse onto the limbs of her violently distressed spouse.

I panic. I can't – I shouldn't be here. I push my car into drive, and go, leaving Glenda naked and thrashing as she is wrestled into submission on the side of the road by the woman she loves most in the world.

Text messages between Lucas Harkin and Reg Holland, 25 August 2022, 8.06 am

Reg: *Are you still on the soup run?*
Lucas: *Yes.*
Reg: *Pack up, now.*
Lucas: *What? Why?*
Reg: *Some horrific news about an attack in New Farm Park. I want the patrons out of there. Police will be crawling any moment.*
Lucas: *I found Frances asleep in New Farm Park this morning.*
Reg: *That makes no sense.*
Lucas: *I suspect it is drug or alcohol use.*
Reg: *Did she explain herself at all?*
Lucas: *Said she'd gone for a run, then just drove off.*
Reg: *She drove there? And then you think she slept there?*
Lucas: *Something like that. Found her on a park bench. What happened?*
Reg: *You need to write all this down. I'll call you.*

At home I peel off my clothes and let the shower melt over me.

What is going on? Where did I leave my mind last night?

I wish I had a touchpoint – anything other than Celine's (Anouk's?!) ferocious protection, and Glenda's stricken look of recognition, hoping that I might prevent her forceful abduction. I wish I had the coin. I wish I had Neve. I wish I had Mary. But Mary is gone, and all traces of her are gone.

I am due to get Neve in forty-five minutes, and my heart has begun to throb in that familiar anticipation. Today is portacath insertion day. We've done this before; I understand the brutal rhythm. We'll head to the children's hospital at 5 pm and she will stay overnight, just in case.

Chemo will begin tomorrow through the port in her chest, if all goes well. I haven't had time to consider the processes too much. Things change so quickly, the plan is improvisational, only ever half-set. Treating cancer is like playing a dirty game of rugby: you just get as far as you can with the ball – dodging and dummying and passing and sprinting – before you're tackled to the ground yet again. There are strategies, sure, but cancer never tells you what its plan is. We might end up doing chemo tomorrow. We might not. We might have our child with us for Christmas. We might not.

The *we* feels bitter, bile-like. There is no *we*. I should remember that.

I switch on the main bedroom television, tuned to the twenty-four-hour news channel, just for some company. It fills the empty corridors of the house, urging me to feel better about my circumstances. *See? There are people worse off than you in this world.* The news flickers on and the dulcet tones of a journalist's affected voice echo through my home.

I rummage in the wardrobe for clothes, watching it from the corner of my eye. There is an aerial view of a Brisbane parkland, taken from a helicopter, and then a woman in a grey blouse is speaking gravely to the camera. There is footage of police putting up tape, and a banyan tree playground, and a park bench, and a sports dugout, and soon my nose is pressed to the television, and I am shaking.

I grab my phone. There is a missed call from Reg. A voice message.

I do not call him back.

Breaking News, 25 August 2022

A young woman was taken to hospital in a critical condition after being discovered in New Farm Park, Brisbane, at 7.12 am this morning.

She was found, grievously injured, by a couple walking their dog. They alerted paramedics and police, who report that the woman suffered a violent assault. Police have requested for anyone who has information about the woman or the assault, to come forward, including anyone who was in the park between 9 pm and 6 am. They will be surveying CCTV footage.

Police Commissioner Alicia Sloane spoke to the press at 9 am.

'Reports of women being injured or killed on the streets of a city we deem to be safe has reached epidemic proportions. We are sick of telling women to make safer choices. It is time we stopped this violence. It's time for clear, decisive legislation, and for justice to be served. We are in the process of identifying the woman in the hope of contacting her family.'

More to come.

Voice message from Reg Holland to Frances Kocsmáros, 25 August 2022

'Frances, we need to talk. There has been terrible news, you may have seen already. The police have involved the mission. Call me. Please. And brief your lawyer.'

The Gospel According to Frances 14:1

Neve eats a Happy Meal nugget – the last supper before surgery – and frowns at the tubular McDonald's playground.

'It's just not very fun on my own, Mummy.'

'I can't *fit* in there, Nevie. It gives me claustrophobia.'

She picks at her food. 'I don't like the playground at hospital. I don't want to go.'

I sigh. My brain feels like scrambled eggs, and I want so desperately to be present with my kid but the stimuli coming in every direction blurs her in my field of focus.

'*Mummy.*'

'Yes, darling?'

'I missed you.'

I look at her now: the short curls that will be gone oh-so-soon just covering her hearing aids. The soft cheeks, bright green eyes. The way her chubby little hand reaches for mine to tug me into her orbit again. She knows I'm distracted. She also knows I starve for her. And I pull myself out of the vortex to look her dead in the eyes and tell her the truth.

'I missed you so much. I always miss you so much.'

'What did you do while I was gone?'

I sigh. *Fuck.* She loves this question. Usually I say, *I worked, and then I did a bit of cleaning, and then I worked some more . . .*

'Well, I went on a magical adventure.'

'What?!'

'Yep. To a treehouse hidden inside a playground. And a forest with a special feast. And I ate the best chocolate mousse *ever.*'

Her eyes widen. I've never seen her so enthralled.

She leans closer, conspiratorial. 'Mummy, did you go to the *Inn?*'

Wait. What?

She stands, the hospital forgotten. 'Let's go! Let's go there now!'

I pale. I don't want to imagine – has she *been there?*

'Where, darling? Where do you think it is?'

'The park, Mummy. Let's go to the good park.'

It is deeply inappropriate for us to go to New Farm Park. There are police at New Farm Park. There is a crime scene at New Farm Park. But this is the last free wish of my only child, before she endures seven weeks of chemotherapy.

So we go.

Inpatient letter, 23 August 2022

Dear parent/guardian of NEVE HARKIN,

This is a letter to confirm that Neve will be admitted into the paediatric oncology ward on Thursday, 25/8/2022, 5 pm, for the insertion of a portacath line. Please ensure the patient fasts for six hours before the procedure – nil by mouth. Inpatient chemotherapy will follow for approximately two weeks, with outpatient chemotherapy to follow. We confirm you are a private patient in the public hospital, and your account details are below.

Please note: there is limited sleeping space for parents in the paediatric oncology ward, with a single recliner beside each bed. Though we encourage parents to stay with distressed children who require comfort, we do not have room to accommodate more than **one parent** *overnight.*

Visiting hours are from 7 am to 9 pm.

Thank you for your understanding.

Paediatric Oncology Unit
Brisbane University Hospital

The Gospel According to Frances 14:2

As we drive around the park, Neve pesters me with questions:

'What will you eat this time?'

'Will you take a nap in the special guest room?'

'Will you climb the star trail?'

I stutter imaginary answers, not knowing how to process her knowledge of such things, or the enthusiasm with which she remembers.

The far end of the park is cordoned off by tape, with detectives and police moving meticulously through the area. The banyan tree castle is miraculously free of all criminal commotion, and no-one else is there. It feels abandoned and derelict in light of last night's wonder, but Neve runs to it in absolute glee.

My mind floats between my child's own magic, and Mary. I look to where police are collecting evidence and shudder at the possibilities. I never wanted this. I never looked for it. But I want that injured girl – whoever she is – to be okay. I *need* her to be.

Neve climbs onto the first ladder leading up into the roots, and I am afraid of what will happen – will the world suddenly shift and change again?

She walks to the bridge, and stretches her arms to the trees.

'WELCOME TO THE INN, MUMMY!'

The playground stays the same – just a playground.

I walk over. 'What do I do?'

'You give me flowers, and I'll give you some yummy food, and then you follow me.'

I pick some jasmine from a nearby bush and hand it to her.

She beams, seeing more than flowers. Seeing more than a playground. Seeing more than a mother appeasing a daughter. Her imagination stretches past every limitation on her body. She knows the Inn because she invented the Inn for herself, and she is thrilled because I have finally seen her imagination as something real and worthy.

I realise, with extraordinary relief, that this is play. Maybe everything last night was just play? Maybe the tragedies reported on the news are play? Maybe Mary is simply a figment of my imagination?

Play I can do. Play is *fine*.

I take the bark chips she would like me to eat and I follow her up the bridge, into the hanging braids that grow from the trees.

'To the guest room, Mummy!'

There is a ladder up to a lookout, and I climb it, curling up on the platform like a caterpillar at her request.

'Now, pretend you're asleep and I'll wake you up and say, "Time for hospital." And you have to say, "No, no, no, I don't want to go."'

We play it out, and I see her system relax, breathing easy in its power. Her little limbs grip and push and climb and slide, and she is a whole child. A whole, healthy human being, perfumed with limitless potential, able to deliver gasps of absolute joy and cries of utmost despair. I want this life for this child. I want her to feast on it.

She comes to me, adorns my hair with leaves, pretending to be the 'doctor'.

'You always get better at the Inn, Mummy.'

I feel her little hands against my temples, taking my temperature, copying the endless checks that will soon be performed on her tired little body.

She slides back down the slide, and takes some of the tiny white flowers to a patch of soil.

'I'm going to plant you an ice-cream tree.'

I see her digging, placing a stick in earth, when suddenly she squeals in delight.

'I FOUND TREASURE!'

She scrambles back up to my apparent guest room and presses something cool and small against my open wrist.

'This is the cure. Now you're better.'

I look at the trinket she's placed lovingly on my skin. It's a two-dollar coin, with words engraved around its rim.

to cure is to kill is to cure

Crime scene notes by Senior Constable Paul Jacobs, 25 August 2022

Perimeter has been walked through, three sets of footprints. Dog faeces. A broken curlew egg – possibly stepped upon? Blood. No weapon found yet.

CCTV footage from the playground shows multiple people in the park from 2 am. Usual rough sleepers, possible drug users.

A person arrived in a car with licence plate 456RTG around 2.12 am, moved out of view of the CCTV and then re-entered and left at 6.40 am. A confused individual was apprehended by two others at 6.45 am, during which a short interaction took place with the person in the car. The two people who contained the confused individual arrived in a car with licence plate 561GND, the registration holder identified as Anouk Neilson, a registered full-service sex worker in legal brothels.

At 10.30 am the car with licence plate 456RTG returned to the playground. A woman and child got out, attended the playground, then left at 11.17 am. The licence plate has been run through the system and the registration holder identified as Frances Kocsmáros. No criminal record but she is known to police due to recent disruptions at a public church service, and a pending intervention order requested by her ex-husband, Lucas Harkin.

The Gospel According to Frances 15:1

At home I sit under the rainwater shower with my daughter, both of us naked, her body curled into my crossed legs on the tiles. I wash Neve's hair, as she clings to her coin even now, whispering to it. 'My treasure,' she croons, like a beautiful little Gollum, and all I can do is nod.

'Today we're learning about the letter D. D, for dog!'

The bedroom's television is turned to ABC Kids now. Neve gets enough bad news in her own life; she doesn't need to see it broadcast. I am desperate to know what has happened, though, and desperate for it not to be real. There is a rock in my stomach, and images from last night parade through my mind like a fantasia nightmare. I wish there was a way to make sense of it. *Who was hurt?*

The water runs down our bodies so smoothly that it allows us to forget, for a moment, that skin can, and will, be pierced.

I comb her curls while she sits on the king-size bed in a towel and watches *Bluey*. Her little hospital bag is half-packed beside me.

'Are you feeling okay, Nevie? We had a big morning.'

She yawns. 'My tummy hurts.'

The meds are on the bathroom bench, and I instinctively reach for them before stopping myself: she's supposed to have nil by mouth.

'Mummy, make it go away.'

'I don't know if I can darling.'

'*Mummy*. It's like someone is sitting on my insides.'

She's arching and crying silently now, limbs folded stiffly around her distended abdomen. It's too much to bear.

I measure out some painkillers with great focus. Tiny bodies need specificity. It's so easy to overdose, so easy to injure in your attempts to alleviate. I think of the streeties, of the lethal overdoses we would see each week at the mission. How many times has a human being died from a valiant attempt at staying alive?

She relaxes back against me once she's swallowed them and I feel her breathing slow and her body unclench. God knows how much pain she was in before I thought to ask. I stroke her forehead, willing her into a nap. Tonight they'll give her something more to help, but it won't be comfortable.

She's almost out, so I turn the television off and carry her down to her bedroom. She nuzzles against me, still conscious, entirely comfortable in my arms. I lay her down upon her bed, which has butterflies stitched all over the quilt in a joyful swarm.

Neve reaches for my neck and strokes it.

'Where will I go when I die?'

I can't hold myself up through that one. I crumple down beside her. I am wet washing falling from a line. I think of every single thing I was taught. I think of heaven. I think of hell. I think of the stars. I think of the mortuary at the hospital, the lot at the cemetery, a tiny vase that might sit on my mantel one day, containing half of her ashes. Where will she go? Where will she go? I don't know; I have never known. I have only ever tried to keep her here.

'It's a mystery,' I whisper, my voice trembling.

'Like a secret?'

'Like a story with a surprise ending.'

'A good surprise?' She clutches her coin, the words catching the light from the kitchen through her doorway.

I think of the Inn. I think of the dhal. I think of Achara's arms around Sylvie.

'All I know is that there will be a warm bed. And a hot meal. And there will be someone waiting there to hug you.'

'Will there be cake?'

'Of course, my love. It will be a party.'

And with that she smiles, and falls asleep.

Email from Lucas Harkin to his lawyers, 25 August 2022

Dear Jeremy,

Attached is the updated outline of events from the church and from the incident in the park where Frances hit me. Thanks for drafting up the letter for me.

My boss has informed me that the girl in hospital is in fact brain dead, and life support will be turned off once she's identified and family is contacted. My colleague Reg Holland says that Frances is implicated and will be under investigation. Is this helpful in a legal setting?

Neve starts chemo tomorrow and I have ensured that I will be staying overnight at the hospital, so I can take any necessary steps from there.

Please read the attached document and let me know if you need anything further.

Thank you,
Lucas

The Gospel According to Frances 15:2

We park on the fifth level of the car park and walk into the hospital hand in hand. It's drizzling now, which feels appropriate. It makes the warmly lit hospital feel like more of a sanctuary in the twilight. I remember staggering in here at a similar time when I was ready to give birth to Neve. I push that memory from my mind. It's too cruel a contrast.

Neve is wearing her little backpack, and holds her soft toy, Peach, and the coin.

They admit us quickly enough, and settle us in the PO ward. We have our own room – a welcome gift. The ward's decor is well intentioned. There are cartoons, cute toys, craft trolleys and colourful wallpaper with interactive art *everywhere*. But you can't polish a turd, and you can't remove the stench of suffering in the oncology unit.

Neve waits anxiously for the nurses in their brightly coloured scrubs. They weigh her, take her vitals and check her meds. They move quickly. She has to be sedated before the insertion, and I must leave her side once in the operating theatre. It will take about an hour. The longest hour.

I help her put on her gown. Her skin is a distinct yellow against the white fabric.

I hold her, unwilling to let go.

'Don't worry Mummy, I'll be *asleep*.'

As she climbs into the bed, she's beaming – a brave face means compliments from the nurses, and later some jelly. I understand. We evolve quickly in this life; we learn how to survive in the harshest of environments.

Our nurse tonight is Greta. She wears fuchsia scrubs with animals printed on them. Greta talks about Elsa while she prepares Neve's canula. Another nurse holds her arm down firmly, trying to seem friendly. Neve's smile falters as the needle is brought to her skin. Sick children do not simply adjust to procedures – the trauma of being a pin-cushion can become exponential, until a blood test is akin to amputation.

Neve screams in my arms as Greta continues her fuchsia-coloured small talk.

'What do you want to be when you grow up Neve? Maybe a *princess?*'

I walk beside her bed as a porter wheels it into theatre. I watch the anaesthetist place the mask upon her quivering face, and I hold her hand as he counts down out loud. I feel her grip on me soften as she goes under. I watch them intubate her. I watch the cannulas snake out of her mouth and nose and think *that is my child, but not how I made her to be.* I blow her a kiss, I leave.

The time feels empty and pointless without her. Greta makes up the recliner chair into a bed for me, complete with sandpaper sheets and a blanket so thin I can see through it. I don't have the heart to tell her I won't be the one sleeping in it tonight. Lucas arrives at 6 pm.

'You know where the parents' room is, yeah? Tea and instant coffee is in there.' This is just another shift for Greta. Neve is just another name on a whiteboard.

My body should be hungry, even if it isn't, so I go in search of food.

The children's hospital is connected via a bridge over a busy road to the main public hospital, where all the takeaway outlets are.

The adult hospital is darker than its paediatric sister. There are no attempts at joy, though small touches of hope – a vase of flowers here and there, or a neutral landscape painting. Everything is beige or grey. When I cross the bridge, I stop at a sign next to the lifts:

Reception	Ground
Food Court	Ground
Emergency	Level 1
Outpatients	Level 2
Ward 3A	Level 3
Ward 4A	Level 3
Maternity	Level 4
Intensive Care	Level 5

I pause. And then I enter the lift and press the button for the fifth floor.

Patient notes, Brisbane University Hospital, 25 August 2022

JANE DOE

Patient seems to be aged 16–25, unknown. She has received blunt force trauma to head. Was still breathing when found. Considered entirely unresponsive, is currently kept alive on a ventilator. Brain-stem death.

Doctors are testing bloods. Options cannot be considered until identification.

Next of kin not yet identified.
No phone.
47 kg/160 cm tall.
Some identifiable body piercings and tattoos – see photos attached.

Rev. Reg Holland (Eternal Fire Mission) – 0423 678 975 – called by police. He is coming in, but he had no patrons fitting exact description. Queensland Police are running fingerprints.

The Gospel According to Frances 15:3

I step into the utter chaos of intensive care. There is no-one left at the nurses' station, presumably due to an alert sounding overhead and a code flashing on a screen.

I wait. I'm not interested in sneaking around, I just need to know.

Soon a frazzled young nurse in a green training uniform appears. He looks at me, expectant. 'Who are you here for?'

I swallow. 'There was a girl brought in, I think. I have a feeling she might be the teenager I've been a temporary guardian for.'

He squints at me in confusion, and I add, 'I work for Eternal Fire. The street mission.'

The young man nods in recognition, seemingly convinced by the circles under my eyes.

'The girl from the park?' he asks, and I nod. 'They haven't identified her yet.'

He calls a supervisor, but no-one picks up the phone. 'There's a lot going on here today,' he mutters in frustration, 'but you should probably go in.'

He takes me to a bed, machines bleeping and whirring and a ventilator pumping. I look at the tiny body in the bed and crumple inside.

'Do you know her?' I am speaking with a new nurse now – an older woman. She is urgent, insistent, but I don't understand the rush. Time has stopped.

'Yes, I do.'

Even if she were alive, Sylvie would look entirely different from the bombshell bride of last night. She is scrawny, her skin prematurely pocked and lined. Her hair – matted with blood – is half black regrowth and half peroxide. Her face is almost unrecognisable due to the violence inflicted upon it, but the beautiful earrings remain. She wears a dirty tracksuit instead of a wedding dress. Her feet are bare, tattooed with tiny dolphins. I want to pick her up and carry her back to the Inn. I want to feed her skeletal frame with bread and sauce and chocolate mousse and hear her speak of wonder upon wonder.

'Her name is Sylvie.'

'Sylvie? Short for Sylvia?'

'Ah . . . yes.'

'Surname?'

'I don't . . .'

'So you are her next of kin, as far as you know?'

I falter. What?

The new nurse is already pulling up her online file.

'We need you to decide whether you consent to the donation of her organs and tissue. She is a unique case – almost everything has been spared. But she's crashed twice now, and if it happens again we'll lose everything.'

I look at the nurse, stricken. 'Actually, I –'

'It could save the lives of seven people, at least.'

I'm in the ICU. I'm in the Inn. I'm cuddled next to an unconscious Neve. I'm under a butterfly quilt. I'm between a lover's legs. I'm in the theatre. I'm at the bottom of the ocean.

The nurse looks to Sylvie's broken body. 'There isn't much in this world that could make this kind of suffering worth it, is there?'

'No, there isn't.'

'So do you consent?'

I nod.

The nurse runs out to get paperwork, leaving me alone by the bed. I sit beside Sylvie and stroke her wrist.

I do not know what I have just done, but I don't care. I do know that someone, somewhere will benefit from this. I suspect the Sylvie I met last night would want that.

There is a sharp rap on the door, and I look up.

It is Reg, and a police officer whose face I know quite intimately from across a laden table.

'Frances Kocsmáros. I'm surprised to see you here.' Reg frowns, flashing a look of warning in my direction. 'This is Senior Constable Paul Jacobs.'

Paul gives no indication he recognises me, or the tragic shell of Sylvie in the bed.

'Ms Kocsmáros, do you know this woman?'

'Well, I . . .'

'I'd be interested to speak to you. Let's step outside.'

The Book of Mary 8:1

Dog waits outside the hospital while I go in to do a wee.

We've been here since 7.30 am, waiting for them.

He is hungry. So am I.

But we aren't invited, not tonight.

In the bathroom mirror I pull out the gift Sylvie chose. The one I took from her body after I laid my hands upon it. Before the couple came with their stupid dachshund and that lady vomited by the tree.

A tiny sleeper, sterling silver. Engraved with the smallest writing.

to be born is to die is to be born

I slip it into my own ear, and nod up towards the fifth floor.

The Gospel According to Frances 15:4

I follow Paul into the corridor of the ICU, baffled.

'How are you, after last night?' I ask him. 'This is so upsetting, isn't it?'

He looks at me like I have slapped him, then stares doggedly at his notes.

'CCTV footage places you at the scene of this woman's assault last night. Are you known to her?'

I gape at him. Is he suggesting I was *involved?*

'I'm known to her in the same way you are,' I say.

'What do you mean?'

'The park . . . ? You were there last night, too.'

He stares at me, incredulous. Like he cannot believe what has come out of my mouth.

'Are you insinuating you stalked a patrolling police officer, Ms Kocsmáros?'

'No! No, we went to the Inn . . . We sat with everyone, with Sylvie. Remember?'

He does not remember. He does not see anything in front of him but a psychopathic criminal. I have to salvage this.

'I'm mistaken, clearly. I was in the park looking for my foster kid, who is pregnant. I found her, but I couldn't convince her to come back, so I drove home.'

'Foster kid?'

'That's right – Mary. Ask Reg. He set it up.'

'And how do you know Sylvia Rathdowne?'

They've formally identified her, then.

'I met her last night. She was sleeping there, in the park. I have an employment history with Eternal Fire; I know how to speak with streeties, know how to work out if people need extra help.'

'And did you see anything suspicious, in your expert "streetie" opinion?'

God, this guy is a cunt.

'No. Everyone seemed calm. It was a warmish night. Nothing strange went on at all.'

He looks at me dead in the eye, and nods, seemingly satisfied. 'That's all for now, Ms Kocsmáros. I'll corroborate with the Reverend.'

I peer back into the room, and enter. Reg is praying over Sylvie's body.

'Heavenly Father, thank you for the life of your daughter, ah . . . Sylvia. Bless her spirit, let her enter into eternal life, let her sins be forgiven as she comes to the gates of paradise. In Jesus' name, Amen.'

I watch him lay hands.

'Did you know her, Reg?'

'Not really. Saw her around a bit. Battered girlfriend situation, I think. Drugs.'

I exhale.

Paul re-enters, holding up a photograph on his phone. He shows it to both Reg and me.

It is Celine. Anouk, yes, but ultimately it is Celine. Her profile page, from Spice Den.

'Have either of you ever come across this woman, Anouk Neilson? She goes by Celine Riot when operating as a sex worker.'

I stare at the page. So does Reg. We both shake our heads.

Transcript of interview between Anouk Neilson and Senior Constable Paul Jacobs, 25 August 2022

Snr Constable Jacobs: *Thanks for speaking with me, I wanted to ask you some questions about last night and this morning.*

Miss Neilson: *Sure.*

Snr Constable Jacobs: *You and two people connected to you have been seen on CCTV footage as present around the scene of Sylvia Rathdowne's murder at 6.45 am at New Farm Park. Can you please explain what you were doing there at that time?*

Miss Neilson: *Sure. When I returned home, I was informed by the nurse and carer who works with us that my partner – um, Glenda: Glenda Lui – that she was missing. He had fallen asleep, which is fine, it's part of his night shift, but he didn't realise she had let herself out.*

Snr Constable Jacobs: *And Glenda needs a carer because . . .?*

Miss Neilson: *She has early-onset Alzheimer's.*

Snr Constable Jacobs: *And you were out with friends?*

Miss Neilson: *I was at work.*

Snr Constable Jacobs: *What's your occupation?*

Miss Neilson: *I'm a residential support worker.*

Snr Constable Jacobs: *Like Peter?*

Miss Neilson: *Kind of, yeah. Except no-one pays you to take care of your own wife, do they? We work in different parts of the NDIS.*

Snr Constable Jacobs: *Can you provide any substantial evidence for this alibi?*

Miss Neilson: *Alibi?*

Snr Constable Jacobs: *Can you?*

Miss Neilson: *Absolutely.*

Snr Constable Jacobs: *Right. And when did you realise she was missing?*

Miss Neilson: *It was maybe 4 am. We went out searching. We live about a kilometre from the park. We found her about 6.30.*

Snr Constable Jacobs: 6.45 *am, I think, yeah. And could she tell you anything about where she'd been?*

Miss Neilson: *She was agitated – angry at us for interrupting her. She thought she'd been to a dinner with new friends. A night in a hotel or something. She described it in great detail. It might have been an old memory.*

Snr Constable Jacobs: *And when you say agitated, do you think there's a chance Glenda could be violent? Especially if confused?*

Miss Neilson: *Not . . . like that. Not if left alone.*

Snr Constable Jacobs: *What if she wasn't left alone?*

Miss Neilson: *I just don't know. Not Glenda, as I know her. She just wants to live with the memories she has. She is very accomplished, very respected.*

Snr Constable Jacobs: *But Alzheimer's means she isn't really Glenda anymore, is she?*

Miss Neilson: *I don't think that's true at all.*

Snr Constable Jacobs: *This morning, did you come into contact with this person at all?*

[Shows driver's licence image of Frances Kocsmáros.]

Miss Neilson: *I did not.*

Snr Constable Jacobs: *Have you ever seen her before?*

Miss Neilson: *No, I have not.*

Snr Constable Jacobs: *That's all for today.*

Text messages between Cressida Charalambous and Frances Kocsmáros, 25 August 2022, 5.04 pm

Cress: *Fran, are you coming in on Saturday night? I'm a staff member down for the matinee and night show. I just wanted to make sure after last night. I'm keen to keep you on but Charlie is on my back to make sure staff are fully committed.*
Frances: *I'm in.*
Cress: *Everything is all good at home?*
Frances: *Everything is fine. I can work.*
Cress: *Amazing, I'll lock you in.*
Frances: *As usher?*
Cress: *On it.*

The Gospel According to Frances 16:1

I finally go downstairs for a meal. There is no food left except old sushi or an almond croissant. I decide on the croissant, because fuck it – I'm a haggard mess of a woman right now and I need butter, not salmonella.

I pick at the pastry as I walk back to the children's ward, my body like lead. It's been almost an hour. Soon I will hold my sleepy, portacath-ed child, ready for months of chemotherapy. We'll have jelly, and I'll sing her to sleep. Then I will do the hardest thing yet in this godforsaken day, and walk out of the hospital alone.

I start to cry just thinking about it. The tears come smoothly, freely, like a sun shower. I cry for Neve, and for Sylvie and for Mary, and I cry at the maternity sign, because I never wanted only one child, and I cry at the lift, because a man is in there holding flowers, and I cry at the paeds entrance, because they've tried so hard to make it look safe, a tiny teddy at the window, welcoming the dying young.

As I enter the ward I sense a heightened, frantic energy. People are calling, running, whispering. I flinch – I know that shift in mood. Something has happened. Someone's child is the reason that nurse no longer wears a poker face. It does not occur to me that it could be my own until I see Lucas sprinting towards me, stricken.

'Why haven't you picked up your phone?'

'What? I've been here – it's only been fifty minutes. What's happened? Has she – has she?'

I find myself clinging to him, already hysterical, the scream sitting on the edge of my throat. *You left for fifty minutes, Frances, you did this, you did this –*

'She's alive, but unstable. They're keeping her sedated. Something happened in the surgery.'

A young registrar we don't know is running towards us now, and she ushers us into an empty room.

'You are the parents of Neve, yes? Okay. Sorry just grabbing up the notes – so there's been a complication. The team noticed Neve's vitals were shifting during the insertion, and we are concerned she has gone into fulminant liver failure.'

I'm desperately confused.

'But this was a simple procedure that she has had before, they weren't supposed to *touch* her liver.'

'There is a small chance she has received a paracetamol overdose. Anaesthetists give children paracetamol intravenously during surgery, but the levels can tip very unexpectedly into poisoning in weakened bodies, especially weakened livers. We are still waiting on toxicity levels to see the damage, but I need you both to tell me – have you given Neve paracetamol in the last twelve hours?'

Lucas looks straight to me, murderous. 'She hasn't been in my care.'

I cry out to defend myself, and stop. I remember what I did, the gamble I took, the writhing moan of the young child. There is nothing left to be said before the room that holds me spins like a gravitron into a black blur.

She was in so much pain –

Electronic medical record transcript: Brisbane University Hospital

Harkin, Neve DOB:15/11/2017 UR:BU1578790

1645. 25/8/2022. Dr Smith. General Surgeon
General anaesthetic and attempted portacath insertion via open cut-down technique.
Unanticipated amount of bleeding from surgical bed. Intra-operative TEG showing gross coagulopathy.
Patient haemodynamically unstable: decision made to abandon procedure and transfer patient to PICU still intubated.

1900. 25/8/2022. Dr Jones. PICU consultant
Liver function tests have revealed transaminitis in the thousands.
1g of paracetamol given 4 x 5 days leading up to surgery.
Parents unaware of paediatric dosing guidelines. Anaesthetics unaware of pre-operative dosing – further IV paracetamol given intra-operatively.

Impression: Acute liver failure due to the suspected paracetamol overdose. Hepatic reserve already compromised in setting of hepatoblastoma.

Plan: Keep intubated and sedated. Consult to hepatology.

0230. 26/8/2022. Dr Adams. Paediatric Hepatologist
Transaminitis now in the tens of thousands.

Liver is not salvageable. I have placed patient as an urgent candidate on Australian organ transplant list. Extremely guarded prognosis if liver does not become available in 48 hours.

I assume Lucas is staying in the recliner in her ward room. He didn't stick around to see me recover. The nurses laid me down on a spare bed, forced a hot tea into my hands. I have not moved in four hours.

It happens more than you think, the surgeons said. *It isn't necessarily anyone's fault, some bodies can handle more paracetamol, some can't. If she hadn't had the cancer, hadn't been fasting . . .*

But it is someone's fault – it is mine. The guilt is a hand against my throat, pressing harder with every passing minute.

She is in a critical condition now. They have suggested we may only have seventy-two hours. *Seventy-two hours.* I thought this only happened to people who intentionally tried to overdose, hoping for a painless exit, perhaps unaware of the agonising death the medicine causes. Not by *accident.* Not in *love.* Not by the one person who would die in the place of that child.

I have not been able to call my parents. I have not been able to look at my phone. I do not sleep. I simply listen to the hospital's ticking clock, knowing it will eventually pull me by my strangled neck to her PICU bed.

I hear movement in the room, a nurse perhaps. Someone shuffling, rearranging things. I squeeze my eyes shut, unwilling to interact. They come closer, aware of me. I notice the rhythm of their gait is slightly off. Like they have four legs, not two. Strangely, the thought makes me relax.

Something jumps onto my bed, licks my exposed hand. Something lays down upon my bent legs and exhales its full weight onto my anxiety. An anchor tethering me to the ground, lest I float away. There is the smell of jasmine, and the sound of waves washing gently upon a beach.

Crash . . . crash . . . crash . . .

CRASH.

There is a sudden hit of air and I start in shock as the room's door opens quickly.

Lucas stands in front of me, panting for breath.

There is no animal on my bed.

'They did it.'

'What?'

'Frances. *Frances*. They have a match. They have part of a liver. For us. For her. We got triaged, prioritised. I have signed the paperwork on our behalf, I decided to accept the conditions of it.'

'What conditions?'

'Nothing important. The donor was an IV drug user, but the organs aren't affected they said. They'll give part of the liver to an adult, and a smaller part to Neve.'

Part of my brain registers what this could mean, what atrocious breach of Hippocratic law I might have committed, but the mother within me rips out that question with her teeth.

Your child before your conscience.

'Do you think it is safe?'

'They say it is safe. It's a miracle, it's a miracle. They are removing all of her cancer.'

The world slows, and now I am standing, holding Lucas's shirt like he himself is Neve, burying myself in the possibilities. The hand around my throat releases, and I take a single breath.

A future, a future, a future.

Organ Transplant notes – Hepatology Unit, 26 August 2022, 4.06 am

Donor: Sylvia Rathdowne
Signed by Next of Kin: Frances Kocsmáros
IVDU but bloods tested negative for Hep B, Heb C and HIV.
No updated information on patient connection to recipient at this stage.
Sign off from Queensland Police regarding criminal investigation, injury and autopsy.
Due to critical condition of recipient, choice was made to prioritise transplant.

Recipient 1: Neve Harkin
Signed by Parent/Guardian: Lucas Harkin
Fulminant liver failure after paracetamol overdose + hepatoblastoma.
Oncologist Dr Simon Yates was informed that a liver had been found.

Partial liver transplant from adult to child, surgery began 3.05 am.

The Gospel According to Frances 16:3

They keep Neve sedated. Lucas and I are not scrubbed up, so we do not get to hold her or whisper to her before she enters the theatre for the ten-hour operation. We view her through a window, our fingers pressed against the glass, willing our love to permeate.

Lucas does not engage with my guilt or attempt to relieve it. He bows his head on the seat beside me in her room, and simply prays.

'Heavenly Father, heal her body, bless the hands of the surgeons, thank you for this miracle –'

He glances at me, as if to question why I haven't bowed my head too.

Beside Neve's bed is the coin, and I reach for it, turning it over in my hands.

to cure is to kill is to cure

I think about Neve's pain. I think about Sylvie, about her mother – wherever she is. I think about the parents in this hospital keening over empty beds where their babies used to be.

'Why did we get the miracle?' I ask. 'What sets us apart?'

Lucas looks up, shocked that I have spoken those words aloud, amazed that he has a chance to *preach* to me.

'The prayers of a faithful church. We petitioned God. Prayer works, Frances. You know this.'

'What about the person who died? Doesn't God care about them?'

'Depends if they were a believer.' He says it with absolute sincerity.

I turn the coin over in my hand, remembering the Table, the Inn, and Sylvie's wedding dress with its long white veil. The way her eyes softened in the glow of the garden.

'I guess that depends how you define believer.'

He forces a smile for me. 'You don't need to fear death if you're going to heaven, Frances.'

'Then why do you pray for Neve to be healed?'

He looks down at his hands. I realise he's still wearing his fucking wedding ring – another crown of thorns, this one in white gold. *What a martyr.*

'Because she's my child. And I'm selfish. I want her to stay here longer.'

It's the first honest thing I've heard come out of his mouth in years. I lean in and take his hand in my own. 'Okay,' I say softly. 'Let's pray.'

We bow our heads, and I hold the Inn firmly in my mind, looking for the words I willingly forgot.

'God, if you're there –'

Script for the final sermon of Frances Harkin, 28 February 2020

This was supposed to be a sermon about Job. I told Pastor Reg and my husband, Lucas, it was a sermon about Job. I'm sorry to say it has turned out a little differently. I hope you can hold me in my preaching today. (** *Do I say sorry? Am I sorry?*)

In 2018, the two-year-old daughter of a very well known American pastor died in her sleep. Her parents were bereft. The grief response from the wider international community that knew of this mega-church was immediate denial. *We will pray for resurrection. We will believe, fast, petition.* So for three days that child lay in the morgue, and hundreds of thousands of people publicly prayed, believing she would be raised from the dead. They prayed all day and all night for a week. There were round-the-clock gatherings, huge events in her honour around the world. She continued to lie in the morgue. Eventually, the family were told she needed to be buried or cremated, that the morgue would preserve the girl's body no longer. She was not resurrected.

You would think the disappointment and deflation of that event would offer enough cognitive dissonance to help some of us Christians engage with the reality of tragedy. Instead, it kind of made it worse. The pandemic happened soon after, and a lot of people in our communities leaned into spiritualism further – denying science, prophesying political events that never came to pass, accepting conspiracies, and relying solely on 'the power of the spirit'. (** *Some may walk out here or heckle – just ad lib if so about respecting body autonomy.*)

I prayed for that little girl to be resurrected. Fervently. I wanted to see God perform the miracles everyone talked about, the miracles I fully believed in. I knew two-year-olds shouldn't just die in their sleep. The injustice did not align with my understanding of His character.

We all know the story of Job, whose faith is tested by God sending him trials. Parts of his life are destroyed one by one – he loses his property, his children die, his body is afflicted with physical agony. His wife suggests he curse God and die. His friends gather around him, accusing him of transgression, before the Lord Himself appears and says 'Don't you know how powerful I am? You understand nothing.' Job gets his wealth and health back. He has ten more kids. But he doesn't get the other children back, the ones killed in the name of faith. And that is how we know a mother did not write this particular book of the Bible.

I prayed for resurrection because I longed for more of a triumphant narrative arc than that from the one true God. Would you really crush someone, simply because you can? Would you allow a man's life to be destroyed in order to prove that he loves you? Would you take a two-year-old, to show how many people would believe for something you never had any intention of doing?

When the child was finally accepted to have died, I comforted myself the same way everyone else did: 'God is powerful. God knows what He is doing. She is with God now, anyway. Safe, healed, eternally held. I cannot possibly understand the mystery until I get to heaven.'

Over the last ten years I have prayed for many people's tragic circumstances with full belief in a miracle. I have told them their marriages would be restored. I have told them they would be delivered from the spirit of homosexuality. I have told them their cancer would be healed. That their bipolar disorder would be prayed away. I am sorry if any of you have received that kind of counsel from me. It was so easy to pray. So easy to see suffering as a way of getting closer to God's miraculous power. So easy to assert power with that kind of claim. Nothing can touch you. Until, of course, it does.

If you had told me my two-year-old would get sick, I would have told you that I couldn't wait to see God perform the miracle of healing her. But she is sick, now. Really sick. And when we found out that news a few weeks ago, I did not react that way at all.

I woke up, when they told me. I knew, right down to my bones, that my faith did not include praying for my daughter to be healed. Not because I didn't want her to survive. Not because I didn't believe in God. I just knew that wasn't how it was going to work. I knew I had to grow up in my faith, immediately. I had to learn how to hold someone in their suffering, without denying its existence. I saw the pain in her, pain that no performative prayer could cure but which the loving arms of a mother could actually soothe. I saw how I needed to advocate, how I needed to protect, how I needed to find the right treatment. I felt repulsed by the idea of dishonouring her suffering by assuming God would remove it. She needed me to suffer with her. She needed me to find a way to physically heal her within the realms of medical research. She needed the comfort of reality.

I still believe in God. I believe in His love for me, for Lucas, for Neve. His joy in our marriage and family. I believe He knows, and He cares. I believe in goodness, in hope, in eternity. I still believe Jesus rose from the dead for me, but I do not believe Neve will.

I know that grief makes us desperate. I also know that in the gift of suffering, miracles don't fit in so well. The exclusivity of salvation doesn't fit in so well. The rules don't fit in so well. The question is more important than the answer. The mystery is more sacred than what I can see.

I am preaching my faith to you today, not my lack of it. I know this is challenging for some of you. Many will disagree with me. But I want you to know that since I've stopped asking God to perform the impossible for me, I'm seeing Him in every possibility.

I'm seeing Him in the night sky. I'm seeing Him in the gift of waking up in the morning. I'm seeing Him in the furrowed brow of my husband as he makes me tea in the morning, even when he doesn't feel like it. I'm seeing Him in the mission, at the soup truck. I'm seeing Him giggling at the bus stop, in tears at the playground, and holding hands on a first date. I'm seeing Him in my daughter's tiny, hurting body. I'm so much more aware of Him, now that He doesn't have to be anything but what is real. Now that the miracle is what He has already given me, not what I am waiting on. And there is great healing in that.

The Book of Mary 8:2

Dog's ears prick to the wind. Listening, listening, listening.

Hearing something, he begins to trot down the street and, as always, I follow. We leave the hospital and traipse into the suburbs. Right, then left, then straight.

Fucking hell, my ankles are swollen. I wish we could hail a cab. I wish I had better shoes. I'd give him a kick with them.

Dog turns back once to growl at me.

'You love me, little fucker.'

He falls back and we walk, side by side, into the dawn.

The Gospel According to Frances 17:1

At 7 am, a nurse advises us that everything is going beautifully. Lucas has been on his phone, and I have been dozing on Neve's empty bed. The silence between us has never been so peaceful.

The nurse tells us kindly to go home, sleep and eat, to return at 1 pm when the surgery is due to finish.

'If there are any complications, we will call you both immediately.'

I'm relieved, in a way. I know the surgery will work. I know the Innkeepers have somehow, *somehow* gifted me her cure. I know it so deeply I can walk out of the hospital without looking back. I will sleep in the smell of her at home, and then I will come back and hold her healthy, healing body. There will be no more cancer left when I see Neve next. It will be gone. It will be over.

I nod to Lucas as we both prepare to leave. 'See you this afternoon.'

He nods back, and gives me a gentle smile as he looks at the light coming in through the window. 'Never have I been so relieved to see the coming of a new day.'

Perhaps they have transplanted the cancer between us, too?

I walk to my car in the patchwork light of the exit signs. I drive through the busy morning traffic. As I pass New Farm Park I shudder, memories of police crawling back into my brain. Sylvie did not give the gift of life freely; it was violently taken by someone. She dances in my mind, a welcome but muted ghost. A locked vault of story, aching to be told.

Sylvie was killed, and because of this, my child will live. I lied about my authority over Sylvie's body, and because of this mindless impulse, Neve's body persists. I push down the ethical shitstorm brewing inside of me. I did not *harm* Sylvie. I was simply the only person present able to identify her. Before they ran her fingerprints

I was the only person they could find who had ever *met* her. But does that really make a difference?

to cure is to kill is to cure

Tragedy must be met with the defiant cultivation of life. I have chosen to cultivate life.

Email from Lucas Harkin to his lawyers, 26 August 2022, 8.08 am

Dear Jeremy,

After the events of the last twelve hours, I would like to move forward with the domestic violence order (I've flagged this with the police and begun the paperwork). I would like to confirm that I will take immediate custody of Neve from the moment the statement is signed.

Am I right in thinking Frances would have to get an urgent court request to turn that around? What happens if she contests it?

Please see my attached outline of events for the DVO. There is evidence to suggest Frances overdosed Neve, poisoning her.

She also has been somehow connected to the organ donor, but police have not clarified details with me.

I am very concerned about her capacity to injure Neve and will fight to have her protected.

Regards,
Lucas

The Gospel According to Frances 17:2

I pull into my driveway, buoyant – perhaps too much so? The kind of elation that teeters on the edge of anxiety, makes you feel the manic balloon will burst at any moment. I don't know how I'll sleep with this much light in the house; this much light bursting out of my body.

I skip through to the kitchen, and drop my bag.

I check my phone again, just in case the hospital has called and I have missed it. Nothing. Blissful, benign nothingness. Healing.

I go to Neve's room, ready to soak in the evidence of her life. No matter where we end up living, we will be living there together. I bury my face in the butterfly quilt, and smell a hope I have never let myself believe in before this moment.

Notes from Senior Constable Paul Jacobs to Detective Devi Ramineni, 26 August 2022

Hi Detective Ramineni,

Please see my notes below.

If you would like any further information, don't hesitate to contact me. I'm quite interested in advancing into this field in the next stage of my career.

Senior Constable Paul Jacobs

> Interviewed Frances Kocsmáros at Brisbane University Hospital, where she was discovered at the bedside of heroin addict Sylvia Rathdowne (formally identified using her fingerprints and criminal record). Frances claimed to have only met the deceased the night before, and that she is a guardian for another young woman. Rev. Reg Holland confirmed she used to work for the Eternal Fire mission and is currently in their employ on a volunteer basis, living in church accommodation.
>
> Later, a nurse informed me that Sylvia Rathdowne's organs were to be donated, and that the hospital had obtained the consent of her next of kin. Upon looking at the paperwork previously signed off on by Queensland Police, I saw the next of kin was listed as Frances Kocsmáros.
>
> In a concerning twist, part of one of Sylvia Rathdowne's organs (her liver) has been offered as a match for the terminally ill child of Frances Kocsmáros, Neve Harkin. This is an extremely serious conflict of interest, one the transplant team generally works hard to avoid. In addition, Lucas Harkin has requested a DVO due to accusations that Frances Kocsmáros is an abusive and negligent parent, and poisoned the child, prioritising her for a liver transplant.

As Sylvie's heart, lungs and other section of liver had already been donated to other patients, we were unable to withdraw the consent. We were also unable to halt the procedure upon Neve Harkin, as interruption would potentially kill the child.

However, I believe this information suggests multiple levels of deception, and a clear motive for murder.

The Gospel According to Frances 17:3

I sleep for an hour, at most. At midday I can't bear it anymore, I don't want to wait for the phone call. I hurriedly pack a few more things for Neve – some toys, the butterfly quilt. On the way to the car I grab a few sprigs of jasmine from the neighbour's cascading bush of it.

As I drive, I pray soft poems of thanks. To God, to the Innkeepers, to Mary, to whomever will accept them.

Thank you for the sky, thank you for the road, thank you for breakfast, thank you for hands, thank you for my heart, to feel this gratitude at all.

Whoever is there – whoever orchestrated *this* – it feels as though they are somehow on my side. And I don't have many people on my side.

It reminds me of when I first met God, so young and fresh and vulnerable at the age of twenty-one. It was always about wonder and relationship, then. I met Jesus, fell in love, decided to commit. But after a few years I felt catfished. As if the person who gave me that wonder never existed at all, and was just a mask for a bunch of desperate men, setting a trap to appease their desire for control.

I made so many decisions attempting to get that wonder back, as if it were being withheld from me until I fulfilled the true picture of a Christian woman. I married Lucas. I quit my arts degree and swapped to theology. I made only Christian friends. I fasted, I studied, I served, I gave away. I changed my political views to fit with the religious rhetoric. I had a child. But the wonder never returned. Not in the same way. Not until now.

Driving into the hospital car park I find myself still whispering thanks. There is a missed call on my phone from the hospital, but I know what the voice message will say. The surgery is complete, and my child is in recovery, ready for the first day of the rest of her life.

Paediatric intensive care nurse June Laidlaw's Obs: Neve Harkin – PICU recovery ward, 26 August 2022

1.08 pm
Temperature: 36.7
Oxygen sat: 97%
Heart rate: 90
Respiratory rate: 25
Blood pressure: 90/61
Notes: Obs in normal ranges. Patient sleeps peacefully

The Gospel According to Frances 18:1

I walk up to the security doors of the hospital. The security guard is a tall man wearing a uniform and a face mask. He looks tired.

'Name?'

'Frances Kocsmáros. I'm here to see my child, Neve Harkin, who is a patient in the PICU.'

His body tenses, as if in alarm. 'You haven't received a call from the hospital or the police?'

'Uh, the police? No.'

'I'm under specific instructions not to let you enter the building.'

The earth tremors.

My chest is erupting, spilling lava.

He makes a quick phone call upstairs, eyes on me as I begin to unravel, clutching the butterfly quilt like a shield.

'Yeah, she's here. Doesn't know about it. What do I –?' He listens, hangs up.

'Let me in to see my child.'

'Ma'am, I'm really sorry, but I can't.'

I arc up, magma on fire. I am every animal that ever had young. Every curlew, crying out.

'Let me in to see my child.'

'That's not possible.'

'Why not?'

'You aren't allowed within one hundred metres of the ward. There's a restraining order, and you are under investigation.'

I go utterly still, the shock settling over me like cement.

'In fact,' he continues awkwardly, 'I need to ask you to leave.'

I don't move.

He touches my arm, shuffling me towards the car park, the quilt trailing against the cement. He is gentle, apologetic.

'Which is your car?'

I cannot speak. He places me on a plastic seat next to the pay machine, as if to wait out a bad trip.

'Will you be okay here?' He fidgets, stricken. 'Call your lawyer, yeah? You can contest these things. Get 'em overturned really easily if they're not true. It's not the end of the world.'

But it is. He is clueless. This is the end of everything.

Letter from Lucas Harkin's lawyer to Frances Kocsmáros's lawyer, 26 August 2022

Dear Ms Ramke,

My client Mr Harkin seeks to advise that he is serving Ms Kocsmáros with a no notice, no contact domestic violence order, effective immediately. As you will see in the attached document, the return court hearing is in two months' time. Neve Harkin is also included as a respondent in this DVO, with the conditions of safe contact from the assailment to be determined in court after the adjournment period.

Lucas Harkin will be taking sole care of Neve Harkin from this date, indefinitely, to maintain the health and safety of the child in her vulnerable state. We will not be discussing the arrangements until we are before a Family Court judge.

This will be enforced by Queensland Police and any breach of this order is a criminal offence.

Regards,
Jeremy Harold

Wedding vows of Lucas and Frances Harkin, 2 July 2012

Minister: Lucas and Frances have decided to write their own vows, in addition to the traditional vows professed in Christian marriages. Lucas will share his first.

Lucas: Frances Irén, my beautiful bride. Words can hardly express what you mean to me, what you offer me, what I dream of when I think of our life together. You are the most alive person I have ever met. You make me a better man. It is an honour to make these vows to you.

I vow, my bride, to ensure every single day feels as good as this one. I vow to write you letters, because I know how much you love them. I vow to keep the tea hot and the beer cold. I vow to love you more than I love myself. I vow to be the first to apologise, every time. I vow to lead you by following you. I vow to take care of you, always, in all things. I vow to raise our children to love and honour you, always. I vow to put Jesus in the centre of this marriage. I vow to pray, to fast, to surrender. I vow to give you all of myself, until death.

Minister: Frances.

Frances: Lucas Joseph, my beloved, and my best friend. They think we are young fools, and they might be right – but even the gospel is foolishness to those who don't believe it. All I know is that this is the first day of the rest of my life, and I want the rest of my life to feel like this. My love, I have written vows – but they are just the beginning. I vow to make as many more as I can write.

First, I vow to accept you entirely as you are. I vow to love every version of you as you change and grow. I vow to give you my hand in marriage, in help, in comfort and in connection. I am yours. I vow to make decisions for us as one, not as two individuals.

I vow to see the image of God in you forever, no matter what is said or done. I vow to stand before God one day, and present my marriage as my proudest achievement in love and service. I vow to walk with gratitude through the ups and downs of life, holding your hand. I vow to see love as a choice I make daily, and I vow to always, forever, choose you.

The Gospel According to Frances 18:2

I am still catatonic on the plastic seat in the car park. People have come and gone throughout the hour. I don't know who I am waiting for. Lucas? Reg? A nurse?

I do not know how my child is. I do not know where my child is. I do not know what I am supposed to do. If I could move, I would call my lawyer. The security guard was not wrong; there are options. But I am currently very small, and these options are on the highest shelf of possibility for me in this moment. I cannot reach that far.

I close my eyes. It has been hours now. Hours of a new liver for my child. Hours of her wondering where I am. The butterfly quilt lies limp, dragged in the dirt of a public hospital. The flower I picked is wilting.

I breathe into my own stillness, trying to block the sounds of cars screeching on the shiny cement of the car park. The light shifts against my eyelids, and I am suddenly hit with a heady floral perfume.

Fucking *jasmine*.

Email from Detective Devi Ramineni to Reverend Reg Holland, 26 August 2022

Hi Reverend Holland,

My name is Detective Devi Ramineni, and I'm investigating the death of Sylvia Rathdowne, who I understand may have been a patron of your mission on occasion.

One person of interest to us is an employee/volunteer of yours, Frances Kocsmáros. Is it correct she is currently a residential carer for a minor patron? We are investigating her involvement in Sylvia's life, and would like to speak to you as soon as possible.

In addition, I would inquire seriously into the welfare of the young person currently in her care (Mary?) and relocate the child immediately.

Thank you.

With regards,
Detective Devi Ramineni

The Gospel According to Frances 18:3

I open my eyes to a peach-lit room, warm and clean. It's like the foyer of a spa – there are pot plants, candles and steaming jugs of tea. I am on a long velvet couch, wrapped in a *robe*. I flinch at the indulgence of it. I want to be wearing a sackcloth and ashes, I wanted to be cold and broken and hungry and bleeding, I want to be dea—

'Frances?'

A hunched older woman in a soft apron walks out holding a towel. She's strangely familiar – something about the curve of her neck. She beckons to me to follow her, and we walk in silence through the foyer to a pair of sliding doors where, in reality, there is usually a lift. They open as a lift might, except behind the doors there is no boxy compartment.

A breeze, a blue glow, and the unmistakable sound of soft waves stretching themselves upon a shore. There is white sand beneath my toes, and a natural beach the size of a large swimming pool. A rock cave arches around it, and steam rises off the clear water – a hot spring. Sunlight pours through fissures in the cave's roof, dancing through the water and projecting soothing patterns onto the rough rock walls.

The woman hands me the towel and gestures to the spring.

'What am I supposed to do?' I ask, entirely at a loss.

'Rest, now.'

She bows her head, and exits back through the lift.

I am entirely alone in the cave. The water is deep, but the sand is clearly visible at the bottom. The smell of lavender wafts from its surface. I check beneath my robe and discover I'm wearing my swimmers. I didn't even know I still owned them.

I am beyond tired, beyond traumatised. I have no instinct now but to do as I am told.

The hot water provides immediate regulation. I am submerged to my neck, and every sense is washed clean. Every thought feels soaked and sanitised. I don't forget what has happened, but I can hold the events at a distance. *You need to work out how to access justice. To access healing. To access your child.*

I float, letting my hair splay like an anemone. I am weightless, where I have been heavy; I am soft, when all I have felt is hard. I drift on the tide of grief, the water absorbing every last urge for control that my body possesses. It is womb-like. Preparatory. A baby before birth, a bride before her wedding, an elder before death.

An hour later, when it is time to climb out, my mind has cleared a little, and my fingers are not even wrinkled. I wrap myself in the towel and begin to look for an exit.

The lift is closed, and the only other door opens to a series of steam rooms, saunas, showers and toilets built into rough-cut stone. In open lockers I see belongings: children's beach toys in one, folded fuchsia scrubs inside another. I keep going, moving through a dimly lit hallway of doors. There are names on some of them, and numbers on others.

At the end of the hallway, there is a door with my name on it.

I've given up resisting, so I walk through.

Inside is a beautiful bedroom. It has curtained windows, thick carpet, soft lamps. The large bed is covered in blankets, and finished with Neve's butterfly quilt. There is even my favourite tracksuit, folded neatly in a pile. On a tiny table beside the bed there is a bowl of broth.

I change into the tracksuit, barely registering what my body is doing. I drink the soup, letting the spices linger. I remember everything: Sylvie's death, the transplant, the withholding of my child. I do not disassociate, and I do not try to forget. But I hold the truth with temporary understanding, and then I carefully place it down. Even when it's over, it is not the end. I will hold Neve again.

I collapse onto the mattress, and for the first time in days I really, truly sleep.

The Word of Dog (Proverbs)

I roast the bones again before I boil them. Celery, carrot, a red onion. Bay leaves. Ginger, for warmth. Lemon, for alertness.
I let it simmer for seventeen years. I let it cool.
I have waited an eternity to feed you back that which you have lost.

They always say the holiest drink is wine. They are wrong.
It is milk from the breast of a desperate mother.
It is perfectly brewed tea.
It is water at midnight.
It is bone broth at the very bottom of the ocean.

Drink. Hold. Be held.

Messages from Ruairí Hickson to Frances Kocsmáros, 26 August 2022

Cress says you're back in tonight. Come see me. I have something for you. (3.06 pm)

It's the hour call, come in now? Otherwise after! (6.30 pm)

The Gospel According to Frances 19:1

I wake up in my car, overheated and panicked. The butterfly quilt lies across my lap. It's 6.35 pm. I have missed calls from Cress. I'm supposed to be at work, because I never told her, never explained the situation, never had a moment. I might be fired for this. Just another thing, another loss.

Where have I been? Another part of the Inn? This time it really does feel like a dream.

I check my phone to try to stop the questions escalating in my mind. People posting stupid recipes, selfies, reels of bad dancing with their roped-in spouses. Then I stop.

Eternal Fire has posted a 'testimony' picture on Instagram of Neve, still sedated in her bed in the PICU. My baby, ripped from my arms and placed into the hands of scrolling strangers. My fingers almost break the phone's screen. I want to climb into the photograph.

My hands grip the butterfly quilt instead. It is dirty, and even a little ripped on the edges. *Where have I been?* I squeeze it, pull at it, bury my face into it and scream.

FUCK

YOU.

When I lift my head, I feel the sudden cool of metal touching my left hand. I look down – tucked into the embroidery is a silver thimble. It is filled with fine white sand, and has tiny words engraved around its circumference:

to mend is to tear is to mend

Instagram post, 26 August 2022

@eternal_fire_qld
Description: A little girl, four years old, sleeps in her hospital bed in the PICU, tubes and cords connected to her. A soft toy bunny has been placed in her arms. Her father sits beside her, grinning.

Caption: *JESUS HEALS. Thank you for praying for Neve Harkin. God has performed the miracle we knew He would and given Neve a BRAND-NEW LIVER. Believe in your own healing, pray for those around you. God is good and He will do it, if you have faith enough to hope!*

Top comments:

@jesusandweightlifting *YES GOD. I claim this testimony in my own life!*

@livelaughlove78 *HE SUPERNATURALLY GAVE HER A NEW LIVER!*

@coffeeandtheword *He is faithful. Thank you, Jesus. What a great dad Pastor Lucas is, after so much hardship. Godly families are blessed generation upon generation.*

The Gospel According to Frances 19:2

I am an hour and forty-five minutes late for the shift. No make-up, and unwashed theatre blacks from the top of my washing pile, but I did manage a shower. I'm a mess, but I'm *here*, as I promised Cress I would be.

Cress eyes me with concern, probably still processing the frenzied phone call I made to her on the drive (*I can't explain it but I am going to come in and I am going to be late and I'm fine, I'm fine, but I will not look fine, and I might have to leave if I get a phone call mid-shift, but I really need this job, Cress, don't drop me yet, please* –), and offers me a mint.

'Honey, do you want to take five just to freshen up in the bathroom?'

The play has already started. The foyer is full of dirty glasses but is otherwise calm and clear. All we need to do is clean and prep for interval.

'Okay, yes. Sure.'

I take a breath in one of the bathroom stalls. I vomit once, twice. My head spins and then stabilises. *What are you doing here?*

I catch myself in the mirror as I exit, and note that I have aged a couple of years in the last few days. It has all snowballed so severely, my body hasn't had time to catch up.

Cress ducks her head in, face contorted with suspicion. 'What is actually going on?'

I look at her, unsure where to begin.

She picks up on the blockage. 'All you need to say is "Neve", and I will understand, Frances. I have kids too.'

Blessed matriarchs. I nod my head and mouth her name, the sound unable to meet the shape of the word.

Cress crosses her arms, as if accepting a mission. 'Is she all right?'

I nod again.

'So it's fuckface then, is it? Making your life hell?'

I don't know how she knows any of it. I've never disclosed my marital breakdown at work. As far as any staff or cast members know, I don't even have any children. But Cress is right – mothers know the hunched shoulders of other mothers. They implicitly understand things others simply do not see.

Cress cracks her neck once, in one direction, and then a second time in the other. Her eyes go grey, and her pupils narrow. I can see why she would be a good actor, now.

'Right. And he's a staff member of that church in the city, isn't he? The mega one, Eternal Fire.'

'Yeah,' I say, wanting to qualify or reduce it. 'But I –'

'Good.'

'Good?'

'Let's just say that the reverend and I have history.'

She checks her own make-up and slicked-back ponytail in the bathroom mirror.

'Do the shift, go visit that cute actor who keeps asking about you, and go to bed. Leave it with me. No woman needs this kind of shit. Especially not a mother.'

We walk out of the bathroom together and she disappears into the office with a formidable smirk.

I survey the foyer, then get to work.

Instagram post, 26 August 2022

@theatre_mama
Tagged: @eternal_fire_qld

Description: A photograph from 2004 of a Caucasian man (then aged 32) at a party at the Brisbane Arts Theatre. He is dressed as Scary Spice, in blackface.

Caption: *Hello, Theatre Kids, it's Theatre Mama back again. Today we have a blast from the past. Who knew that the Reverend Reg Holland from @eternal_fire_qld was a member of the theatre community back in the day? Or that he was dropped from* Much Ado About Nothing *for exposing his genitalia to those present in the women's dressing room? Or that he had a real interest in racial mockery of women of colour?*

This church gave money to the homophobic 'No' campaign during the Marriage Plebiscite. They literally paid for someone to write 'NO' across the sky.

If you are one of the many people who donate to this institution and support the apparent 'holy works' of this man and his congregation, I encourage you to reconsider where your money is going.

Donate to Indigenous and Black womxn, donate to sex workers, donate to the LGBTQI+ community, donate to women's shelters. Do not donate to Eternal Fire Christian Church.

Let's expose the men on this staff and get them out of leadership.

Theatre Mama xoxo

843 likes. 167 comments.

Top Comments:

@turbulenttheatreco *WTAF?*

@millierenoir *This is disgusting. I donated last Christmas during their yearly appeal – never again.*

@humptydumptydyke *I like this post better than all your other reviews put together.*

@ginathelma *TEAR THEM DOWN. DESTROY THE JOINT.*

@garymccosker89 fucking leftists have forgotten how to have fun.
@theatremama (reply to @garymccosker89) stick your limp white dick up your own arse Gary, see how much fun that is

The Gospel According to Frances 19:3

At interval, Cress asks that I take over ushering for the second act. After seating the audience I slip into the usher's chair and allow the darkness to drift over me like the water of a hot spring. I remember the beach cave and the bedroom. Another strange hallucination, or a secret comfort that I never knew existed?

Ruairí steps on stage in a wedding dress and veil. The audience laughs, before realising they aren't performing drag or comedy, but simply the role of a woman yet again.

Their voice projects out into the darkness:

'The first time he hurt me, I thought it brought us closer together.'

I realise I am gripping my pants, hands sweating profusely, waiting for the words I already know are coming. I know that dress. I have admired its lace and tulle, I've seen the way it fell on the tiny frame of the woman who wore it.

'The sixteenth time, I thought perhaps it was because he wanted me to hit back. Passion, you know. But that was never the point of hurting me. The point was always power. When I was high, there was nothing left to take. The power was entirely out of his reach. When I wasn't high, it was handed to him on a silver platter.'

They speak just like her. They have somehow found her essence. They breathe and pause like they have memorised footage.

'But there is something you find, in that place. It isn't some kind of meditative Zen thing. It isn't justice – fucking hell, I wish. It isn't the high or the reconciliation or whatever. It's knowing there's always a bit of you untouched. A bit that won't be addicted. A bit that won't be broken. A bit that can't ever be hurt.'

They smile at the audience, removing the veil.

'Sylvie, twenty-four years old, Brisbane.'

Letter from Eternal Fire pastors to the congregation of Eternal Fire Christian Church, 15 June 2017

Dear Eternal Fire congregants,

We felt in the current climate we needed to address the Same-Sex Marriage Plebiscite taking place in Australia, and our position on the vote.

As Scripture states, Christian marriage is between a man and a woman, to the exclusion of all others. Marriage between two people of the same sex, or between more than two people, is not within God's vision for the covenant that represents Jesus and the Church.

As Christians, we live in service and worship to Jesus. Marriage is worship – a sacrifice at times, and a discipline we revere and protect as a community.

While God loves all people, regardless of orientation, it is the position of this church to vote 'NO' in this plebiscite. We believe it is wrong to change an ancient tradition, and we believe in the religious freedom to only officiate weddings within our biblical value system.

To read more about our values and standards, please go to our website: www.eternalfirecc.com.au

Yours in Christ,
Senior Pastor Damien Rowling, Senior Pastor Reg Holland and Pastor Lucas Harkin

Cress asks no questions when I walk out of the show again, five minutes into the second half. She just hands me a tea towel and traipses in herself, a bit of a swagger in her step.

I dry champagne flutes and then move on to the white wine glasses.

An hour later the audience slowly trickles out into the humid night. I watch the foyer empty, one eye on the stage door for Ruairí. I have questions, but I don't know if I'm in the right headspace to ask them.

The other actors duck out, nodding in the direction of the bar then skipping off into the night, their hair out, make-up removed, bodies soft under tracksuits.

Ruairí exits last, showered and cooled down, red hair slicked back.

'Frances Kocsmáros. Fucking *finally*.'

I glance at Cress, stacking chairs in the corner. She releases me with a quick nod of the head.

'Do you want a drink?'

They ask so innocently. Like this is just a normal night, a normal shift. And it is, for them. They don't see me standing in the ruins of my life.

'Sure, Ruairí. A drink it is.'

They offer me their arm, and I loop my hand through nervously. I am not a mother, not tonight. I am not grieving. I am not in shock. I am not under investigation by police. I am not confronted by supernatural portals in the darkest moments of my life.

I'm a woman in her thirties, wearing zero make-up, who has just been asked out for a drink.

Ruairí and I sail out of there, and walk to the theatre's local, Stage Name. Stage Name offers alcohol, hot drinks, nachos and cake – entirely understanding the assignment of a post-show haunt for artists and audience alike. There is often live music, comedy and drag. We squeeze into a booth at the back, the light red and golden, a lamp on every table. They order a tea. Fuck. I was going to ask for whisky. I order a hot chocolate instead.

The drinks arrive promptly.

'So, Frances, tell me about the last ten years.'

I flinch. And I remember. *Tonight, I am whoever I choose to be.*

'No wait,' they say, grinning. 'Let me *guess.*'

I prod the marshmallow into the froth of my drink, and nod. 'Go right ahead.'

'Last I remember, you were training part-time with the Butoh program while at university. I reckon you got into a little dance company in, like, Berlin or something. You did a couple of major, hectic years in Europe doing body-specific, devised art practice, loved it. Then something really shit happened. Maybe an injury. Maybe you got your heart broken or you lost a visa. So you travelled to London, started working in something creative but less physical, like design maybe. Or as an agent's assistant. Or at the Natural History Museum. And you were poor as fuck but you ate really good food and went to incredible parties and met fascinating people. And you had other goals, so after a couple of years you came home.

'Maybe you had a partner or two, thought things might go further but they wanted dogs or kids and you weren't ready for settling down or compromising like that. Maybe you started running queer arts programs for at-risk youth. Then you began your PhD in something fierce, like the social acupuncture of feminist dance. Now, you live on your own in some exposed-brick apartment and write articles here and there for bougie arts publications and earn a bit of cash ushering theatre, which is a dormant love of yours since you spent first year at university doing amateur plays with your weird friend Ruairí.'

I smile at my handsome, bright-eyed date, the familiar stranger who only sees the person I should have been, not the person I chose to become.

I raise my mug to toast them in the hazy midnight light. 'You know, it's almost uncanny how close that is to the truth.'

Voice messages from Rosemary Kocsmáros to Frances Kocsmáros, 26 August 2022

'How did the portacath go darling? Did you start chemo?' (9.09 pm)

'Please call me back, I get worried. I'd love to come and bring Nevie some games. It's terribly hard on her.' (10.03 pm)

'I'll drop in tomorrow, yes? Your place or BUH?' (10.15 pm)

The Gospel According to Frances 19:5

Ruairí and I fuck in the surprisingly ornate bathroom at Stage Name. It's all tongues and fumbling hands until we're up against the wall tiles, shadows merging behind the sandalwood candle burning on the vanity. We're in the magic of mood lighting and memories, and we have nowhere else to be but entirely in this moment. They lift me up, their fingers learning and steering me easily, and they growl into my shoulder. They're so *energetic,* I'm so *sober.* It's wild and rhythmic; we move like we're dancing. I don't remember queer sex being like this, but I like it, I want it –

They pull off my shirt and step back for a moment, staring at me. *A mother's body, squashed and stretched, breasts that have been milked four hundred nights, now drooping in exhausted retirement –*

'You are fucking perfect, Fran.'

They kiss me, their hand entering me again, finding something honest within me, and I tremble with the intimacy of it.

'Do you need protection?' As soon as the words come out of my mouth I remember that I'm not in a brothel.

Ruairí pulls back abruptly. 'Um. What do you have in mind?'

I hold their chin in my hands with some added force, bite the side of their cheek gently. God, they're beautiful . . . 'Just keep going, ignore that I said that, I kind of forgot –'

Ruairí laughs, bites back. 'Forgot what? That I don't have a *dick,* Frances? Well, that is presumptuous, but lucky for us, I'm biologically structured to not get you pregnant and fuck up your wild and wonderful life with a kid.'

They kiss my nipples, move down to my thighs to lick and suck instead, but their words linger, poisoning whatever sweetness sits on our tongues.

My life *is* my kid. My entire world is my kid. There is no reality, no future, no Frances without her. Ruairí doesn't know about that wild and wonderful life.

My body has gone limp, cold and numb. Ruairí realises something is wrong. I can hear their voice asking kind questions, feel their body retreating out of respect, but all I can see is Neve clutching Peach in her hospital bed, looking up at me with love and trust as she is wheeled away forever.

The Book of Mary 9:1

We finally make it at midnight. My feet are raw, cut up by glass and gravel. I stand in the room that has carpet – instant relief.

God, there are so many *things* here. But things become very important when you cannot touch the person they represent, and worthless once you can. We'd all trade the things for the person. I guess.

I poke my belly with my finger. The baby sticks its leg out like a mini fuck-you.

Do I want to hold you the way she wants to hold her daughter?

I don't know.

Dog is rummaging in the kitchen and barks at me, but I don't go. I don't want food. I'm feeling grumpy, tired. A bit over being a holy vessel. Nobody asked me.

He trots in and finds me looking at little dolls and pictures. He tries to nuzzle and I push him off.

No it isn't hormones, you fuckin' animal. I'm sick of being used. I'm sick of taking care of people. I want someone to take care of me.

I look at the butterfly quilt. It's been dragged through mud or something.

Perfect, already soiled.

I know it's wrong, but I want to pretend, for a moment, that someone's made a bed up especially for me.

The Gospel According to Frances 19:6

Ruairí orders me an Uber and waits on the side of the road with me, their hand stroking the back of my arm. I'm mortified, for every possible reason. They don't ask for an explanation, don't offer any small talk. My hands won't stop shaking.

As the car pulls up they hug me awkwardly, then laugh. 'I almost forgot.' They produce from their backpack an old polaroid photograph: Ruairí and me, no older than eighteen, high as kites on a dance floor. Them with long red hair and a backwards cap. Me in overalls and face paint.

'I found it in my old stuff at Mum's. I thought it was amazing.'

'Yeah. It is.'

'See you at the theatre next week?'

'Yeah, yeah.'

I crawl into the back seat, clutching the evidence of our little selves, so innocent to the wider currents of living and dying and surviving.

I don't look back at my friend as the car moves off into the dark morning.

Email from Reverend Reg Holland to the Parish Council/Senior Leadership Team, 26 August 2022

Dear Team,

First, I want to apologise if the photograph released caused any distress. My past is imperfect, and in this PC world we must live in it is even more fallible. I believe ALL LIVES MATTER, and understand that the fancy dress depicted in that photograph is no longer considered appropriate. It is only by the grace of God I am saved. I claim no righteousness but His. I am but a sinner – and yet in Him, I am able to walk as a saint. I hope you will understand this was in a season of wandering, and that now, as your pastor, I operate according to a different moral code. The other accusations are lies and I will be publicly defending this persecution.

Obviously we are working hard this evening to remove the injurious social media post and its subsequent 'reposts' on multiple platforms, but it may not be possible. Please do not worry about our church financials or the upcoming appeal; the body of Christ is not so easily deceived, and God is our provider. I understand we've taken a few public hits recently, but the world is set on finding reasons to discredit the truth. Jesus' church will prevail.

'But we have this treasure in jars of clay, to show that the surpassing power belongs to God and not to us. We are afflicted in every way, but not crushed; perplexed, but not driven to despair; persecuted, but not forsaken; struck down, but not destroyed' (2 Cor 4:7–9).

Let's not forget the miracle that just took place in the lives of Lucas and Neve Harkin! Keep your eyes on Jesus!

Rev. Holland.

The Gospel According to Frances 20:1

I drag myself inside, preparing to throw my body under water. I drop my keys on the kitchen bench, turn to the hallway and freeze.

There is a light on in Neve's room. A light that was not on when I left.

I'm so feverish with fatigue and adrenaline that I grab a knife from the drawer and edge towards the ajar door, unsure what my body will do.

'Hello?'

There is no sound from within the room. I pull the door open with my foot, the glare from the lamps blinding me for the smallest moment before I take in the scene.

There are two small figures huddled beneath the butterfly quilt on Neve's bed – a pregnant teenager, and a dog. They stir, startled, as I stand over them with the knife.

The rest of Neve's bedroom is in a state of disarray, as if it has been searched. Toys, books, clothes are strewn everywhere. The pictures she has drawn are half-ripped off the walls.

'What the actual *fuck*, Mary?'

'Whoa, calm down.'

'GET OUT.'

I am trembling with something like anger or amphetamines.

How dare she.

Mary scrambles out from under the quilt, and Dog stands on the bed, tongue lolling from his mouth like a maniac.

'We didn't mean anything by it. I didn't know which bed was mine.'

I am so repulsed by her right now, and equally ashamed at my own repulsion.

'Her bedroom: it's –'

'It was Dog, he just went mental. I dunno why. I tried to stop him, I tried to –'

'You let a dog tear my daughter's room apart?'

'I'll just fix it.'

I'm agog at her stupidity.

'This can't just be *fixed,* you stupid little bitch. None of this can be fixed. Not Sylvie, not Neve, not Lucas. Not me.'

Mary trembles. She's no longer my Puck-like guide in the midst of magic. She's a kid. A fuck-up. A failure.

'You turn up here, try to move in, take me to a crime scene, and then *disappear.* I thought you had died. My child is actually . . .' I attempt to gather the words but give up. She doesn't deserve details. 'You think you can come back and sleep in my daughter's bed? Who the fuck do you think you are?'

Mary shrugs, eyes down and shoulders hunched.

'I'm no-one. I'm just trying to do my job. Trying to take care of this baby.'

'YOU HAVE NO JOB. THERE IS NO DIVINE MISSION, YOU IDIOT. YOU ARE PSYCHOTIC.'

'Wow, tell me what you really think, Frances.'

'You've screwed up your life, and think you can just screw up other people's to make yourself feel better about it. You don't *know* anything. You don't *have* anything. And that is no-one's fault but your own.'

I'm out of control now, a cartwheeling firework of hatred, burning whatever I come into contact with. The fury feels righteous – like finally someone has to listen.

'Maybe, yeah. But you don't deserve any of the shit you do have.'

'*What?*'

'You think I don't know how fucked your life is? What you do when your kid isn't here? How you live two lives? How you just give up, over and over?' She spits the words, face red.

'You know nothing about my life.'

'I wish I didn't, Frances, but I do.'

'You don't. You're a charlatan. A homeless piece of trash. And that baby you're growing? That is just a normal, fucking *nothing* baby, a product of your own slutty negligence, whose life is probably going to look exactly the same as yours if it isn't put in the foster system the second it is born.'

Dog barks then, and I turn to the animal and charge, as if I'm going to kick him.

Mary screams out and flings her body between us, and I suddenly catch myself in the midst of the violence.

'You're wrong,' she cries. A ripped solar system mobile dangles above her head, as Dog chews on Saturn anxiously.

I breathe in the carnage of the room: Neve's belongings rearranged haphazardly, and my own livid intent rendering a pregnant teenager a sobbing mess on her floor.

My mind rails, defensive. The waif has been sleeping in her bed – *her* bed. The bed I retreat to in order to keep her safely in my body.

'How did you get in?' I hiss.

'It isn't hard to get into places if you need to,' she mutters, her body shaking. She is trying to stand now, her belly popping out more than ever. 'Not everyone remembers the Inn, you know. But you do. It means you remember how to hope for something.'

Mary slowly picks up one of the drawings and holds it tenderly, as if to place it back on the wall. It is a picture of a family – a mummy, a daddy and a little girl. I know this picture. I know what Neve wanted me to write on the back of it.

'I don't remember, Mary. I refuse to.'

I grab the picture from Mary's hands and I rip it into pieces. Then I grab another picture, and do the same.

Mary stares at me, tear-streaked and unmoving. Then, suddenly, she picks up a lamp and throws it to the ground. It breaks.

It's on.

We both grab at paper, at shirts, at dolls, at furniture. Mary climbs onto the desk and throws the books onto the floor. We rip and tear in a frenzy of anger. We pull out the clothes, pull down the bunting. Dog jumps around at our ankles.

She screams as she throws a plastic baby across the room. I bellow like I am in labour, ripping pages from books. We destroy, and destroy, and destroy. We spit and rage, we punish ourselves. I take the butterfly quilt, its threads now loose, and with a piece of broken glass I shred the embroidery.

Mary watches, shocked into silence.

I collapse onto Neve's bed, staring at the pieces of my child.

Mary sinks down upon the carpet, Dog beside her.

We sit in the wreckage; the curlew egg now smashed upon the grass. The silence stretches on and on, like a perfect, cloudless sky, until –

'How long did it take you to set her room up?' Mary stares at the ceiling, unseeing.

'The whole four years.' I look around at all the things Lucas and I chose together, the things I chose myself after he took half, and the things Neve chose for herself. 'It started simple – like a cot and table – but it grows as they grow. You need more and more as they learn to interact. Developmental toys, baby sensory stuff. And books. So many books.' I pause, immediately regretting the material goalposts I've just implied. 'I mean, you don't – you don't need *that* much. At least, not at the start.'

Mary nods, thoughtful. 'I'm gonna make him a room. I want to do it – to bring him home somewhere. Put him in a bed. Have toys above his head.'

'Of course you –' I start, then correct myself: 'Maybe you will.'

'I dunno. He deserves a fucking room. He's the son of God.'

I flinch. I haven't heard her say it like that before.

She sees the question in my eyes and grins, and for a moment I think she's going to tell me she's joking.

'I didn't fuck Jesus.'

'Yeah, I believe that. But I still don't believe you're a virgin.'

She raises her eyebrows, shrugs.

'I still don't believe you're *not* a virgin.'

I almost choke at the shade of it.

'I have had *sex*, Mary.' I blurt, before I suddenly remember I'm talking to a minor. 'I mean, I have made love –'

She raises an eyebrow, like she knows. My interaction with Ruairí lingers on my skin – tongues, desire, trauma, shame. *You haven't though, have you? Not in a very long time, if ever. You don't know how.*

Mary rubs Dog's belly, the cheeky grin fading. 'You act like immaculate conception is the part that's hard to process. Even after the Inn. But "Mum" . . . that's the really fucked bit. That's the impossible part.'

I sink further into the bed and close my eyes. I say nothing, because she's right.

'I want to be able to do it. I want to feel it. I want it to be easy. But I think I'm going to be a bit shit,' she whispers, as if hardly daring to admit it.

'What makes you say that, Mary?'

'My mum was shit. Didn't really care. Didn't really notice me. Had her own stuff to deal with. She gave up.'

My imagination paints a clear picture of how Mary has become a product of the system – a system I have hated since the start.

'So you want to keep your kid? Despite the challenges? Despite the options you have?'

She stares me, confused. 'Don't you?'

I clutch the ripped-up butterflies, thrown by the question. I have given up too, I realise with a jolt. Lost my child and climbed straight into bed to revert back to one myself.

'Of course I want to keep my kid. I'm her mother.'

'Exactly.' But Mary looks worried. Afraid.

The words that came flying out of my mouth in anger now seem sharper and more injurious than I ever intended. Taking them back would be like picking shards of glass from her skin.

I reach out to touch her hand. 'I personally never had the maternal instinct that other girls had,' I say softly. 'I wanted to foster or adopt or something, because it was righteous and Christ-like – not because it was actually something I yearned for.'

'Law instead of love. Religion instead of relationship. You wanted to be good. But it doesn't work if your heart doesn't care.'

'Yeah.'

The words start tumbling out before I've even thought them. 'Not having any kids felt selfish, self-indulgent. But having them also felt selfish . . . and stupid; anti-feminist. I thought motherhood was just this generational game that we all lost, no matter what choice we made. Systemic misogyny, where the patriarchy kicks us out of the running in the workforce by filling us up with sperm. The sentence of womanhood, right?'

Mary chortles, running a hand through cropped hair.

'I love womanhood. Being a woman is bloody incredible. Someone was like: *Let's make the most badass piece of creation ever invented. Let's give her boobs and lips and cankles, and hair she can do weird stuff with, and the ability to laser a fuckboi just by looking at him, and then make her so strong that she can basically do anything, even while bleeding, or broke, or exhausted, plus build babies inside her body, and force them out the same hole she poops out of, and then feed the little babies off of milk made from her own body parts until they've grown up.* Seriously, wow.'

'I think we're going to need to clarify a couple of things you just said, but first up you will not have this baby out of the same hole you poop out of.'

'A dude at the mission told me I was going to tear so bad that the vagina and the anus become one.'

'That is not what's going to happen to you.'

'But it does happen?'

'No.' I hesitate. 'Not *every* time.' *Maybe this kid is a virgin?*

'See? Women. What the fuck. Beasts.'

I regroup, trying to stifle the bewildered laugh that wants to steal out of my poker face.

'Yeah, we are. We're amazing. But regardless of everything you just said, we're also considered the most disenfranchised and oppressed group of people in the world. The system is rigged – or it feels rigged.'

'So you decided no babies?'

'Well, for me, when I was thinking about starting a family, the church made that feeling of disenfranchisement worse, because suddenly I was the *helper,* and my husband was my *head,* and my role was to nurture, not to lead or create or pioneer. I loved being a loud woman, but I taught myself to be a quiet woman so I could love God too. I was told Jesus was a feminist over and over again, and yet motherhood felt like another way to silence me and the women around me. Because when you're that fucking tired, how do you have time to make much noise?'

Mary listens. Dog listens.

'You really loved God, didn't you?'

'When I thought I knew God, I really loved God, yes. I knew a lot about Him. I studied Him, even preached when they let me. But I just liked talking to Him. I liked asking Him for advice. I liked receiving that advice. I found it one of the most satisfying relationships I had ever had.'

'And then what?'

'I had a child, and realised how you are supposed to treat people when you really love them.'

Mary nods, back to the original topic. 'So you adopted?'

'No. I fell pregnant by accident. We'd just moved into this house.'

'Did you tear through to the anus?'

'I'll get to that bit.'

'Hurry up then.'

'Well, I found out I was pregnant – there'd been a slip-up with my pill, we weren't planning it. But Lucas was so happy. He bought me seven pregnancy tests and made me do them back to back, then ran around the house looking at them under different lights with this big smile on his face. I couldn't really believe it. Couldn't feel excited. Was expecting to have a miscarriage, but the pregnancy just kept going. I thought I was going to be a really awful mother, too.'

Mary inches closer. 'Were you?'

'No. Actually, I was really good at it.'

'But you were so scared?'

'It was an illogical fear. I mean, at first the fear was that my kid wouldn't like me, or that they might be troubled or suicidal or something. I was scared of *that*. Of the teenager, already! Of my kid rebelling, rejecting life, or God, or me. Those fears are so foreign now, knowing how innocent that child was. How I just omitted the purity of childhood and expected the worst for later on. And yet the purity of childhood is all I've had of her. It's the whole point.'

'Maybe she'll end up being pregnant at fifteen too?'

'If it means she makes it to fifteen, I damn well hope so. Bring on the grandchildren.'

Mary grins, all teeth and dimples. 'So tell me about the vag bit.'

'Well. It was long. It was a twenty-hour labour, and Lucas was stuck at the church dealing with a pastoral issue or something; he was the only person on at the mission that night, and she'd come two weeks late so we'd kind of given up on her coming out at all. I did it alone, but I didn't really, because she did it with me. She had to go through the trauma of it, through that claustrophobic journey from one world to another. And the only person she knew on the other side was *me*.'

'Did it hurt, though?'

I chuckle, actually remembering it now. 'I thought God was going to give me a pain-free labour.'

Mary brightens. 'Oh, really?'

'I believed it. I had read about it online. Supernatural healing, ecstatic labour. I was going to have orgasms instead of contractions.'

'And is that what happened?'

I can see the corners of her mouth curl up.

'Umm . . .'

We stare at each other, faces straight, before exploding with laughter. We are doubled over, cacking ourselves.

'The contractions were relentless. She came out really slowly – her head kept popping in and out . . . it was *terrifyingly* painful.'

Mary holds on to her belly, in hysterics, tears streaming from her eyes.

'Her head . . . popping out . . . like an orgasmic poo . . .'

'Like a poo the size of a watermelon.'

I catch my breath, in between fits of giggles, with Mary still caught in one of those rigid silent laughs where she can't even get noise out.

'But I will say this . . .' I compose myself a little, trying to meet her gaze. 'The pain was very spiritual.'

'Why? What do you mean?'

She is still now, listening intently. I don't know if I'm speaking to a waif or an angel, or both.

'I don't really talk about this stuff anymore; it's a part of my life I've decided isn't quite healthy for me.'

She picks up the ripped pieces of Neve's picture, looks at the little girl scrawled in pink pen. 'Like healing?'

'Yes, like healing. Except I learned a lesson about healing when I was in labour. I learned that sometimes God – if God is there – gives us different kinds of healing.'

'Like healing for cancer, compared to healing for a broken leg?'

'Not quite. Different kinds of presence, is what I probably mean.'

Mary snuggles up to Dog, as if settling in for a story.

I persevere, unsure where I'm even going with this.

'So, there's one type of healing, where you feel pain but God takes it away completely, like it never happened, and you can get up out of your wheelchair and walk. Miraculous and immediate.'

'Yes, I've seen those on YouTube,' she says. 'The church loves those.' She is playing with her septum piercing.

My God, does the church love those.

'And then there is the kind of healing that happens when you feel pain, but God doesn't take the pain or the sickness or the injury away. Instead, He just stays with you while you're in it, and

He feels it with you. And He doesn't make it stop, but He doesn't leave your side. You endure it together, and there is a comfort in that.'

'So God's pushing the wheelchair?'

'No, God's in that wheelchair with you.'

'Ha. Squashy.'

I smirk. *Yeah.*

'The second one doesn't sound like healing,' I say. 'Sometimes it doesn't feel like healing, either. But it is. Eventually. Especially in birth.'

She seems to know so much already – so much about life and death and magic and hunger and human beings – but somehow I need her to know this. Mother to mother. The blissful grief of it. The terrible trap of learning how to fall in love. I want her to go in without fear. I need to pull out one shard of glass at a time.

'You got up to the bit where her head was popping in and out of your vag.'

Fucking teenagers.

'She came out after an hour of actual pushing.'

'Was she beautiful?'

'She was perfect.'

Mary smiles in satisfaction, hands rubbing her belly.

'You loved her straight away?'

'I didn't expect to recognise her, and I didn't expect her to recognise me, but the moment we met was like a reunion. You've always known your child, Mary – I didn't realise that. When they finally placed her on my chest, I saw it. She knew my voice, and my smell, and my breathing – I was safe for her. I realised I was her home, and if that was parenting, I would give it *everything.* I would never, ever lock her out, or let anything unsafe in. I would always leave food in the fridge and the porch light on.'

I grip the bed, my heart in my mouth. There are butterflies in my hair, in my stomach, in my bloodstream. *Where is my child?*

'Mum packed up my room when I moved out to marry Lucas. I hated that. I was never going to do that to my daughter. I wanted her to feel like she was always welcome to come back home. To come back to the safe place. To me.'

I look around her destroyed bedroom. I look at the tangible chaos of my pain. The helpless, rabid, primal thing that will not be touched, will not be tamed.

'And did you tear?'

'Pretty badly. Third degree.'

'Did that bit hurt?'

'It was the second kind of healing. Enduring it together. Labour is functional pain. Pain with a purpose. Tearing is less so, but par for the course. In comparison to what happened later, it didn't hurt at all. It was the best day of my life.'

I feel for my own abdomen, so empty now.

'I didn't even know what pain was, back then. I do now.'

I take the scraps of paper from her hands. The torn shapes of little Lucas and Frances, in rainbow colours.

'It isn't a question of whether I failed, because I know I did. It's how. How did we not protect her? How did anything else break in, with that much love on every side? How did cancer, or religiosity, or abuse, or hate, permeate her world at all? Who would sit by and allow that? Is there anything else in the world I could have done to shield her?'

Mary's body softens against the carpet. 'Is this the second kind of healing again?'

'No. This time God left me on my own. This time there's no healing at all.'

Dog shuffles to the foot of the bed and licks my ankle. Mary has a hand on her belly, and looks down as something wriggles around in there. She must be, like, eight months? She glows, as so many young mums do. Like they'd be incredible caregivers, if only we'd let them. If only we valued it.

We lie there in the darkness for a long time, the fur of the animal up against me, reminding me I am alive.

Mary's breathing evens out, deepens. After half an hour I get up, the blood rushing from my head. I scoop up the dead weight of the pregnant girl from the floor, trying not to grunt, and place her in the empty bed. I survey the room. Dog is already snoring, chasing something in his dreams.

'Goodnight, Mary.'

'Grrnigh . . .'

I leave, touching nothing, and wander down the hall to the main bedroom. I look at the untouched bed, so neatly made, a towel rolled on the end of it. I take off my shoes, and slide between the sheets.

I remove a tiny thimble from my pinky finger, and place it on the bedside table.

to mend is to tear is to mend

Image description: A drawing in black pen on paper by Neve Harkin (aged 4) of two adults and a child. The adults have love hearts inside their chests.

Caption: *A picture of Mummy and Daddy and Neve. Mummy loves Daddy again, and we are back together as a family so I never have to miss anyone.*

The Book of Mary 9:2

In the morning Frances sleeps in, and then Dog and I fix up what we can. Well, I only help a little. I'm getting a bit fat.

Baby has been kicking a lot since we slept in a bed. Even some hiccups. Cartwheels, handstands, twerking. I'm proud. Rest looks good on us.

Dog curls close to my belly.

I am not alone.

Ward round notes: Dr Simon Yates, 27 August 2022

Patient Neve Harkin (4 years 9 months) received her liver transplant twenty-four hours ago and for the first twelve hours post-surgery was progressing excellently.

In the past twelve hours, she has become febrile, and the team are watching closely for signs of infection. They have kept her sedated. Also running ongoing tests for hepatitis and HIV due to the donor's status.

I have spoken with Lucas Harkin, and have been informed Frances Kocsmáros has been denied access due to allegations being made against her. I have flagged this as highly unusual and problematic due to the unpredictable state of Neve Harkin's health right now, and the possibility of things going wrong very quickly.

I will be consulting with the hepatologists closely to ensure we are across her blood counts and oncological status also.

The Gospel According to Frances 20:2

I wake late, refreshed. I'm in our bed. *Except it isn't 'our' bed anymore, Frances. It's just your bed, now.* I slept so well. God, I missed this mattress. I stretch out, taking up space in the middle of the bed instead of just one side.

The mayhem of the night before comes back to me. I let it play through my mind like a film, cringing at the flashes of Ruairí between my legs and trembling at the memory of Neve's room. I am somewhat comforted by the image of the little woman curled up in the single bed, arms wrapped around her belly. It settles the sadness of it all. I am here, in this day, and I know what I need to do.

I shower properly, dress with intention and pad downstairs. It is silent. She must be sleeping still.

I put on the kettle, thinking the sound might stir her.

After making a pot of tea, laying a table with two settings and rummaging in the fridge for something resembling food, I creep down the hallway and knock on the door.

'Mary?'

'Yes?'

I breathe a sigh of surprise and relief. I half-expected her to have disappeared again, and I realise in that moment that having her here is an anchor to living – an anchor I have been missing.

She emerges from the room, Dog trotting behind her. I peer in to survey the damage in the light of day, and do a double take.

The room is perfect. Not just tidied – it's exactly as it was before the carnage. The lamp is unbroken, plugged in, the glass giving no suggestion of ever having been smashed. Neve's illustrations are not in pieces; they're whole, untouched and stuck back on the walls. The dolls are in place. The solar system mobile dangles elegantly from a hook on the ceiling. The books are unripped. The butterfly quilt is entirely clean and perfectly intact.

Of everything I have seen so far, this somehow scares me the most. I stagger back, almost tripping over Dog.

I'm scanning the fractures of memory in my mind. Did I imagine last night? I recall it so clearly, we trashed it, we were frenzied, upset . . .

'What happened?'

Mary just shrugs, picks her dirty fingernails.

'The first kind of healing, I guess.'

The faintest glimmer of a smile. Then she waddles off into the kitchen, Dog right behind her.

Frances Kocsmáros's phone notifications, 27 August 2022, 10.04 am

Rosemary Kocsmáros: 3 missed calls, 6 text messages

Darling I'm heading to the hospital okay?

They won't let me up to Neve's ward?!

Call me back.

I'm coming over to your place immediately.

I just saw Dr Yates. Very strange.

ETA is 20 minutes.

—

Unknown caller: 2 missed calls, 1 voice message

'Hi, Frances, my name is Detective Devi Ramineni, I'm investigating some allegations and would like to speak to you. Please call me back urgently.'

—

Reg Holland: 1 missed call, 1 voice message

'Frances, as you may have seen, things are, ah, heating up, and I'd quite like to talk to you about someone called Cressida Charalambous?'

—

Brisbane University Hospital: 3 missed calls, 1 voice message

'Hello, Frances, this is the PICU at BUH. We would like to give you a progress update on your daughter. Please call us back as soon as possible.'

—

Dr Simon Yates: 1 missed call, 1 text message

Frances, call me back ASAP please.

—

Fiona Ramke: 2 missed calls, 2 voice messages

'Hi, Frances, I've received a bunch of documentation from Lucas's lawyers. Don't panic, but we need to talk immediately.'

'Me again, Frances. If you get a call from the police, know that you do not have to say anything without me present.'

—

Ruairí Hickson: 2 text messages

I hope you're okay, beautiful.

We've got three more weeks of shows, then I'm back to Sydney. Hope I see you.

Letter from Frances Harkin to Lucas Harkin, 15 September 2014

Dear Lucas,

It felt easier to write what I wanted to say. I wanted to talk about the stuff that came up in our fight the other night and the way I handled things. I'm really sorry. I love you, and I didn't really recognise us in that moment. I felt really triggered by what you said about mutual belonging, and my body not being mine and your body not being yours. I felt pressured, and cornered, and angry in a way I haven't been before. I felt like you were kind about it, up until the moment you realised I was going to say no. It hurt me. I know what you're sharing is scriptural, and I want to honour it, but it challenges me deeply.

The thing is, I want to be open to you, and I don't know why my body isn't aligned with how my heart feels. I prayed, and I asked what was going on – if Holy Spirit could maybe help me sort through it. It came to my heart that maybe it was something to do with sin I wasn't aware of, maybe a way in which I've opened a door to other spiritual influences in our relationship. I feel like I have prayed through so much of my past, but I don't know if I've done it fully. While praying, God reminded me of how adultery happens in the mind – how even thinking of someone else during sex is ultimately the same as a physical betrayal.

This made me think about the porn stuff, first of all. It made me feel frustrated and resentful. I know you fight the urge so much, but I don't <u>*want*</u> *it to be a fight. It makes me feel so small, and whenever you touch me it feels like your hands have already touched someone else. I kind of thought God was just reminding me of how you've wronged me . . . but then I remembered I wasn't being that honest with myself, or with you.*

I want to confess something to you: when we got together, I had made a deal with myself that when it came to thoughts of homosexuality I would take every thought captive. I would resist any opportunity to masturbate at all – but most pointedly to ensure I never masturbated to the fantasy of a woman. I worked really hard to keep my thought life pure. When we began having sex I felt like I could sustain this, but for the last few months of our marriage I feel like images are creeping in, fantasies and ideas that I previously never allowed. It isn't anyone specific or anyone we know. I have no idea where it has come from. It is just a female body, with my body. I <u>*want*</u> *to have sex with you . . . but to orgasm I have to think of a female body. And I wonder if it has created a distance between us, resulting in this kind of resistance I am feeling to your touch. I wanted to share with you the scripture I felt the Lord give me this morning.* Ecclesiastes 3:5 – 'There is a time to embrace and a time to refrain from embracing.' *I think I need to refrain before I am able to fully step into our sexual relationship again. I want our marital bed to be pure. I want to offer you something healed and whole, and I plan to go to the inner-healing counselling to cultivate the fullness of that healed and whole self.*

This is not me trying to avoid sex. This is me trying to save it – to sanctify and protect it. I hope you can understand. I hope we can pray and discuss this together, safely and lovingly.

I love you. Forever.
Frances

The Gospel According to Frances 21:1

My mother is in my kitchen. Standing in my kitchen, staring at Mary and Dog like they're bits of shit on a toilet seat.

She arrived near hysterical, which is actually quite unlike her. Barrelled in like I should be expecting her, which – upon actually charging my phone and reading the messages – I probably should have been. The barrage of hell that has greeted me through that tiny metal box this morning should have destroyed me – and on any other given day, it would have. But something about last night shields me. The sting of terror is gone. The brutality is expected, welcomed. *What else have you got? I have little miracles everywhere.*

Mum is insistent on panic as a motivator: 'I don't think you understand how serious this is, Frances.'

But I do. I just cannot combat this the way she wants me to. I cannot win this with fear or tantrums or even legalities. I will lose. I'm set up to lose, a mouse baited into a patriarchal trap. They will find discrepancies in my story. They will say I am in the midst of a drug-induced psychosis. They will say I've killed Sylvie to bring my child back from the brink of death.

'Mum, I *will* call Fiona Ramke back.'

'She needs to get you in to see Neve. Simon seemed to think she was becoming critical, the liver may not be taking, you need to fight –'

'Yes, I know. But there are things I need to do first to allow that to happen.'

'I feel like you don't care, you have stopped caring about your own daughter, you won't even try –'

'Stop.'

Mary's voice rips through the room like the shard of glass through the quilt. 'Frances would die for Neve.'

Mary is quivering with defiance as my mother looks at her in shock. Her words wrap around me like a scarf. *Yes, I would.*

'And who are you?' Mum spits, venomous enough to do the job here and now.

'No-one. And no-one would do that for me. But you'd do it for Frances, and Frances would do it for Neve.'

Rosemary flickers with emotion. I realise that this is the curse of motherhood, after all: to watch your child in pain is the most powerful of tortures. The irrepressible urge to hurt in their place is the most potent of loves.

I have nothing to say to my mother. She cannot understand. She has never lost me – not like this. She does not know what it is to be paralysed by devotion, so she does not know how to lead me out.

I know I could call the lawyer. I could sit through the list of possibilities, hear how a judge might discern truth, waste precious time filling out paperwork.

I could write down every single thing Lucas has ever done to me, exhaust my mental state to its inevitable collapse, and submit myself to the lion with the promise 'it has no teeth'. I know they would all assure me he doesn't have a case, but they are not the ones who will be dismembered limb by limb the moment we all discover that he does. That he has worked very hard to build one; to ensure I am punished for the sins I have committed. After all, *God is on his side.*

It is not justice. The men win because the men don't know how to lose, and we are afraid of what will happen if they do.

The witch within me wants to eat their throats. The child within me wants to hide from them. Hide in fantasy and miracles and kindness and false hope, like every other person who has ever tried to believe in a deity. Hold that same deity to account for their failure to steward power. Ask for a better lot.

I do not want my real life, and I do not want to confirm my founded fears, and so I will not call the lawyer. I will not make a failed attempt at justice.

Instead, I will go and find the Innkeepers.

Instagram message from Celine Riot to Theatre Mama, 27 August 2022

I'm a FSSW (full service sex worker) who saw your viral post about Eternal Fire. I decided you might find this information interesting.

Just block out my name, yeah?

Attached: IMAGE

Description: A receipt.

$450 from [REDACTED] to Celine Riot: Consultancy Services

The Book of Mary 10:1

I know what she wants to do, but I know it isn't possible. You can't force their hands. You can't just *knock*. I know this better than anyone.

Oh well. She's on her own pilgrimage to the bottom.

All we can do is follow.

Emails from Fiona Ramke, 27 August 2022

Dear Frances,

Can you please call me? I would like us to discuss the DVO and the Family Court mention. Would you like to contest it? I feel you should. We can organise urgent court proceedings considering your circumstances.

I'm available all day.

Fiona

–

Dear Frances,

Please call me before 2 pm. They are likely to bring you in for questioning today, if not place you under arrest. There may be a warrant to search your property. I can't imagine they would have a case to press charges – at least, not yet.

You don't need to say anything; in fact, I urge you not to.

Please call me.

Fiona

The Gospel According to Frances 21:2

We drive to New Farm Park. It's been raining, and Dog's head is out the window, taking in the sweet petrichor. I can't imagine anyone being in the park after the sudden deluge, and feel relief in the privacy.

We park the car near my original bench. I flinch as I see the playground, and my senses instinctively reach for Neve. *This is your path back to her. Keep focused.*

I get out and edge towards the giant trees with play equipment seemingly growing out from their insides. Is there another version of this place, where the Inn stands proudly?

'If you can hear me, I want to talk,' I whisper into the age-old branches and roots, the wild bridges, slides and swings strung between them.

Mary stands by the car and yells at me, impatient:

'They can't let you in like that.'

I shrug. I have nothing left to lose. I shout at the trees:

'FUCKING SPEAK TO ME, IF YOU WANT ME TO BELIEVE YOU ARE REAL.'

Mary rolls her eyes at me like I'm an imbecile, but I hear a muted shuffle from near the toilet block. She and I both go very still.

'Fuck off.' The sound is coming from the *toilets*.

'It's Jasper,' Mary groans, almost collapsing against a nearby tree.

She says it with such a level of exhaustion that it makes me ask gently, 'Do you . . . *know* Jasper?'

'Ugh. Jasper travelled alongside me for a bit. Was involved in bad shit, tried to get me involved too. Made promises he couldn't keep.' She shrugs. 'I don't like him. Not anymore.'

I go towards the men's block quietly.

It's a dark, damp, brick structure, with a little bit of light trickling in from some patterned holes in the concrete blocks. There is a stained urinal, graffiti, and two cubicles. One is closed.

'Jasper?'

A cough, from inside. He does not come out.

'It's Frances. From the . . . dinner.'

'You mean the organ-harvesting cult?'

His face peers out from behind the wooden door. Real-life Jasper is gaunt, greasy-haired and pimple-faced. He wears a fraying hoodie and sneakers with holes in them. He's a far cry from the handsome young man who sat, ate dhal and gave sharp chat at the Table only a few nights ago. His expression is untrusting, but open in its recognition. I realise he has probably assumed he was hallucinating.

'I'm relieved you also remember,' I say to him, stepping a little closer.

'You're the woman who wore that blue dress, huh? You look heaps different.'

No shit, kid. Look in the mirror.

'Why are you here?' He's suspicious, afraid.

'Can we talk outside?'

'Are the pigs out there?'

'I'll check.' I take a quick look then assure him: 'All clear.'

He follows me out, squinting in the sunlight. I lead us to the park bench, and he eyes Mary, plodding along one of the playground bridges with Dog at her heels.

'What the fuck is she doing with you?'

'She's staying with me for a bit. Until the baby is born. She's helping me sort out a bit of a pickle I've found myself in.'

He shuffles, doesn't take his eyes off her. She's deliberately ignoring him.

'She's real pregnant now, eh?'

'Yeah, she's getting closer. Eight months or so.'

He nods.

I push a bit harder, curious. 'Are you the father, Jasper?'

He spins towards me, angry. 'No. I'm fucking *not*.'

Mary flips him the bird from across the playground. I realise I don't have time for the soap opera.

'Jasper, do you know how to get into the Inn?'

'No. I didn't ask for it, last time. I was just having a real shit night, and it happened.'

We're standing by the road, looking over to the sports bench with its little tin shelter.

He pauses, his breathing changing – he's nervous. 'Is Sylvie okay?'

I'm not sure if he's taking the piss, but his eyes are clear, focused intently on me.

'No, she's not.' I clear the lump in my throat. 'She died.'

He bends over, vomits.

A few metres away, Mary groans.

Should I put a hand on his back? I'm unsure.

'Jasper, we could . . . we could go to the police?'

He looks at me in abject horror.

'You don't get it at all, do you?'

He pulls out a small object – a key. And it's been engraved with tiny writing that winds itself in an infinite circle.

to speak is to be silent is to speak

Jasper presses the key into my palm and it sits heavily in my hand. 'I didn't do anything –' He stops, overcome.

I shudder to think of Sylvie, softly dreaming in her wedding dress, torn from her peace.

'What *did* you do?' I ask Jasper.

'I hid. While it happened. Until all the police were gone. Until the body got taken. Until everything stopped. I just hid. Didn't sell anything for days. Didn't eat.'

'Did you recognise the police officer – Paul?'

He grimaces. 'Yeah. Fucktard.'

'Do you have history with him?'

'He came in that night, like he was a buyer.'

'He bought drugs off you?!'

'Kind of. He bought some, then after he paid he told me he was a cop and he wanted to have a chat. And I was like, *fuck, I'm sprung*, and I ran, and he chased me and I panicked and I lost him, and then later he was at the fucking *dinner*. But we didn't speak there. And the next day, he's looking over her body.'

I take this in slowly. A senior constable buying what – ice, heroin? Then investigating a murder in the very park he spent the night in, with that drug in hand? In my mind I see his face contorting in the ICU as he interrogates me. What a hypocrite.

'Can you tell me who hurt Sylvie?'

He gives me a scared look. 'But the police –'

'The police think it was me.'

Jasper runs his hands over his face, stricken.

'Can you . . . can you come to the Budapest?'
'If necessary.'

I'm surprised. I know the Budapest.

I signal to Mary that we're leaving. She refuses to look at Jasper, just dawdles towards the spot where we parked.

He averts his eyes from her belly and kicks tufts of grass with his sneakers all the way to the back of my car.

Fucking teenagers.

The Book of Mary 11:1

I don't like the Budapest. I don't want to see any of them. I am starting to feel like crawling back into the Inn, curling up like this kid in his womb. I'm so tired. So grumpy. Fuck, I need to lie down. If only I could wrench open the door, ask for some kind of rest. A holiday. A ten-year sleep. I don't want to help Frances and I don't want a baby and I don't care what the Innkeepers say about kids who will change the world. Fuck him. *I'm* a kid.

I'm done. I'm hot, I'm fat, I'm swollen, I'm itchy. Get it out of me.

Fucking Jasper. He called me a whore the last time I saw him properly. Like that's an insult.

I want to punch everything. Ughhhhhhh.

If this is a miracle, it's a gross, painful miracle and I quit.

The Gospel According to Frances 21:3

Mary shifts uncomfortably in the front seat as we drive the short distance to the Budapest.

'Can you hurry up? I feel car sick.'

I stare at her, seeing the adolescent. Being a teenager is hard enough without her added complications. When I was sixteen I was worried about having enough spending money to buy red frogs from the tuckshop at school.

'Are you all right?' I ask.

'Just feel anxious.'

'She doesn't like seeing me,' Jasper pipes up from the back seat.

'I gathered that.'

We continue to drive in silence. I've taken plenty of patrons to the Budapest in my time, and retrieved a bunch too. It's an odd kind of boarding house – an accredited residential service on paper, but a riot inside. Some stay for a few years, but most don't last longer than a week. An old bugger called Buck runs it, and mostly just ensures no-one breaks any of his windows.

It's an old Queenslander – utterly prime real estate considering the location and the architecture – and has a huge wraparound verandah from which its residents watch the street and finesse their heckling.

When we pull up, there's an altercation in progress. The bear-like figure of Gregory (who is supposed to be in Eternal Fire's rehab rooms; even *I* know this) has pulled a pocketknife on a young whippersnapper called Imogen, whose eighteen-year-old skin has been turned into the texture of beef jerky by her ravenous ice consumption.

Imogen paces – a tiny bull before an unkempt matador.

We sit in the idling car, unsure if the situation is going to escalate.

They stand off, spitting profanities at one another, until Mary has had enough of it. She flings open the passenger door and storms out, Dog at her heels.

Jasper and I scramble to follow. My heart is pounding, and he hangs back, genuinely afraid.

Mary walks right up to Gregory, furious, and slides the knife from his hands with a superhuman ease. She passes it straight to me, as if she simply cannot be fucked holding another hundred grams of extra weight. I remember this part of pregnancy all too well.

'You got me kicked out of rehab, fuckhead. I hope an animal bites your dick off while you're sleeping.'

As if on cue, Dog growls, and Gregory finally has the sense to look nervous.

'Fuck off, Mary. You weren't even on drugs.'

Imogen walks away, muttering something to herself about Dog speaking in tongues. Gregory turns too, and wanders onto the hostel's front verandah, disappearing into the shadows behind the lattice.

'Where's Buck?' Mary yells after him.

'He's dealing with Achara.'

I look at Jasper, who does not meet my eyes.

Voice messages from Dr Simon Yates to Rosemary Kocsmáros, 27 August 2022

'Rosemary, it's Simon. I can't get through to Frances. Can you call me back? It's about Neve.' (2.54 pm)

'Rosemary, sorry for the phone tag. I've got clearance for you to be at Neve's bedside. Just don't speak to Lucas. When she's conscious Neve is asking for her mother, but we can't get Frances in here yet. Have them page me when you arrive at BUH. Tonight will be pivotal.' (3.17 pm)

Excerpt from transcript of interview between Detective Devi Ramineni and Lucas Harkin, 27 August 2022

Det. Ramineni: *Tell me about how you met Frances Kocsmáros.*

Mr Harkin: *Ah, I was attending Eternal Fire Christian Church – I think around 2011 – when I met Frances. She got saved, quite dramatically actually, and we, ah, connected and started dating. In 2012 we got engaged and then married six months later.*

Det. Ramineni: *She got saved?*

Mr Harkin: *Um, became a Christian. She'd lived very differently, and then met Jesus and repented and changed her life up.*

Det. Ramineni: *Right, right. So would you say a big part of your relationship was based on your mutual beliefs?*

Mr Harkin: *Definitely. That was a major priority for me. But we connected in other ways, too. We both loved music – she was a dancer, back then.*

Det. Ramineni: *And what was your experience of your marriage to Frances?*

Mr Harkin: *It was tense. Not always, obviously. We realised we had different values about some things pretty early. She was frustrated. She acted out, rebelled. Didn't like the boundaries of our life. I felt she had a temper.*

Det. Ramineni: *A temper? Did she ever physically hurt you?*

Mr Harkin: *No. But she would yell sometimes. Withdraw, stone-wall. She would withhold sex. And I think she had some mental health problems.*

Det. Ramineni: *What mental health problems?*

Mr Harkin: *Well, it was okay for the first couple of years. We both started working for the church after the first year together – I was ordained, and she was a street chaplain. But we fell pregnant in 2017, and after we had Neve she got more touchy, and anxious, and she'd suddenly change her mind about things. Said the birth had changed her. Like, she started questioning my choices, or suggestions.*

She criticised our employers. Kept asking whether we were happy, or believing the right thing. Started getting paranoid. And then Neve was diagnosed and she really closed off and decided she didn't believe in hell, and . . . well, she took on a progressive theology, which is not uncommon, but she would start preaching it from the pulpit. Or making pastoral decisions that didn't fit within the church ethos. And sometimes she'd talk about leaving the church altogether. Then she decided to leave me.

Det. Ramineni: *Did she ever see things or hear things that weren't there?*

Mr Harkin: *Well, kind of, yeah. We are part of a church that believes in the gifts of the Holy Spirit – so, like, hearing from God, healing and praying in tongues. Things happen – miracles – and that's normal. But it all has to happen within a biblical framework to be considered spiritually appropriate. She would get visions and dreams though – dreams she thought were meaningful, or real. And I don't think they were always from God.*

Det. Ramineni: *Right. What about with Neve? Did Frances have any strange ideas about Neve or her condition?*

Mr Harkin: *She didn't believe in healing. Refused to, especially after we divorced. Even with all the visions. And then really recently, around the time of the poisoning and the transplant, she suddenly changed her mind.*

Det. Ramineni: *Interesting that she didn't believe in healing. Do you think she* wanted *Neve to remain sick? Is that why she administered the paracetamol overdose?*

Mr Harkin: *Like 'Munchausen by proxy'? It has occurred to me. Or, she wanted to control Neve's prognosis . . . to ensure she died, to prove me wrong. To punish my faith.*

Det. Ramineni: *And did you question her sudden change of heart when the transplant became available?*

Mr Harkin: *I thought it was possibly a manipulation. That, or maybe my prayers had been answered. That she'd realised God was working to care for Neve. Now I am aware of what she did, I don't know. Guilt?*

Det. Ramineni: *And do you think it's at all possible Frances would do something illegal to obtain health or healing for Neve?*

Mr Harkin: *She does not operate within a framework of righteousness, so yes, perhaps.*

Det. Ramineni: *You recently took out a DVO. Why?*

Mr Harkin: *Even before the poisoning she attempted to attack me at a healing church service for Neve. She has been involved in unpredictable and immoral behaviour, and I am going to the Family Court because I believe Neve will have a safer life with me.*

Det. Ramineni: *Right. We have evidence Frances lied on transplant paperwork. We are trying to ascertain whether she physically attacked Sylvia Rathdowne as well. Do you think that's possible?*

Mr Harkin: *Is Neve implicated in that at all?*

Det. Ramineni: *We aren't going to remove your daughter's liver, if that's what you're asking.*

Mr Harkin: *I'm sure you understand our situation is still unstable, in any case.*

Det. Ramineni: *I do know that, and I'm very sorry. I understand time with your daughter is critical, and I don't intend to take up much more of it. Do you think Frances is capable of grievously injuring another person?*

Mr Harkin: *Unfortunately, yes. I do.*

The Gospel According to Frances 22:1

When we enter the Budapest, I half-expect another magical shift, to find ourselves somewhere comfortable, clean and welcoming. The reality is just as I recall it, and far from the ideal: a hallway of termite-riddled walls, stained carpet and four little rooms with padlocks. A communal kitchen and dining area sits in the middle of the house, with labels and instructions on everything, courtesy of Buck. No art, strictly fluorescent lights and plastic furniture. But it's a home. It's better than a toilet block.

There is a soft murmuring from the back room and we follow the sound to a final door, currently ajar. I knock and, when there is no response, peer in.

Buck is a lanky, elderly gentleman with a long bushranger beard and a grey ponytail. He straddles a chair, facing Achara, who is deathly still, curled up against the wall on their single bed. Achara, like the others from the Inn, is a far cry from the ethereal sage of the night garden. They're grey-skinned, bald, their face blistered and bruised. They're naked, but for a sheet wrapped around them like an unravelled toga.

Buck barely acknowledges us, and mutters to Achara gently, 'You will need to come back to us soon, otherwise we'll have to take you to hospital again.'

I cough, and Buck turns, his face tensing in surprise at seeing me.

'It's been a long time since the happy-clappy Bible bashers have come over this way.'

I cringe. 'That's not really what I do anymore, Buck. I'm here with these two' – I gesture to the teenagers – 'and I know Achara. I thought maybe I could chat with them.'

Buck laughs bitterly. 'Chat away, woman. Old mate's been catatonic for the last two days. Deep in an episode.'

I take in Achara's state again, and edge a little closer. Mary and Jasper hang back, as if far too aware of how dangerous a situation this is. Jasper keeps his face down, out of view.

Achara holds out their hand to me, the first movement I've seen them make. At first I don't understand, until I realise their eyes are on the pocketknife I'm still holding.

'What are you doing with that?' Buck asks sharply. 'We don't allow knives –'

Achara reaches for it again, body suddenly alert, muscular; the masculine within them all too apparent.

'My gift,' they rasp.

Gift? I study the knife, and in the sunlight streaming through the window I see that it too is engraved.

to kiss is to pierce is to kiss

Achara looks at me, eyes black. They smile slightly then vanish into oblivion once more. It isn't them. The person on the bed is a curdled, perverted version of the Achara I met. I don't feel safe, and neither does Buck.

'Go outside please, everyone. Achara's not well.'

'You should call the hospital,' I tell him firmly, forgetting this is no longer my job.

'It's on the cards, but they don't handle my folks well. Especially the schizophrenics.'

'They need meds.'

Achara has begun kissing their own knuckles, softly at first, then harder and harder and harder.

Mary grunts irritably in the background, and I spin to her, done with the petulant mood: 'Can you just offer a *bit* more understanding, please?'

But Mary is pressed against the wall, face contorted as she puts pressure on her lower back. There is bloody water running down her legs. She pants and writhes.

I move to her, place a hand on her belly. It's rock-hard.

Jasper's eyes are wide. 'What's happening, what's going on?'

Buck looks at me like, *What the fuck have you brought into my hostel?*

Her contraction ends and she opens her eyes. I take her hand.

'We should go, Mary. Now.'

Excerpt from transcript of interview between Detective Devi Ramineni and Reg Holland, 27 August 2022

Det. Ramineni: *Reg, I understand you've been under public scrutiny recently.*

Rev. Holland: *It's all lies, absolutely ridiculous.*

Det. Ramineni: *Nothing you've participated in is directly breaking the law.*

Rev. Holland: *Sure, but in my community there are significant ramifications.*

Det. Ramineni: *Is there anything you can tell me about Celine Riot?*

Rev. Holland: *I don't understand the relevance of this.*

Det. Ramineni: *We've been made aware that Frances Kocsmáros is also a client of Celine, and that both Celine and Frances were placed at the crime scene.*

Rev. Holland: *What?*

Det. Ramineni: *Does that mean anything to you?*

Rev. Holland: *Ah . . . no. I don't know who Celine Riot is.*

Det. Ramineni: *Right. We are hoping to find some answers around the death of Sylvia Rathdowne and we think Frances may have been involved. I understand she was removed from the church premises recently after causing a scene. Is there anything else you can tell me about her divorce from Lucas Harkin, or involvement in the church's programs?*

Rev. Holland: *It's complex.*

Det. Ramineni: *This could potentially assist the public profile of the church. It may indicate that someone reasonably unstable is trying to defame or slander Eternal Fire's mission.*

Rev. Holland: *She certainly doesn't like us.*

Det. Ramineni: *What does that mean? What does that look like?*

Rev. Holland: *Well, she no longer holds to a godly morality. And she wants to restrict Neve from experiencing the joys of church community. And she wants to stay in church housing, you see, but since she no longer works for us –*

Det. Ramineni: *She's in church housing?*

Rev. Holland: *Yeah, she is. And she was going to get kicked out of there by the board, so I . . . well, she begged to take on some volunteer work. So I said yes. I wanted to be generous.*

Det. Ramineni: *What kind of volunteer work?*

Rev. Holland: *I allowed her to help out with a patron who has high needs. A teenage girl, pregnant.*

Det. Ramineni: *Right. So she's helping this girl in what way?*

Rev. Holland: *Resources. Organisations. Accommodation. The girl has been sleeping in her spare room.*

Det. Ramineni: *She isn't a social worker, though. Is she a registered residential youth worker or foster carer?*

Rev. Holland: *No, but she's done a lot of that stuff through our street outreach program. She has a blue card.*

Det. Ramineni: *Have you done a welfare check on this young girl? Do you understand she and her baby could potentially be at risk?*

Rev. Holland: *I have been trying hard to get information but Frances won't return my calls.*

Det. Ramineni: *Do you know if there is a CYJMA child safety case open on this girl? Or a DHHS one from down south? If there is any plan for the baby?*

Rev. Holland: *No.*

Det. Ramineni: *I'll look into it. What's the girl's name?*

Rev. Holland: *Mary. It's just Mary. Um . . . Detective?*

Det. Ramineni: *Yes?*

Rev. Holland: *What would you do with information about Celine Riot?*

Det. Ramineni: *I would use it to build a case against Frances Kocsmáros.*

Rev. Holland: *Can this information be publicly accessed?*

Det. Ramineni: *Not unless you take the stand as a witness.*

Rev. Holland: *Okay. God spare me.*

Email from Reg Holland to Lucas and Frances Harkin, 2 March 2015

Dear Harkins,

It was a big session today. I pray you're both feeling okay, and have had some space to think and journal. Well done on being so honest with one another.

After what we discussed, I think it would be wise for us to line up another counsellor for Frances, on top of our marriage counselling – a mature Christian woman who can help with some of these stickier issues of headship, submission, marital relations, and thoughts about homosexuality and divorce. A mentor of sorts.

It's easier to hear these things from another woman, sometimes! Frances, you might feel more understood!

I think Sandy Jerrybrook could be a good fit: she runs the marriage course and is trained in inner healing as well. She has a real passion for helping restore marriages into the image of Christ and the Church, and had a daughter successfully go through sexual orientation restoration therapy, who is happily married now.

Remember, you are one. What God has joined together, let no man separate!

In Christ,
Rev. Reg Holland

The Gospel According to Frances 22:2

We drive slowly. She's only in early labour, so there's no dramatic screaming or pushing. Every five minutes she just focuses a little too intensely on the road, gripping the car seat just a little too tight, her breathing elongating. I'm quite impressed at how she's handling it, but it's too early in the pregnancy for this baby to be born. Perhaps not vitally – but enough to raise concern. I take the quickest way to BUH; I know the route well enough. Jasper attempts small talk from the back seat.

'Oi, are you okay?'

'Suck my arse out, Jasper.'

'Cool, sorry.'

We pull into Emergency and I help her out of the passenger side. She can walk easily enough, but a contraction comes on just as we reach the automatic doors and she grimaces for a hot minute.

Jasper wanders over behind us, unwilling to sit bored in the car and miss all the drama.

The security guard by the door nods at the three of us in understanding, and raises an eyebrow at the unkempt dog trotting behind us.

'Can I check ID?'

I baulk. 'This is a public hospital. She's in premature labour.'

'Yeah, sorry, we're under strict security due to a criminal investigation.'

Mary, to my surprise, pulls out a plastic card from inside her bra. It's a school ID for Dandenong High in Victoria. The name beneath her young, curly-haired photograph is 'Penelope Lingard'. *What?*

Jasper, meanwhile, pulls out the shabbiest, fakest 18+ card I've ever laid eyes on. The guy in the photograph has a *beard.*

The security guard just shrugs.

As Jasper slips it away in his jacket, I notice he's pocketed the knife, too. *Not the time to address that, Frances.*

'My mum needs to come in with me,' Mary (*Penelope?!*) says pointedly, gripping my wrist with an unexpected strength.

The guard awaits my driver's licence, patient and oblivious.

I don't know what to do, because I know who they are looking for.

I pull it out, hand it over.

He double takes, and stares at it as if it's a lotto ticket.

'One moment, ma'am.' He reaches for his walkie-talkie.

'She's here. At emergency. With a young woman and a young man. And, ah, a dog.'

I know what is going to happen before it does. It's too predictable, too perfectly contrived. I can already see the panicked look on Mary's face as the unmarked car swerves around the driveway to Emergency.

A woman with long black hair and a sharp jawline steps out of the car in one smooth movement, and makes her way over to me. She says the words, all the right legal words, but I do not hear them.

Mary screams words too, a contraction winding her, punching down through her body, and I can't hear that, either.

I don't fight, I don't go limp, I just close my eyes and imagine jasmine flowers dotting my path to the detective's back seat. My feet are bare, my child is laughing. Jasmine in my hair, jasmine in my mouth, jasmine, jasmine, jasmine –

I open my eyes, but there is no other world. The car is driving into the night, and out the window I see two helpless teenagers being ushered inside by nurses, and a dog left alone on the sidewalk, barking and barking and barking.

Excerpt from transcript of interview between Senior Constable Paul Jacobs and Anouk Neilson, 27 August 2022

Snr Constable Jacobs: *Now we seem to be on the same page regarding your description of your work, can you please talk to me about your relationship with Frances Kocsmáros?*

Miss Neilson: *She's a client.*

Snr Constable Jacobs: *Anything more than that?*

Miss Neilson: *I'm a professional.*

Snr Constable Jacobs: *Understood. Did she mention anything about her relationship with her ex-husband or her child's terminal illness?*

Miss Neilson: *Her ex, yeah . . . I didn't know she had a child.*

Snr Constable Jacobs: *Did you ever provide her with illicit drugs?*

Miss Neilson: *Please clarify what you mean by illicit.*

Snr Constable Jacobs: *Cannabis.*

Miss Neilson: *Medicinal, maybe.*

Snr Constable Jacobs: *Reg Holland suggests you are dealing alongside your brothel work.*

Miss Neilson: *Does he, now?*

Snr Constable Jacobs: *Did Frances buy drugs from you?*

Miss Neilson: *Just a casual spliff between friends.*

Snr Constable Jacobs: *Purely professional relationship, don't you mean?*

Miss Neilson: *Or that.*

Snr Constable Jacobs: *Why did you lie on the record about the nature of your work?*

Miss Neilson: *I don't trust male police officers.*

Snr Constable Jacobs: *If you're working legally, you have nothing to worry about.*

Miss Neilson: *I help young women who aren't working legally to access safe abortions. It's in their best interests for me to protect them.*

Snr Constable Jacobs: *Do you help them access illicit drugs, too?*

Miss Neilson: *No.*

Snr Constable Jacobs: *Right. And when you saw Frances on the morning of 25 August, had you spent that night together?*

Miss Neilson: *No. I spent that night with other clients. One of whom was Reg Holland.*

Snr Constable Jacobs: *Did Frances speak to you at all about her previous employment?*

Miss Neilson: *In the army?*

Snr Constable Jacobs: *The army?*

Miss Neilson: *She told me she was in the army.*

Snr Constable Jacobs: *The Salvation Army?*

Miss Neilson: *No, the army . . .*

Snr Constable Jacobs: *What else?*

Miss Neilson: *That it was hard, like being brainwashed. I got the impression she was traumatised. That she regretted it.*

Snr Constable Jacobs: *Regretted what?*

Miss Neilson: *Hurting people.*

Snr Constable Jacobs: *Are you aware that Frances is in the employ of Reg Holland?*

Miss Neilson: *The pastor? No.*

Snr Constable Jacobs: *Interesting. Can you look at this for me?*

[Shows photograph.]

Snr Constable Jacobs: *Do you recognise this person?*

Miss Neilson: *Yeah. But . . .*

Snr Constable Jacobs: *What?*

Miss Neilson: *It's complicated.*

Snr Constable Jacobs: *I'm not interested in your involvement in illegal soliciting outside of a brothel, if that's your concern.*

Miss Neilson: *Then yeah, I know her.*

Snr Constable Jacobs: *What's her name?*

Miss Neilson: *Penelope.*

Snr Constable Jacobs: *And how old is she?*

Miss Neilson: *I couldn't tell you that. But . . . young. A teenager. Too young for this work. Not soliciting willingly. She was coerced.*

Wanted a termination, but I lost track of her location before the appointment.

Snr Constable Jacobs: *I'd like to ask you more about your abortion services. You understand the abortion laws in Queensland are restricted by gestational dates and medical clearance, right?*

Miss Neilson: *I'm not sure I'm willing to discuss this right now.*

Snr Constable Jacobs: *What do you gain from helping girls to access abortions?*

Miss Neilson: *Nothing. These girls are vulnerable –*

Snr Constable Jacobs: *Vulnerable, huh? In a job you claim to* love.

Miss Neilson: *I'm trying to make it safer.*

Snr Constable Jacobs: *I don't believe you.*

Text messages between 'Celine Riot' and 'Mary' dated 17 January 2022, surrendered to Detective Devi Ramineni

Mary: *Hey sis.*
Celine: *You good?*
Mary: *Can you talk?*
Celine: *Not right now. Client in shower.*
Mary: *Ok.*
Celine: *Problem?*
Mary: *Client just left early and T hasn't come back to pick me up yet.*
Celine: *How much time left in the booking?*
Mary: *40 mins.*
Celine: *This is it then. You dressed?*
Mary: *Yeah. What about the ticket?*
Celine: *I've emailed it. Greyhound. How far are you from Central?*
Mary: *30 minute walk.*
Celine: *You'll make the 2 pm to Newcastle. Go now. Don't hesitate. No paper trail. Call me from the bus.*
Mary: *I don't have shoes.*
Celine: *Find a church when you get there. They'll fix you up.*

The Book of Mary (Genesis)

I run and run and run and run and run, like he's behind me. He's not.

I'm out, I'm off the chain, I'm out of the kennel, I'm a leaf in the wind. I need no-one. No-one needs me. Doesn't matter that my rags haven't come. I'll close up my pussy like a flower and I'll go become a nun. I'll be a president. I'll be an Olympian. I'll be a ballerina. I'll be a child. I'll be a child. I'll be a child again.

I am going to jump in front of the first train that pulls up at Newcastle station. I'm going to get out of this, out of the body, out out out out out. I can feel myself coming down. Vomity. There is no hit after this except the last.

I get off the bus. I'm a leaf in the wind. Ready, ready, done.

But there's a dog there, at the station. Grinning at me.
I'll pat him. Just once.
Then I'll go.

Part Three

The Book of Mary (Bethlehem)

I am the sea and I am the empty promise and I am a world of nests beneath undisturbed earth. I have been a closed fist every day before this day and now I am a palm, opened. Place the gift upon it, and may I never crush it. Held softly, held momentarily, the children come to us as birds alighting on a branch before they go, they fly, they cry out –

I go, I fly, I cry out.

I think I will die.

I think I am the one being born.

I think this is the closest I have ever been to the truth.

The son of God is most rightfully the son of a mother.

Messiah, born through a torn, tarnished cunt.

The second kind of healing, they say.

The Book of Jasper 1:1

Fuck.
Oh fuck.

The nurse gave me a gown and shit, and called me Dad. Lol.
I don't like blood.

Fucking hell, it's a pussy. Is that a poo?
It was a poo.

Now it's a head coming out of a pussy. Shit, it's like the alien movie.
Wow, it's fully, like, alien.

Oh fuck, I'm gonna vomit.

This is the most beautiful thing I've ever seen.

Everyone's looking at the kid. It's not crying or nothing, it looks all small and blue.

They take it away in a fish tank. Yelling and stuff.

She's so ugly when she cries. Also kinda pretty. Should I hug her or –
I dunno.

Excerpt from transcript of interview between Detective Devi Ramineni, Senior Constable Paul Jacobs and Frances Kocsmáros, 27 August 2022

Snr Constable Jacobs: *I want to inform you that you have a right to know why you have been arrested and what offence or offences you are suspected to have committed – in this case, the murder of Sylvia Rathdowne. You have a right to contact a lawyer, and we understand you've contacted Fiona Ramke. You also have a right to contact a friend or relative, and you've left a message for Rosemary Kocsmáros. You have a right to an interpreter – yep, didn't think so – and to, ah . . .*

Det. Ramineni: *Medical treatment, if needed, and privacy from the media.*

Snr Constable Jacobs: *Yep. Thanks, Devi. We would like to make sure you understand that you are not obligated to answer any police questions, but whatever you do say will be recorded and may be used as evidence in a court of law.*

Ms Kocsmáros: *I understand.*

Det. Ramineni: *I would like to ask what you were doing in New Farm Park on the evening of 24 August and morning of 25 August.*

Ms Kocsmáros: *I will not be making a comment.*

Det. Ramineni: *Is it correct you were stalking the movements of people sleeping rough in the area?*

Ms Kocsmáros: *I will not be making a comment.*

Det. Ramineni: *Is it true your child Neve Harkin was being treated for cancer, when you gave her a dose of paracetamol that was unsanctioned by her medical team, which meant that she overdosed?*

Ms Kocsmáros: *No comment.*

Det. Ramineni: *Is it correct that due to that overdose, she went into liver failure, and was urgently in need of a liver transplant? And in the time following her overdose you orchestrated for*

Sylvia Rathdowne's liver to be transplanted to Neve Harkin upon Ms Rathdowne's brain-stem death?

Ms Kocsmáros: *I will not be making a comment.*

Snr Constable Jacobs: *Here's a tissue, if you need one.*

Det. Ramineni: *You'll feel better if you confess, Frances. We can help solve this. Were you involved in Sylvia's assault?*

Ms Kocsmáros: *No.*

Snr Constable Jacobs: *Would you like to speak to us about your relationship with the young woman you know as Mary?*

Ms Kocsmáros: *No comment.*

Det. Ramineni: *Would you like to speak to us about Eternal Fire Christian Church, and your relationship with Lucas Harkin? He has accused you of domestic violence and child abuse. He says you are mentally unstable and aggressive. Would you like to comment on that?*

Ms Kocsmáros: *No.*

Det. Ramineni: *What about your relationship with Celine Riot, also known as Anouk Neilson? From discussions with her, she seems to think you have a violent past.*

Ms Kocsmáros: *What?*

Det. Ramineni: *What did you tell her?*

Ms Kocsmáros: *No comment.*

Det. Ramineni: *Are you aware that Mary is also a sex worker?*

Ms Kocsmáros: *No, she's not.*

Det. Ramineni: *She is also a drug user.*

Ms Kocsmáros: *She's not. I would know.*

Det. Ramineni: *Would you, really? Go into that for me.*

Ms Kocsmáros: *No comment.*

The Gospel According to Frances 23:1

I'm in a small cell, stark but clean.

There's a toilet, a sink and a plastic pillow on a hard bench. *Like the streeties.* The air conditioning blares; it is freezing. I am only wearing a t-shirt and jeans, so I curl up to try to conserve as much body heat as possible.

There are no bars, but there is a thick perspex wall both imprisoning me and exposing me to the supervising police officer. It's Paul Jacobs.

They can only hold me for eight hours since I was just brought in for questioning. I haven't been charged yet, but Devi seems quietly confident about whatever information she has gathered.

Fiona Ramke yelped and protested down the line on receiving my phone call, a practised performance of disgust for my benefit. I wanted to reach through and shake her: *I don't care that you think this is ridiculous. I know it is abhorrent. Just tell me how to fix it.*

Mum did not pick up her phone. I left a very vague message, giving her a number on which to call back.

The shame is like bile in the back of my throat. The humiliation and physical discomfort is a throbbing reminder of my status. *Your inability to prove your innocence means you are less than human.*

I have wondered so many times if the complications of my life are my fault. Because I am broken, as others have suggested.

My initial embrace of spirituality could easily be put down to my desire for an owned change in trajectory: the belief that if I could become a more palatable human being, perhaps I could cultivate a simpler, more blessed life.

I didn't do any research, didn't lay the religions out side by side and evaluate their efficacy as ideologies or walks of life. It coincided with my friend wanting to visit the little church on the corner, where they played acoustic guitar and all had tattoos. She wanted to laugh at it. And we did laugh at the pews and the liturgy and the priest and the song lyrics. But I felt the music through my body the same way I do when I dance. I felt the prickle of electricity, the otherworldly presence, the whisper of a full moon through the window of a sleeping house.

It would never have been enough to actually convert me. It would have been a passing thought, a dalliance, a cheeky one-night stand with God . . . But I met a man that night, too. He sat in the pew in front, and turned to us at the end with this curious look on his face.

After, we went to eat dumplings with him and a group of others, and he sat across from me and answered every single question I had.

He was so direct, so unexpectedly sharp in a room full of softness. I was attracted to Lucas's sharpness, then. It reminded me I was alive. I did not know it would press deeper into my skin with every passing day, until I woke up sliced in two.

I used to believe my life could be written perfectly – free of heartache – as long as I followed the script. I learned the lines, put on the costume. Played the pilgrim of prosperity by going full method. I almost believed my own performance, until the house lights came up on an empty theatre.

I am a pilgrim of suffering, now, even in my awareness that my walk towards it has only just begun. Suffering sits as the inevitable destination of my journey, not a trap I must avoid or an antagonist I must outrun. There will be loss, and there will be cold, and there will be pain, and there will be loneliness. But it is not because I am bad. Even if I am bad.

I feel the raised goosebumps on my skin and rub them for warmth, like I might do for Neve. I remember 'The Little Match Girl', how she lit each match and basked in the fantasy of warmth, comfort and food, before perishing in the Christmas Eve snowfall. I read it to Neve, thinking it was a fairy tale. She loved it, of course.

I don't know which are worse: the fairy tales that tell the brutal truth, or the ones that give you false hope of happy endings.

Through the perspex I watch Senior Constable Paul Jacobs organising my fingerprint paperwork. I close my eyes, and try to sleep.

Letter from Lucas Harkin to Frances Harkin, 18 September 2014

Dear Frances,

Thank you for your letter. I've spent a long time reading it, rereading it, and talking it over with my accountability partners. I'm sorry we haven't discussed this in person yet. It has affected me deeply, and I wanted time to digest it and then respond appropriately.

You have managed to communicate this decision through a lens of 'Scripture', but I personally find that a bit of a stretch. I can't help but feel that 'refraining' has been taken out of context. 1 Corinthians 7:4–5 says: 'The wife does not have authority over her own body, but the husband. Likewise the husband does not have authority over his own body, but the wife. So do not deprive each other, except by mutual consent and for a time, so you may devote yourselves to prayer. Then come together again, so that Satan will not tempt you through your lack of self-control.'

Is it mutual consent if you've just let me know your decision? Don't we need to come to this decision together?

First, my use of pornography is something I deeply regret and have been working extremely hard on, while still committing to being intimate and open with you. It is a very natural, masculine urge – from the testosterone in my body – to have sexual arousal and desire. It is entirely different for men, as you know. I have sexual energy I can't control. If it doesn't get to manifest in my marriage, where is it supposed to go? The Bible talks about this – it talks about sexual desire as a fire. Even when we do have sex, you are often very practical instead of passionate, and it happens maybe once a fortnight. That isn't something that can meet the fire I have to manage. If you don't want me to watch porn, you need to be offering me more in our sexual relationship, it's that simple.

A homosexual urge, however, is not a natural urge. The Bible talks about same-sex attraction as an abomination. I am distressed and uncomfortable that this kind of 'fantasy' has entered our love-making, that you have opened our home to this kind of thought life. It will imprison you.

I spoke about this to Pastor Reg, as the leader of our men's group. He has said he would be open to enrolling you in the Discipleship Healing program in a few weeks' time. There is a big deliverance session at the end. He sent me a prayer script as an example. He thinks it would be good for us both to go, for us to be prayed for as a couple, and for us to see if we can help clear this urge from you spiritually. It really does sound demonic. As you know, it isn't you, it's what you have allowed to become attached to you.

If we must 'refrain', I would like us to prioritise this kind of prayer ministry. The course begins on 15 October, and will take up three nights per week for four weeks. We need to nip these things in the bud, Frances. If we ignore it, it will only rot us to the core. Jesus loves marriage. He loves our marriage. We're captains in God's army, and He will not let Satan infiltrate what He has built between us.

I love you. I know Jesus has us.
Lucas

Eternal Fire Discipleship Healing Ministry: Deliverance Prayer, 15 October 2014

Thank you, Father, Son and Holy Spirit for your power over all sin, for your power over every spiritual entity from hell. You are light, and all darkness shall flee. You are the one God, and your word is life to me.

In Jesus' name, I ________ (name), come before you to confess that I partnered with the spirit of ______________ (homosexuality, fornication, adultery, paedophilia, bestiality, masturbation etc.). I have committed the following acts of ______________________________________ . In these sins, I have allowed a foothold for the Devil to lie to me, and I have believed those lies. Please forgive me for accepting anything but your truth. Please reveal these lies to me now, and help replace them with your word.

Holy Spirit, please come now. I bind any spirit that is not of God, any words that are not of God. I come against the spirit of ______________________, and destroy its chains on my life by the powerful blood of Jesus.

Spirit of ________________, you are no longer welcome in my body. Get out, and go into the pits of hell. Leave me now. Thank you, Jesus. Fill me with your truth, your light, your fullness. May the doors and windows to my soul be locked. Protect me, Lord, from every temptation. Thank you for your sacrifice, thank you for your love, thank you for setting me free. I praise you, Jesus.

Amen.

Text messages between Rosemary Kocsmáros and Ted Kocsmáros, 27 August 2022, 7.17 pm

Rosemary: *Call me now.*
Ted: *I'm in a meeting – is it Neve?*
Rosemary: *CALL ME TED. NOW.*
Ted: *Can't you just text?*
Rosemary: *Frances has been arrested. She's in the police watch house. Might be released tomorrow. Unsure if she'll be charged or if they will allow bail once they do. Fiona Ramke is calling me shortly. I cannot fucking look at Lucas Harkin.*
Ted: *Okay I'm calling you.*

Midwife notes: Moneth Ramos, 27 August 2022

Penelope Lingard (aged 16) gestation 35w4, came in at 4.07 pm, with broken waters and contractions 4 minutes apart. 3 cm dilated.

Internally monitored from 4.30 pm, baby's heart rate 92. Choice was made by OB not to slow or escalate labour, progressing quickly.

7. 03 pm: 8 cm dilated.

Stage 2: 46 minutes.

Monitoring showed distress, forceps were used.

Male baby delivered 8.13 pm.

2.6 kg, 41 cm.

APGAR 2, not breathing. Paeds called, taken to NICU.

Stage 3: Placenta delivered 8.42 pm, showed signs of deterioration and failure.

Mother had 2nd-degree internal tear and fair haemorrhaging (200 ml of blood) but recovering well.

Not sure who teenage boy is but useless.

NOTE FROM ADMINISTRATION: Child safety requested they be notified upon the birth of Penelope Lingard's child, due to her refusal to consent to pre-birth services. They flagged immediate investigation to ensure a safe environment for the newborn.

The Book of Mary 12:1

I'm learning how to express that golden stuff out of my nipples and into a syringe. A midwife called Moneth is helping me. Moneth loves boobs. Loves breastfeeding. Loves it all. Has given me so much information on boobs I think I want more boobs. Everyone deserves boobs. I want to breastfeed now; I don't like squeezing them like they're pimples. I think someone gave me Endone, but I don't know for sure. I'm very spacey. I haven't seen my baby. Moneth says soon, soon, soon. Very soon. Make the milk come in, make sure he has something to drink. I give the little syringes of gold stuff to her and she takes them down to him and tells me he is beautiful, he is breathing, he is doing beautifully. I keep asking to go down, to touch him and hold him. Soon, soon, soon, soon, soon, says Moneth.

A lady comes in with a folder and an ID around her neck and she doesn't smile like Moneth smiles; she is built like she is made of Lego. Behind her comes a woman in a suit and it's the woman who took Frances in the car, and I don't think I should be talking to them right now, I should be holding the baby, or maybe Moneth should be helping me with milk, or maybe we could get Jasper or Frances – where is Frances, where is Moneth, I don't want to talk, I don't want –

The Gospel According to Frances 24:1

My first thought upon waking is that I've grown used to the firmness of the plastic bench. With my eyes still closed I stretch out, my body deeply rested. *It's actually quite soft, isn't it?* It takes me a moment or two to even register the smell of jasmine. My eyes flicker, body tensing.

The room is ridiculous in contrast to where I've just been. Thick curtains, ornate furnishings, a high ceiling. It's dark outside my window, but I can tell I'm in a room on a high-up floor. Art adorns the walls – impressionistic landscapes and still lifes of bursting flowers.

I'm lying in a four-poster bed with a blue velvet duvet, wearing heavy linen pyjamas the colour of lemon butter. There is a card on the wooden bedside table, along with a tall glass of water.

'Choose a costume. Don a mask. Join the party.'

The invitation does not evoke in me the magical curiosity I suspect the Innkeepers intend it to.

All this is a distraction, while you hide away, refusing to answer my questions.

I can't be angry that I'm here – I did ask to see them. I can do nothing but lean into it, play the game, and find the people responsible for destroying my life.

I climb out of bed and survey the room – there's an antique wardrobe in the corner. Costume it is, then. There are around twenty outfits to choose from, all of them more or less my size. Some of them are standard: an astronaut, a Viking, that yellow Kate Hudson dress from *How to Lose a Guy in 10 Days*, a Power Ranger

. . . Then some are strangely specific. The outfit I wore to the year ten formal. My wedding dress. My mother's old work uniform. As trivial as the decision might be, I find myself deliberating – *No. Maybe? Ew, of course not. That isn't quite me . . .*

Eventually I come across a three-piece suit with a tail coat and bow tie, the kind of thing you might see on Fred Astaire. It makes sense, somehow. I've always wondered what it would feel like to wear a traditional suit. To dance in something like that. More than anything, it is the correct attire in which to face God, and punch Him in the face. I put it on.

I move into the bathroom – again an entirely luxurious space, complete with heat lights and a claw-foot bath. There are cosmetics, creams, hair appliances and concoctions arranged neatly next to the sink. A series of costume masks have been laid out on a silver tray. I slick my hair back with gel, and choose a lightweight, mahogany-coloured mask made of silk. It slips over my nose and eyes, clings to my face like it belongs there. I feel handsome, and brave. Like a mother.

I pace a little in my new garb, getting nervous. The room echoes as if part of a much bigger building. I wonder how many rooms there are, and where the party will be held. I drink the glass of water and slip on some black dress shoes. There is limited time. I have to get back, get to Neve somehow.

I walk out through the heavy door into a long, carpeted hallway with stone walls and ceilings. It looks like a hotel, a very nice hotel . . . Really, it looks like a *castle*.

There are doors dotted along the hallway, and another opens as mine closes. Someone in a Peter Pan costume, complete with green felt mask and brown felt shoes, steps out onto the carpet with trepidation. They turn to me and yelp, jumping in recognition and relief.

'Fuck you, Frances Kocsmáros. I knew this dream would get good.'

I hold my grief in the back of my throat as Ruairí Hickson skips along the hallway and gently takes my hand.

The Book of Jasper 2:1

I walk and I don't know the way but Google Maps says fifty-six minutes and I've only got three per cent battery left and I don't wanna steal another phone.

I have it in my pocket. I have it ready.

Just let me in. Just let me explain.

Text messages from Lucas Harkin to Frances Kocsmáros, 27 August 2022

I would only do this if it were absolutely necessary, but I have been told that we may lose Neve tonight, and you should come to her bedside at BUH. (8.06 pm)

Rosemary just told me you've been taken into custody. I don't know what to say. (10.10 pm)

The Gospel According to Frances 24:2

Ruairí and I run down the iron staircase hand in hand, both in shock.

'Why, why, why are you here?' I whisper in awe.

'Drunk and disorderly behaviour. I was walking across the Story Bridge *gregariously*, and they nabbed me and said I deserved a night away to think about it and *calm down*. What about you?'

'I was in the wrong place at the wrong time.'

'Sounds juicy.' They kiss my hand. 'But you don't have to worry about it on the astral plane.'

We reach the ground floor of the castle and follow the muffled sound of live music and excited chatter to the ballroom. It is an expansive, theatrical space, decorated like a Dionysian revel. Food tumbles off tables, lights cascade from the ceiling. There are places to eat, to dance, to recline. There are at least one hundred people in the room, their energy magnetic, and they're all wearing costumes and masks. There is eating, sipping, dancing, conversation. For a group of assumed criminals, they are very well behaved.

A group of guests discuss a piece of artwork in the corner. Others relate anecdotes over cheese and olives. A small, dedicated band plays covers of recognisable songs, oblivious to who might be engaging or not. The lead singer is a drag queen with a wild, soaring voice, dressed like Princess Diana. She has a sprig of jasmine in her coiffed wig. I'm seduced by it all. In awe of the *scope*, until I remember why I'm here and the information I need in order to get out again.

I turn to Ruairí with the intention of explaining – even if just the bare bones – but they're staring at a table of food. I follow their eyes to where a scruffy tail wags from beneath a tablecloth.

'Is that a dog?' Ruairí's bright green eyes go wide, their body pulsing with the stimulation of the room. 'This place is crazy.'

Dog lifts his snout to the table and pulls a few plates down to the ground, snaffling the food like he has never been fed in his life.

'Frances, if this turns bad, you have to make me drink water, okay?'

Ruairí imagines they're still tripping. *If only.* I tuck a little wayward lock behind their ear, and pull the jaunty Peter Pan hat further over their curls.

'Promise me you'll have the best night of your life, okay, Ru?'

'What do you mean – where are you going?' Ruairí demands, pulling me close. 'I want you in my weird dream.'

I point to Dog, now pulling all the mortadella off a cured meat platter like a champion.

'This is my wake-up call.'

Dog looks up, as if in recognition.

I'm coming, you mongrel.

He does not wait, but trots off through a side door which has been left slightly ajar.

I retrieve my hand from Ruairí's, and I follow.

Radio exchange between Senior Constable Madonna McKenzie and Detective Devi Ramineni, 27 August 2022, 10.38 pm

Madonna: *Devi, a kid has just come into the station asking for Paul Jacobs.*
Devi: *Paul's on.*
Madonna: *He's not here. Went for a break about an hour ago.*
Devi: *Right. Can the kid wait?*
Madonna: *He's got something here I think you should look at. But he's jumpy. I'm worried he'll bounce if we let him overthink it.*
Devi: *What's he got?*
Madonna: *He says it's a used weapon.*
Devi: *From which crime?*
Madonna: *The murder of Sylvia Rathdowne.*
Devi: *On my way.*

The Gospel According to Frances 24:3

'Where are we going?'

I yell the question in vain, but I know he hears it. He scampers ahead of me through what looks like a commercial kitchen, strangely empty. The rooms don't seem magic here – not like the Inn that first night. There are more shadows; no softly lit, silly distractions. Are we back to reality? Dirty plates and saucepans are scattered about, abandoned. *Like me.* It's the servants' passage. The back way.

I'm reminded of when the detective drove me into the watch house. I had expected a bright, accessible entrance, like the Emergency Department at the hospital. But no, of course not. You drive down beneath the giant Roma Street building, and you're brought up through the back way, into rooms where every single piece of furniture is bolted down. *You could tip it upside down,* I'd thought at the time, *and nothing would fall away.*

I realise Dog and I are descending together, beneath the castle, further and further into the bowels of the watch house. I would have thought the Innkeepers would be in the highest tower – a souvenir of those hierarchical, biblical beliefs yet again.

We're in the servants' quarters now, following a stark, narrow hallway with wooden walls. There's no light except for flickering fluorescent bulbs every few steps. It's claustrophobic. *Just get to the Innkeepers. They're going to make all of this go away. They will end the nightmare.*

We start passing doors – *cell* doors – with names scratched on them in chalk. *Madonna. James. Devi. Hal.*

The final name makes me stop.

'I'm not looking for him.'

Dog turns, tongue lolling in his usual grin.

'Good,' mutters a gratingly familiar voice.

I flinch automatically. Because the final name is *Paul.*

Excerpt from transcript of interview between Detective Devi Ramineni and Jasper Berlusconi, 27 August 2022

Det. Ramineni: *You've come to the station with a pocketknife.*

Mr Berlusconi: *Yeah.*

Det. Ramineni: *Why?*

Mr Berlusconi: *It was used . . . with Sylvie.*

Det. Ramineni: *By you?*

Mr Berlusconi: *No.*

Det. Ramineni: *By who?*

Mr Berlusconi: *I . . .*

Det. Ramineni: *Sylvie was killed by blunt force trauma to the head. Not stabbing.*

Mr Berlusconi: *This is what killed her, though.*

Det. Ramineni: *How do you have this information?*

Mr Berlusconi: *I was in the park.*

Det. Ramineni: *What were you doing there?*

Mr Berlusconi: *I was sleeping. Trying to sleep.*

Det. Ramineni: *Was it wielded by a woman in her thirties?*

Mr Berlusconi: *It's complicated . . .*

Det. Ramineni: *Nothing I can't take, kid.*

Mr Berlusconi: *It wasn't Frances. That's all I wanted to say. It wasn't Frances.*

Det. Ramineni: *I think you know exactly who it was. You're going to tell me.*

Mr Berlusconi: *I can't. But . . . can you come with me?*

The Gospel According to Frances 24:4

Paul Jacobs sits in his very own cell, dressed in a Spider-Man costume, mask pulled off. He is alone, holding a flute of champagne, the glass shaking a little as he lifts it to his mouth. He clutches something tightly in his other hand.

My chest swirls, thunderous and heavy. I'm unsure if I'm in control of my body or the words about to come out of my mouth.

Paul looks up as I stand before him, and he swallows his champagne slowly. The jarring irony of the circumstance almost makes me laugh.

'Remember me now, Cunt-stable?'

He opens his hand. In it is a Matchbox car. A miniature silver LandCruiser. There is writing engraved on the bonnet.

to mourn is to dance is to mourn

Paul looks younger here, somehow. Less confident. He closes his hand around the tiny toy car and searches my face for understanding.

'Yeah. I have received a few of these now,' I say, steely.

I remember the coin, the thimble and the key, all of which were left in my jeans pocket before being seized by Paul and the officers in the watch house. I wonder where they are, then instinctively feel for the inner pocket of my jacket. *There, safe*. I pull them out as if to provide more evidence of my innocence.

to cure is to kill is to cure
to mend is to tear is to mend
to speak is to be silent is to speak

Neve's coin sits heavy in my palm, like a weight intended to drown me. *Is she laughing, watching TV, eating jelly? Is she asking where I am?* The ring floats into my mind, and I swat it away like a fly.

Paul leans over to see the tiny artefacts in my hand. They look like Monopoly pieces together like that. He shrugs, dismissive.

'I was simply doing my job –'

'Did you hurt Sylvie?' The accusation comes out before I can censor it.

Paul's eyes darken in outrage. '*What?*'

'You bought drugs from a teenage boy that night.'

'I was *undercover*.'

'Bullshit. You aren't a detective. You paid for the drugs and you didn't arrest him.'

Paul downs the rest of his champagne in one go. God, I wish I had a glass of it now, too. This is messy. Inappropriate. Does it count as harassing a police officer if it's within an alternate reality? Fuck.

He gives me a steady look.

'I still don't know for sure that you did not kill her, Frances.'

'You think I could do that?'

He shrugs. 'The love of a child leads parents to do very strange things. Grief leads parents to do very strange things.'

'You know nothing about it, Paul. You know nothing about my grief.'

'You're right.' He's gripping his Matchbox car now, running his fingers along it like it's soothing.

He stands up and moves to the doorway. His quarters are small, cramped, but this isn't a jail cell. I realise this place, devoid of all bells and whistles, isn't a place of punishment. It must be where the cops rest. There's a single bed in the corner, the cover mussed as if he's been lying on it, trying to sleep.

He inhales, offers me his hand. I resist the urge to spit on it.

'Come back to the party, Frances.'

'I can't. I need to find the Innkeepers.'

'They aren't down here.'

'I am not here to party, I need help.'

He raises an eyebrow at me and gestures to his own Spider-Man costume. 'Do you actually think we have a choice?'

Excerpt from transcript of Frances Harkin's third phone call to 1800RESPECT, 29 April 2020

Linda: *Hello, 1800RESPECT, this is Linda speaking.*

Frances: *Hello, my name is Frances.*

Linda: *Hello, Frances, are you safe to talk right now?*

Frances: *Yes, I think so. He's gone out.*

Linda: *Would you like to share with me what has been going on?*

Frances: *Um. Well I don't know if I should be calling. I'm just confused. He hasn't hit me or anything. It's just been . . . it's bad. We had a fight. And I feel a bit scared.*

Linda: *What are you scared of? Do you think you're in physical danger?*

Frances: *No, no, he'd never do that. I don't know.*

Linda: *What was the fight about, Frances?*

Frances: *We're under a lot of stress. My child is very sick. We're part of a community – a Christian community – and he is very involved. I'm not as involved right now. They've asked me to stop working for them.*

Linda: *Right.*

Frances: *But, um, it's become clear we believe a lot of different things right now. Which is hard, but I thought it would be okay. And this afternoon we got into an argument about our child, and how we could best take care of her. He doesn't believe in certain levels of medical intervention. Nothing crazy, but he doesn't believe in abortion, vaccinations, that kind of thing. And she is about to be very immunocompromised.*

Linda: *Is this something you argue about a lot?*

Frances: *I used to agree with him, but I don't anymore. And I get that that's kind of unfair, because he signed up to a certain kind of person, and I'm changing, and he says he didn't agree to marry this new version of me. That he doesn't recognise me. That I'm breaking the covenant that way.*

Linda: *The covenant?*

Frances: *Like, our marriage.*

Linda: *Okay.*

Frances: *And I said that I maybe wanted to put her in childcare a couple of days, so I could go back to university and pursue another career. But we can't afford that unless she is vaccinated, because of the subsidy . . .*

Linda: *I see. What did he say?*

Frances: *He said it was selfish. That doing that wasn't promoting the Gospel, wasn't demonstrating Jesus to people. That subjecting her to the dangers of vaccination just because I wanted to work was not putting her first. That my highest calling was as a missionary and a mother.*

Linda: *He doesn't want you to work?*

Frances: *Well, he wants me to apologise for what I did and repent, so I can work for the church again a couple of days a week. Otherwise be a stay-at-home mum.*

Linda: *What does he want you to apologise for?*

Frances: *I preached a sermon that was considered heretical.*

Linda: *I see. And in this fight today, what made you feel scared?*

Frances: *It was kind of a normal fight, until Neve walked in. She's little; she's only two. She was crying, because we were yelling. And he picked her up, while she was crying and reaching for me. So I asked him to hand her to me, so I could comfort her . . . Fuck, sorry . . . sorry for swearing . . .*

Linda: *Take your time . . .*

Frances: *And he held her tightly and started to move away when I moved towards them. He wouldn't let me touch her, even while she was screaming and reaching for me. And I said, 'Please give me my child.' And he said, 'She is not just your child. I am the spiritual head of this household. I decide what happens to this family. I decide how we deal with our child. You can be close to her again when you calm down and remember that.'*

Linda: *Then what happened?*

Frances: *I lost my shit. I began screaming. I tried to get her back. He ran out of the house with her, and drove away. I don't know where they are now.*

Linda: *Do you think your daughter is safe, Frances?*

Frances: *I don't know, I don't know.*

Linda: *You can ask the police to check on her, if you're willing to tell them you are actively concerned he will hurt her.*

Frances: *He won't hurt her, not like that –*

Linda: *It might be the only way to get them involved. Otherwise he is legally allowed to be with his daughter; it isn't legally considered abduction.*

Frances: *I can't call the police on him, he'll –*

Linda: *He'll what?*

Frances: *He'll . . . destroy me.*

Linda: *Frances . . .*

Frances: *Yes?*

Linda: *What do you want?*

Frances: *I just want my kid to be okay. I just want to be with her. I just want her.*

Linda: *Do you think you could make better decisions for her if you weren't being told what to do?*

Frances: *Some days – and I know this is terrible, I don't mean it . . . Some days I pray he dies in a car crash on the way home. So we can be free. So I can make her life better.*

Linda: *Frances –*

Frances: *Please don't think I'm some crazy woman –*

Linda: *Frances, you are allowed to leave him if you want to. You will get support.*

Frances: *I . . . Oh shit, they're home –*

The Gospel According to Frances 24:5

Paul leads me back through the dark underbelly of the castle, through the kitchen and into the entrance hall. He remains silent, like he's escorting me formally. I feel the power dynamic reassert itself, somehow. I'm angry that the police are allowed in here, where the rest of us get to actually *retreat* and feel human. This is our space, not theirs – even if they're only given the servants' quarters.

'You don't need to march me around like I'm going to escape my holding cell if you don't.'

He turns to look at me, surprised. 'At least you get a proper *bed* here,' he retorts. 'Cops get treated like the help.'

'You deserve it.'

'That's ludicrous. We give our lives over to this job, to protecting people.'

'Protecting who? *Who?* Because no-one protected Sylvie. No-one protected Jasper. No-one protected Mary.' I can feel hot tears now, the edge of rain. 'No-one protected me and my kid.'

Paul's jaw tightens in anger. 'Do you think I am some kind of superhero? Some kind of god who *allows* people to get hurt?'

'No I think you're the reason people get away with it. You're supposed to listen when someone tells you the truth. Help them.'

Paul is sweating in his costume. 'People *lie* Frances. They don't offer me the truth, they offer me their excuses. And if you were lied to again and again you'd become pretty suspicious, too. Pretty jaded. Pretty sick of the damage.'

'You *are* the damage. You're just a selfish, power-hungry pig.'

The words land on him hard. He shakes his head, fist to his mouth. He's fighting *tears*.

'Why are you so convinced you are the only one who has ever lost anything?'

He pulls a hankie out of his Spider-Man jumpsuit to wipe his face, and the tiny Matchbox car falls out of it, spinning along the ground towards me.

to mourn is to dance is to mourn

I pick it up, hand it back. A peace offering, perhaps.

'What does that mean?'

He grimaces. 'Like you care. Besides, you have enough to carry.'

I rattle the pocket containing my collection of 'gifts'.

'What's one more?'

He stumbles over to a couch in the dim entrance hall, and sits. I remain standing. His face is so open. The clenched fist unfurled. His vulnerability makes me uncomfortable, like I'm witnessing someone who is unknowingly naked.

'You want to know about damage?'

He chooses his words carefully.

'James was a cricket fanatic, but also top of his grade. Wanted to know how everything worked. Made things, built things, constantly. I couldn't believe that something *I* made could in turn make something else that had never existed before. Got totally besotted with the joy of fatherhood, you know? He was this joyful clown, always so naughty but not combative. Never angry. He thought he was immortal. He was going to study mechanical engineering, then travel the world and play cricket on every continent, he said. We played a lot of cricket. It was our thing.'

I am watching those dark circles under his eyes. The ones I know too well, the ones I apply concealer to daily. Circles of sleepless grief.

'He went to a party in his final year of school, took something someone gave him, tried to have a wild old night. Didn't realise he was high, perhaps. But driving home, he steered headlong into oncoming traffic. I was actually called to the scene. I had to phone his mother while I held his body.'

My skin begins to feel very cold in this castle of play and dance and music and food. The party is heating up in the next room. The mirror ball is on now, the lights a moody blue above people dancing to the band. Princess Diana sings a soaring Mariah Carey ballad. Tiny ovals of light speckle Paul's face as he composes himself.

I sit down beside him. He moves closer, to speak into my ear, and I feel the heat of his body and breath. He smells like the beach. *Salt and spinning clouds.*

'He was on ice when he died. Someone gave it to him at a party. I don't believe he had ever taken anything like that before. I *know* he hadn't.'

We hold one another's breath, stuck in the ferocious cruelty of it all. He exhales, and does not let himself stop.

'Losing a child is the most humbling, most destructive of human thresholds to have to cross. The worst thing. It brought out the worst parts of me. Things I did not know were there. I wanted to die. I didn't function for quite a few years. Got divorced, because we just reminded one another of him. Plateaued at work. Rejected every call from every friend. Finally decided to start living again when I realised I could try to let it lead me. Could fight for something. Maybe intercept teenage boys going that way.'

'Jasper?'

'I have been trying to speak to Jasper for a long time. I want to find out who is supplying these kids, destroying their futures. I want to help him. I was trying to help him.'

I would look at him, but I don't know if I want to break away from this intimacy. The truth, so close to my ear. The truth, of someone else's hurt, of someone else knowing what it feels like, of someone else angry and starved of the only thing they have ever loved *that* much. It's like a mirror, like a poem, and inside of someone else's pain I see myself, and I see myself surviving.

Paul takes my silence as disbelief.

'You don't have to trust me. I'm a pig . . . but I understand.'

I place a hand on his arm, swallowing my own cracks of trauma.

'Thanks.'

In the background, the band starts up a soaring nineties anthem by the Cranberries. Through the doorway we see people spin across the dance floor in their costumes, fast and colourful. A woman in her seventies costumed as Madonna; a tattooed man in an *Alice in Wonderland* pinafore; a couple dressed in matching Mario and Luigi costumes, kissing defiantly between screaming out the song's lyrics.

I realise that for some of these people the watch house is the last stop before incarceration. This is their final night of freedom – not freedom to destroy but freedom to taste pleasure. To have romance, and brightness, and curiosity. To feel their body's rhythm. To experience a normalcy that can only come when all the other shit is taken care of, like a bed, and food, and a relaxed nervous system – when someone else foots the bill.

This is the party that promises it wasn't all your fault. This is the party that promises to remember your name in the morning.

The party that reminds you that beneath the horrors of anger and violence and survival, there is still a child inside, with eyes wide at every wonder on this earth. That the child is innocent, and the child remains, even after you commit or are accused of atrocities. Even if you're taken to court and sentenced in the morning.

Then there are also just wayward art hooligans like Ruairí, who simply needed a place to sleep it off. I see them grin as they throw themselves into the fray with a willowy girl dressed as Catwoman, their bodies grinding and spinning to the mood of the room, and I give a mental shrug. *Actors.* The rogue doesn't owe me anything.

Paul follows my gaze. 'Do you know her?'

'Them. Yes. They're an old friend. They told me they got pulled in while walking drunkenly across a bridge.'

Paul watches Ruairí for a moment, then nods lightly. 'Right.'

We sit together, watching the revelry, side by side, consciously still while the music whisks the room into a frenzy.

He looks at his Matchbox car one more time, then slips it into his pocket.

'Would you like to dance, Frances?'

I'm taken aback.

He seems earnest, but there's a hint of a smile, and I'm surprised to find my hand accepting his as he leads me into the ballroom, into the pulsing mass of revellers in costume.

My senses are hit, overwhelmed, dizzied. For a moment I'm unsure if he's going to pull me into some kind of waltz, but he releases my hand, slips his Spider-man mask over his face, and *spins*.

Paul begins to move to the music like he's fucking Nureyev. He swerves like Prince, like Beyoncé, like David Bowie. He *flies*. It is entirely unexpected, and entirely thrilling.

The crowd around us parts to watch him duck and turn and jump and thrust. Peter Pan/Ruairí grins at us from a few metres over, Catwoman wrapping her tail around their neck. Paul has lit a match under the room, and soon everyone is throwing themselves onto the dance floor with total abandon, like the music is a pool of sparkling water. The ugly are beautiful tonight, the poor are rich, the criminals are the cream of society, and they dance like they're at their own weddings.

I have sudden flashbacks of my own wedding day – the silk, the scowls, the stress, the fumbling sex. I remember sitting on the toilet and whispering to God to *help me*. I remember dancing, dancing, dancing. I remember that Lucas didn't. Refused.

I loosen my bow tie, electricity crackling in my chest. Every villain looks like a hero in the right light.

Fred Astaire stretches out her arms, bends her knees, and jumps in.

The Word of Dog (Psalms)

Mortadella (the meat of pig)
Burrata (the milk of the new mother)
Focaccia (the body broken)
Champagne (the blood spilled)

Feast, beloved.

The Gospel According to Frances 24:6

The night ends with games. We're all joyously drunk, delirious with play. Murder in the Dark with criminals, ironically, feels entirely safe. It is the final activity around 2 am, every light in the castle turned off, and with the night's stragglers either hiding in corners, stifling giggles, or searching the halls with torchlight, hoping to catch costumed guests.

Fred Astaire, Spider-Man, Catwoman and Peter Pan are hiding behind a suit of armour, squashed like sardines. We danced and danced and danced. Our bodies moved like animals, like memories, like fire. I felt every age at once: seven, twelve, sixteen, twenty-three, twenty-eight, thirty-five, eighty-nine. We danced like it was our last night on earth. When the games began, the four of us scurried onto the second floor together, the sprinkled light catching us as merely a blur against the night.

It is a secret pleasure to be sad with someone who is also sad. It is a lovely betrayal of that sadness to be happy with them, too.

Who is this woman I have become in the darkness?

Tucked behind the decorative armour, Paul entwines his fingers with mine without uncertainty or clumsiness – as if we've done that one thousand times. Ruairí and Catwoman are curled into our laps, blissing out. This is not reality. We will not remember this in the morning. He won't look so wide-eyed and cheeky; I won't look so beautiful or brave. Ruairí won't look so young and handsome, and Catwoman won't look so effortlessly flexible. We'll be back to the bottom of the barrel, where Paul will help to charge me with a crime I did not commit, and I will have no alibi worth saying out loud.

Murder in the Dark. Murder in the Dark. Murder in the Dark.

If only we were children, in costume, and all this shit was just a party, a dance, a game.

I lean over and fall into the bodies of my friends, melting into shadows, into whispers, into hope.

It is my last night, after all. The world has already ended.

The Book of Jasper 3:1

I was there, see, in that toilet. And I was sleeping there and I was sleeping on my drugs and just waiting for the morning. I don't use. I just get my cash that way, right? And Sylvie bought from me; she bought junk and used quite a bit, and this time the hit had worn off, it had got shabby, and she came down and was having withdrawals, big ones. We'd . . . I'd seen her that night and she'd been fine, she'd been so content. But she was sleeping there – over there on that sports sub bench, and she came over scratching for a hit, but I didn't have any.

So I'm here on the ground – just here – and Sylvie comes in and she's all wild and angry and shit, and she starts to get physical and a bit pushy. She's not big and I don't punch chicks, I didn't touch her, but I was like, *Okay, Jasper, you gotta run now, you gotta get out, this bitch needs a hit you can't give her,* and I knew my supplier was around, I'd seen them that night. Like, I couldn't afford it, but I couldn't afford not to have any, she wouldn't leave me alone.

So I promise Sylvie, I'm like, *Come on, we'll go to the rosebushes, go chat, go get you some smack.*

Here, come here – it's these rosebushes here.

And Sylvie settles a bit, so we go, and we see my guy there, but this is where it gets weird. Because my guy isn't always my guy. Not always okay, right? Is sometimes good, sometimes not so good. And when I went over it wasn't good . . . My supplier is curled up in a ball, can't move, can't speak. And Sylvie thinks I'm fucking with her, right? So she cracks it, and she starts searching the guy for drugs, and she can't find any, just this little pocket-knife. So she starts to kick the body of my guy and scream, and

I'm like, *Girl, let's go, we'll find more tomorrow.* We walk back to her dugout, 'cos that's where she sleeps – just over there, yeah.

Yeah, so here she has another wave of it and asks me for some more and when I say no she punches me in the face . . . And I go down, and she kinda loses it and goes to jump over me, the knife in her hand, ready to cut me or stab me – like fully ready, arm back – when my supplier comes up from behind her with a tree branch and just takes her over the head. She went down straight away, on top of me, right here.

Oh, there's the branch. See? Near the playground. That's the blood.

And my guy just went back to this stiff state, and I was like fuck fuck fuck, and I went back to the toilet and I hid.

I say guy but they aren't a guy; they're like a mix. I dunno. But they were just trying to save me. They didn't want Sylvie to die. They just didn't want me to die either.

The Gospel According to Frances 24:7

The other three have already passed out in the four-poster bed, dawn leaving a pink wash on the wallpaper, life glowing through the open window. I refuse to sleep. If I sleep I'll go back. I don't want to. I will lie here, wrapped in warm bodies, drinking in stillness, and I will not close my eyes, I will not, I –

There's a knock at the door and I sit up, surprised.

'Hello?'

Silence.

I stand, slipping on the linen pyjamas quickly.

The knock sounds again. It is gentle, patient knocking.

I open the door cautiously.

Before me stands Achara, wrapped in a red silk gown, black hair in a slick bun, make-up immaculate.

'Thank you for holding my room for me. I've been wandering in the wilderness awhile.' They smile, eyes crinkling in apology, in sympathy, and in grief. 'It's time to return, Frances.'

I look at the bed, where Paul has begun to stir.

'Return . . . how?'

Achara doesn't answer, just kisses me on each cheek and bows low. They turn back to the hallway, indicating for me to close the door behind them.

I run back to the bed, burrow into the sheets, into the soft and open arms of the others in the drowsy morning light. Someone kisses my eyelids, and the limbs of the three other dreamers tangle with mine contentedly.

I lie there for the shortest breath before I fall asleep.

When I wake, it's a new day.

Report by Detective Devi Ramineni on the arrest of Achara Saelim, 28 August 2022

At 4.30 am on 28/8/2022 we arrested Achara Saelim at the Budapest residential hostel in New Farm. Saelim has been charged with supplying dangerous drugs (Section 6 *Drugs Misuse Act 1986*) and the murder of Sylvia Rathdowne.

Evidence for these charges was supplied largely by Jasper Berlusconi, who has also been charged with supplying dangerous drugs (as a recruit of Saelim). Due to Berlusconi being a minor, and his cooperation in confessing and providing essential evidence, he has been released on bail.

It is also apparent that Saelim is an unmedicated schizophrenic currently in a catatonic episode. They are biologically male and, according to sources, non-gendered. We are considering sending Saelim from the watch house to a mental health facility before they go before a court.

Previous suspect Frances Kocsmáros has been released from the watch house and all current charges have been dropped.

The investigation into Sylvia Rathdowne's organ donation without consent has been paused.

The Gospel According to Frances 25:1

I stand in the cold cell as Paul unlocks the perspex.

Last night feels like a dream, and my release just as surreal, but the punishing reality of what I must walk back into pushes on my brain and body like a hangover. Neve. Lucas. Mary.

In the station's foyer, a bleary-eyed Ruairí is already curled up on a plastic chair, eyes shut, while Paul processes my paperwork. Ruairí will have no recollection of what transpired in the night, of this much I am certain. They are barely conscious, the larrikin energy finally crashing hard into the ground.

Paul, in contrast, is pure professionalism. He does not meet my eyes, discreetly explains my rights and what charges have been dropped, and apologises for the inconvenience.

I nod numbly. *Does he remember?*

He returns my belongings to me in a plastic bag, and asks me to check all is there before I leave. I search his face for the dance, for the secrets, for his son. Nothing. In the bag I find my phone (*fucking hell, it's like a bomb's gone off in there*), my keys, my wallet . . . the coin, thimble, Jasper's key . . . and a tiny Matchbox LandCruiser.

to dance is to mourn is to dance

I look up, and for a moment Paul's eyes reflect the spinning lights of a mirror ball, as he pushes open the door and lets me walk free.

The Gospel According to Ruairí 1:1

Where is the sunlight here? Why are all the pieces of furniture bolted to the floor?

Every time I look in the mirror I see a different person. I waited for the moment when I might just recognise my own face, my own skin, and every day it gets further away from what I thought skin was supposed to be.

I am not bolted to the ground.

I went to the bridge because it's a metaphor for transition. *I'll cross the bridge*, I said. *I'll cross the bridge and I'll be there on the other side, and it will tell my body that soon it will be on the other side, too. The secret rite of passage. I'm suspended in between bodies*, I told myself. *But not forever.*

I got halfway across, and looked out into the water. It felt to me like the destination was gone in that moment, that only the river existed, that the bridge was not necessary. Why exist on either shore? Why exist on the exhausting spectrum of a bridge, when I belong in the water?

I play so many roles. This was only ever just another one. We must scrub off characters in the shower after every performance, otherwise we take them home with us.

Wash her away. Wash him away. Wash them away.

They had seen me on the CCTV and they ran over.
I got scared. Punched someone.

I wasn't going to jump. I was going to dive in.

Article in *The Courier Mail Online*, 15 June 2014

TEENAGER DIES AFTER HEAD-ON COLLISION ON BRUCE HIGHWAY

A 17-year-old Brisbane boy driving home from a party on the Sunshine Coast has died after his four-wheel-drive swerved into oncoming traffic and crashed into another vehicle. The driver and three passengers of the second vehicle are in a critical condition.

Acting Inspector Devi Ramineni called on anyone who may have been at the party or been a witness to the accident to call the police.

'We are trying to piece together a serious situation. A child has died, potentially under the influence of drugs. We need to understand where our children are accessing these drugs, who is supplying them, how we can prevent these deaths.'

It is understood the boy – who cannot be named for legal reasons – is the son of a police officer.

The Brisbane State High and West End community are grieving, and principal Gerard Pope has called for better drug and alcohol education in the public education system, asking the state government to fund an ongoing program.

Report by Senior Constable Paul Jacobs on the arrest of Ruairí Hickson

> Ruairí Hickson was found standing on the external railing of the Story Bridge at 12.07 am on 28/8/2022, under the influence of drugs and alcohol. It was understood that she/they were attempting to take their own life by jumping from the bridge. They punched a police officer on arrest.
>
> They were held overnight in the watch house for their own safety, and have been referred to psychiatric and rehabilitation services. They have not been charged.

Frances Kocsmáros's phone notifications, 28 August 2022

Rosemary Kocsmáros: 3 missed calls, 4 text messages.

Darling we need to speak urgently.
Yesterday 7.19 pm

Okay I got your message.
Yesterday 8.31 pm

I've tried calling back the watch house but they don't answer outside of work hours apparently.
Yesterday 8.45 pm

Don't panic, but when you get this, please come straight to hospital.
2.54 am

Fiona Ramke: 3 missed calls, 1 voice message
7.09 am

'Frances, the charges have been dropped, as I'm sure you know. Lucas Harkin's lawyer has contacted me to say that Lucas will leave Neve's bedside so you may have an opportunity to say goodbye to her.'

Reg Holland: 1 text message

Praying for you, Frances. Trust in the Lord!
Yesterday 10.04 pm

Lucas Harkin: 1 text message
4.16 am

Frances, I'm so scared. I think she's going.

The Gospel According to Frances 25:2

I am running, lungs stretching and tearing, the air is scalding. *Let me be fast enough, just stop time, let me be fast enough, let me breathe in enough air.*

I've run out of everything.

The doors of Emergency are open. There is no security. I run through them, into a room of people waiting to be pieced back together.

'Ma'am, do you need assistance?'

I know where the PICU is, I've run these halls in my sleep.

There is a stray dog in the corner of the waiting room, curled up on a hygiene pad.

I catch my breath, and then I bolt.

The Book of Mary 14:1

My milk is in. Leaking, squirting, jet-streaming. I feel like I have two fake tits, hard as oranges. The milk is a watery blue now, perfect for making him fat. I pump it, give it to the nurses, who give it to the baby. The baby has been claimed by the state. There is a court date tomorrow, they said. Or we could 'work something out between us'. They want to negotiate my consent to give him away. The son of God, not even held against skin. The son of Mary. Consecrated, set aside, put behind the plastic veil of a humidicrib.

They lied then. The spirit of God must be contained in a building, not the human heart. He has to be given a home with four walls, a home other than me and my arms. He's too holy for his whore of a mother.

They said I can keep bringing milk to him in the NICU if I remain clean.

I've always been clean. By the blood.

I don't cry. My breasts cry for me. He drinks my sadness. He drinks my love.

to be born is to die is to be born

I wish I could do either.

The Gospel According to Frances 25:3

Neve's body is attached to every machine imaginable.

Mum is already there by her side. I enter, and she grips onto me as if I am her parachute. I let her fall away. It has been days since I have seen or touched my child. I hover over Neve's body, the PICU nurse watching closely, as if I might suddenly turn and do something violent.

Neve is yellow, limp, and there is a crust forming around her intubated mouth. My bright and precious child. A shadow of life.

Dr Simon Yates comes in. He's gentle, he speaks softly to me about livers, about *acute graft rejection* about *infection* about *metastases*. He can see I am not listening.

He takes my hands. 'You are tired, Frances. But I need you to hold on just a little bit longer. This is touch and go. We have tried so hard. And we haven't given up, not yet.'

But I have given up, because it is right to give up, and he knows that. My body loses its footing as I heave and retch and sob upon the shoulder of a doctor who knows and cares but cannot perform miracles.

He eases me into the chair next to Neve's bed, his own emotions in check, ever the professional.

'Just let her be with her mum. Let that distance heal. Just be here, now.'

He asks the PICU nurse for a word, tugs my own mother away for a cup of sugary tea, and closes the curtain. We are alone with breath and body. We are back to our first moments outside of the one womb. My child and I, water over perfect skin, together forever again.

Report by Department of Children, Youth Justice and Multicultural Affairs, Child Safety social worker Anneke Dowd regarding Penelope Lingard and her male baby, 28 August 2022

We've received information from representatives of various agencies, including Detective Devi Ramineni from the Queensland Police Service and Reverend Reg Holland of the Eternal Fire Street Mission, of the minor's circumstances and parental capability. We have made the assessment that as Penelope is unable to provide accommodation, ongoing financial support or stable health to this child, it is appropriate for the child to be placed into state care on an 18-year plan.

The baby was born at 34 weeks, six weeks premature. He is currently requiring CPAP and oxygen support, and will be in the NICU and special care nursery until 38–40 weeks. An initial court date is scheduled for Monday. A foster carer or adoptive family will be organised while the child is in the NICU. The mother is being encouraged to express and pump breast milk for the child, but we have concerns about the mother viewing or holding the child. The mother and child have both tested negative for drugs at this stage, but the mother apparently has a history of drug use and illegal soliciting. Penelope will be discharged today.

The Gospel According to Frances 26:1

I stir in the seat beside Neve's bed. I didn't realise I had fallen asleep. My hands reach for her before my eyes catch up, and feel warmth – *she's still there*. But there's something else, something tapping the window of my senses, saying, *wake up wake up wake up, you idiot*.

The smell of jasmine.

There is music playing in the background. Vivaldi's 'Spring'. Weird. I force myself out of the comfort of sleep to face whatever strange reality I'm in now.

I'm back in the bedroom I drank broth in, after the hot spring. It's soft, pastel-coloured and full of light. I'm in an armchair, my feet raised. But Neve is not on the king-size bed beside me. The person whose leg I have touched twitches in his sleep, drooling in a way I remember all too well, his body burrowed into the blankets in exhaustion, like he hasn't slept in days. Which he probably hasn't. Because the person curled up beside me is my ex-husband Lucas.

I stiffen. I've been invited to the Inn again – in *this* moment in time – but it is time I don't have. I was waylaid by the debaucherous watch house ball. I never spoke to the Innkeepers, never even saw them. Now my only priority is to return to Neve.

I move my hand away from Lucas's sleeping body. He stirs, reaches for whomever was touching him, for the comfort of presence. When he settles again, I stand.

As I walk towards the door, I notice I am wearing a dress of peach-coloured satin that shimmers and ripples in the morning light.

What am I doing here?

My feet are in leather sandals, and my hair is braided around my head like a band of flowers. I have fine gold jewellery in my ears and on my wrists. It's so *feminine,* so elegant. It's a bit perturbing. I wonder if I'm supposed to be going to an event.

It doesn't matter. You cannot be anywhere but with your child.

I have a purse with me – gold mesh. I never have a purse.

Inside I find the coin, the thimble, the key and the Matchbox car. My gifts.

Like fuck they are.

I do not look back at Lucas's sleeping form as I walk into the hospital's secret world. Instead of the hallway I've stepped out into a stairwell. It's beautiful, nothing like the hospital car park's ten flights of fire exit stairs. Here the steps are carpeted. They have wooden banisters, soft lights on each landing.

The stairs only go up. So up I go.

Text messages between Frances Harkin and Kelly Linden, 4 May 2020

Frances: *I'm sorry to send you a message out of the blue, but I think I need some advice.*

Kelly: *Oh, sure. Are you okay? Is it personal advice or lawyer advice?*

Frances: *Lawyer advice, I guess?*

Kelly: *Sure.*

Frances: *I'm trying to leave my marriage. I just . . . I don't know how to do it safely.*

Kelly: *Okay I'm going to call you. I can't represent you, but I can talk you through your rights.*

The Book of Mary 15:1

I wake up feeling sick. I know what it means to cross over. I know it means I've been invited. But for the first time I don't want to go.

I know the Inn, I work for the Inn, I stay at the Inn, in its many iterations. It's all part of the same system, and I'm just another little cog in that system. Another vessel. Another virgin slut for another saviour, right? A disposable body to bear a man who'll change the world. Someone's world, but certainly not mine. I'm not even allowed to touch him.

Fuck the Innkeepers. Frances was right.

I look around, finally. I'm in a room with crocheted vegetables and fruits strung up like bunting. What the fuck? There are bright colours, and wallpaper with little squiggles on it, and lamps in the shapes of giraffes. There's a tiny chest of drawers. There's a mobile, with Australian parrots flying in a circle. There's a cot. And inside the cot I see blankets, wrapped tightly, and out of them sprouts black hair and the tiny curled-up hand of a . . .

Oh.

I go over. He's stirring, bringing the hand to his mouth, sucking it. Gives a little cry. Sucks again. Going to give himself a hickey like that. He starts to really cry out. What do I do?

Pick him up.

I pick him up. He smells like baby. My baby. He smells like *me*.

When I hold him in my arms he calms a bit. He's so small, so soft and limp. Like a bag of rice or something. So fierce. He nuzzles into my chest, looking for food. Smells it and starts to really scream now. *Shit, I have no pump.*

Except I *am* the pump. I am a food machine.

You can feed him. You can do it.

I sit back on the bed I've been sleeping in. It's soft, with a heap of pillows piled up as if ready for me to lean on them. I have no idea what to do but somehow this baby knows. I take my shirt off, let him throw his little head sideways. He wiggles to my nipple like a caterpillar, latches on like he's never been fed in his life. I guess he hasn't.

I feel a weird prickly tingling in my tit and then it kind of releases, like a tap has been turned on, and the other nipple is jet-streaming everywhere and I'm soaked in milk but the baby is sucking, sucking, sucking and the relief is fucking blissful. His body relaxes, tiny fists unclench. *I DID IT. I FUCKING DID IT.*

Eventually he's sleeping, sucking, dreaming, sucking, curled into me like he's back in the womb. Back home. In his own room.

You are perfect. You are magic. You are mine. And I am yours.

The Gospel According to Frances 26:2

I pass a handful of doors, all numbered. It doesn't seem appropriate to try them.

There are two unmarked doors on the top landing. One has a carefully engraved handle – the round, bulbous kind that you turn – and a keyhole. It is locked. The other has a beautifully polished copper handle – the long kind that you push down. It's unlocked. As I push the door open, the smell of jasmine hits again, along with a sharp draught of fresh air.

I step out onto a flat roof. It reminds me of a terrace on a Tuscan hillside. There are flowers in pots, jasmine and bougainvillea cascading down walls, terracotta tiles underfoot. A long table sits in the middle of the space, set with cutlery, glasses and platters of food, with olive leaves for decoration. At the centre of the table is a cake, topped with rose-coloured whipped cream and sugar petals in the shape of a mandala. Four candles are nestled within it, and in front of those candles sits a healthy, wholly effervescent Neve.

'Mummy!'

She stands on her seat and waves both hands in glee. She's dressed in a lavender fairy dress, all tulle and wings, with flowers in her hair.

I find myself running, the light wind pressing the satin dress against my body. I feel it all. I feel it all, right down to my bones. My arms grab her, hold her. *She's real, it isn't a dream.*

'I've been waiting so long for you to get here, Mum.' Her face is so alive, so enthralled. *My Neve.*

'I know. I'm so sorry I'm late.'

She runs a chubby hand down my face and along the billows of my dress. 'I love this. It's perfect.'

I'm confused. 'Perfect for what, Nevie?'

'The party, Mummy. We're having a party. For me.'

My heart goes wild with panic. No we're not. We're not, I refuse. I will not have it, I will not celebrate it, I will protest – I will find the Innkeepers and I will beg and plead and punch and kick them and steal the book in which they've written this and rip out all the pages. I'm not going to pretend I don't understand. Neve is almost gone, and this is her farewell.

But she's here, Frances. Right now.

The voice is mine, but a part of me I haven't heard in a long time.

This is what she wants.

My grip on Neve lessens ever so slightly.

She brushes her hair from her face, no hearing aids, no yellow skin. A perky grin. 'There is a big bath here, Mummy, and a beautiful lady who makes me peanut butter sandwiches whenever I want, and the puppy is here too, and he keeps changing shape, and there are the Innkeepers, who –'

I'm there, ready to catch whatever she is about to say, but she trails off, eyes wide, staring at something behind me.

'DADDY!'

I'm crushed. My one private moment with my child, and of course he has to burst into it.

I turn to see that Lucas is dressed decadently now too, in a pale blue buttoned shirt and cream trousers. Neve, delighted, takes him by the hand and drags him towards me.

The three of us gather around the table, the hostility of our parental conflict permeating even *this* reality.

'Frances. What is this?'

'If you're looking for someone to blame, you might have to talk to the Big Man, Lucas.'

I see Neve's face falter for a moment, looking between us with anxiety, waiting for the explosion.

No, no, no. This is not right. I regroup. Meet Lucas's eyes. I realise what I've interpreted as cruelty might actually just be fear.

'Are we in heaven?' he stutters, wide-eyed, reaching for Neve's shoulder as if to steady himself.

'No,' I say. 'This is a place that opens up for people who need it. And I think we need it today.'

Lucas takes it all in. He leans over to admire the beautifully decorated cake.

Beaming, Neve points to the olive leaves adorning the table. 'I picked these myself.'

'Oh yes?' replies Lucas gently. 'Where from?'

She giggles and shrugs.

So many secrets.

'Everyone is invited to the party. We have to make *art* while we wait.'

She takes us each by the hand and pulls us to another part of the lush rooftop, where a low table is covered in craft materials – a child's dream. I notice the view from the roof does not look like Brisbane's CBD. It boasts rolling hills, streams, meadows. Horses graze on green grass. This is everything Neve would ever want in a party.

The two of us paying attention to her in the same place, at the same time, is all she has ever wanted.

She makes herself comfortable at the art table, so desperately and fiercely alive.

'Daddy, you make invitations. Mummy, you make crowns. I'll make the *gifts*.'

Lucas and I do not hesitate. We sit either side of her, and we begin.

The Book of Mary 15:2

His skin is on my skin. I have decided we will never be apart.

Dog comes trotting in, his fur freshly washed, all fluffy, like some show dog. They do it as a joke. He never stays in that form for long when they're around.

I do not look at Dog. I only look at the baby.

Dog does not try to come to him, doesn't try to sniff him or lick him. Doesn't notice I don't have a shirt on and wouldn't understand it anyway. Doesn't act jealous or weird. It's a relief.

I feel myself starting to cry and I didn't realise I could do that anymore, to be honest. I have big, hot tears, and they are the slimy horror, and the stinging fear; they are the relief of him with me, and the pressure of him coming out of me, and the scream of him being taken so far away.

I cry all over him, my tears splotching him, and he doesn't wake; just lets me christen him like this.

'What's his name?' Dog has changed now. Typical.

'Gabriel.'

'Gabriel. The angel of good news.'

'Yeah.'

'I like it.'

Dog wanders off to his own room, his hands brushing over Gabriel's furniture and toys with curiosity.

I lay the baby Gabriel on the bed and pull my shirt over my chest.

I have to find the Innkeepers.

The Gospel According to Frances 26:3

Lucas has had to make about six different invitations, for whom he has no idea. I have made strange crowns out of flowers and pipe cleaners and tiny foam stickers. Neve thinks they're all *perfect*. She has made the gifts: elaborate drawings, none of which we are allowed to see. She has wrapped each of them up inside themselves, and taped them down with stickers in the shape of farm animals.

'Now we place them around the table.'

I wonder how she knows this, whether she's done it before. There is a system she recognises and obeys, the strange flow of a young child who understands a ritual, and pours into the next transition like water from a cup. Someone has been brushing her hair, washing her face, feeding her meals here, all while she has lain in an induced coma in BUH. *Who has been taking care of her?* It can't have been Lucas; his shock upon seeing this place was genuine.

I'm unsure if I feel protective or grateful. Nurses have cared for Neve for more nights of her life than I care to reflect on. I'm used to that pang of handing your heart to anonymous hands, however compassionate they might be. This feels different, personal. Someone here *knows* her. Loves her.

As if on cue, the door to the stairwell opens slowly, and a little boy – no older than five or six – steps into the sunlight, squinting. He has black, scruffy hair, brown eyes and skin, and a toothy grin. He's wearing a shirt and shorts and his feet are bare. It's a far cry from the regalia Neve's somehow manifested for herself and her parents.

'Neve!'

Neve squeals and jumps up from the low table, grabbing an invitation out of Lucas's pile – a primitive drawing of a flower, complete with Neve's name.

She embraces the boy, hands him the invitation and gestures to the table. 'Are you coming to the party? It's my turn.'

'Yeah, all right.'

He must be another patient, I guess. Another poor kid in PICU whose parents don't know if he'll live or die. They must all visit this place.

Neve tugs him over to us by the hand, radiant. Thrilled to have her friend close. Delighted to share in it all with us.

'Mummy, Daddy. This is my friend. Everyone calls him Dog.'

Recorded conversation between Frances Harkin and Lucas Harkin, 12 June 2020

Frances: *You've been tracking me?*

Lucas: *What do you mean?*

Frances: *With that app. You've been stalking me.*

Lucas: *No, that's in case someone steals your phone, Frances. It's normal security.*

Frances: *You're lying.*

Lucas: *Why are you being so paranoid?*

Frances: *I'm not.*

Lucas: *Did you go somewhere you don't want me to know about?*

Frances: *No, I took Neve to an appointment.*

Lucas: *How's Kelly going?*

Frances: *What?*

Lucas: *Kelly, your ex-girlfriend. Who you were on the phone to for fifty-seven minutes last night.*

Frances: *What the fuck?!*

Lucas: *Suddenly you swear a lot, you know.*

Frances: *Are you recording this? Why are you holding your phone like that?*

Lucas: *I won't let you make me the bad guy. You're being crazy and evasive. You need to know – I need to be able to show you –*

Frances: *What is happening to you?*

Lucas: *To me? I've stayed exactly the same, while everything about you has changed. I'm afraid you'll run off with our child at any moment, you're so volatile right now. Calling your lesbian exes, talking about studying or going off on big trips for Neve's sake . . . I need to protect my family.*

Frances: *This isn't a family, it's a dictatorship.*

Lucas: *I would die for you, Frances.*

Frances: *No, you wouldn't. Don't say that.*

Lucas: *You are my wife. We are one.*

Frances: *We aren't one.*
Lucas: *The Bible says –*
Frances: *I don't care what it says.*
Lucas: *What?*
Frances: *I don't want this. I want to leave. I am leaving.*
Lucas: *To go where?*
Frances: *I'm done.*
Lucas: *Divorce is not an option for us.*
Frances: *It is what I am choosing.*
Lucas: *You don't get to make that choice.*
Frances: *I do. I already have. I have my bag at Mum's. Neve is already there.*
Lucas: *Frances, please, don't –*
Frances: *Do not come near me right now. Don't block me –*
Lucas: *I would never hurt you. Babe, I want to save this –*
Frances: *Don't. Just don't.*

Dog sits with us as we continue to craft. He grins at me occasionally, but gives most of his attention to Neve.

She chooses a crown for him (green pipe cleaners, pink bougainvillea, a yellow cow sticker) and a gift, and shows him where he'll be sitting.

They chat and giggle, somehow old friends.

When the little boy puts his crown on, Neve excitedly declares they should play a game, and they spend the next fifteen minutes being Kings and Queens, with Neve bossing him around like he's her brother.

Lucas and I simply watch on flabbergasted, our hands subconsciously still making creations in an attempt to ease any awkwardness.

'She could have been prime minister,' he says eventually, staring at her bouncing around, giving orders with an olive branch in hand.

'I'm unsure how suited to the democratic process she would be. I suspect it would be Queen Neve or nothing.'

He chuckles. He *chuckles*. As if we're back on our old couch, trying to have a glass of wine while Neve makes us laugh in the background. As if we're exhausted from another day of working together, rolling our eyes at Reg together, berating Gregory for lying together, unstacking the dishwasher and folding the clothes and dreaming about holidays and adventures and schools and futures and shit TV shows and the plans of God together. *Together*. But we aren't together. We've never been further apart.

The man who told me he would die for me has attempted to destroy me. He has done everything in his power to hurt me. He has robbed me of my peace, robbed me of my grief, robbed me of my last days with my child. He has lashed out in reactive spite, unwilling to accept I could have a different experience of our marriage from him, unwilling to believe I could change my mind, unwilling to believe he was ever short-sighted or selfish or cruel in the name of love.

Sure, tell me I'll be kicked out of heaven, mate. But the truth rises eventually. The truth has risen, in me.

Somehow, after all I've inflicted and all I've endured, in this moment I still feel the wonder. I still feel as if someone, somewhere is attempting to tell me that they think I'm all right. That they love how that eight hours of sleep looks on me. That my choices will not break me. That I'm inherently kind, even if I wasn't just then. That I should eat the cake, because who knows when the next chance will come. That the girl I like has a crush on me, they're sure of it (*look at how she turned back around to see you*) and that the song is perfect to dance to (*just start the party, just close your eyes and move*) – and that my instincts are right (*take your kid to hospital, don't be ashamed, you're doing your best, it's all you can do*). That someone, somewhere is thinking of me today, because today is difficult, and I am known and I am loved.

I am not sure I could ever forgive Lucas for loving the Bible more than me and Neve. And that's the difference, isn't it? If he had loved God more than Scripture, perhaps it would have all flowed on. Maybe I could have tasted his tenderness and sacrifice, accessed his vulnerability and strength. Maybe I could have loved him, and he could have loved me. But instead we dutifully loved the same old collection of poems and stories and diary entries and receipts, bound together and called 'biblical law', and assumed that this shared love meant marriage. The Bible gave me the boundaries I wanted, and it gave him the purpose he lacked, as if somehow the scrunched-up notes of floundering humans might translate to the infallible blueprint of life. It showed us the truth about a handful of lives, no doubt about it – but that truth is ugly. That truth states that life is absurdly difficult and death is inevitable – even for God. That we will look for God everywhere, everywhere, everywhere, except exactly where we are. And wherever we hurt most, is the place that God will be. If God were to exist, of course.

The day Lucas and I separated was the day I decided not to read the Bible anymore, and decided to write my own.

I've been staring off the roof, into the rolling hills of this mysterious hospital world. I look at Lucas and see that he is pensive, too. He has stopped making craft, and is staring at Neve with a distinct yearning. I know that yearning.

'Are you all right, Lucas?'

He shrugs, scratches at the stubble on his chin, hands clasping his jaw as if they might stop words or feelings from escaping without permission.

'I just miss it.'

'What?'

'Our life. The good bits. I miss it.'

'Was any of it good, really?' I ask, because I want to know. I don't remember.

'There were moments when I thought, *Even if none of this is real, even if the worst possible things in life happened, even if it all ended tomorrow and there was nothing there on the other side . . . it is worth doing this life with you.* And now the worst possible things *have* happened, and it *will* end tomorrow, and I don't have you. I don't have her. I don't have anyone.'

He is crying, I realise. Lost, searching tears.

'You have God.'

'Fucking hell, Frances. You think God betrayed *you?* How do you think it feels to have grown up in a system that never even gave you a choice? I have been deserted.'

I'm taken aback.

'Lucas –'

'I didn't even get a testimony. I never got to have a wild, juicy before story, then live this reformed good-boy life. My before-meeting-Jesus story was like: "Lucas didn't turn up to youth group one week, I wonder if he's backslidden?" That's as much as I got to repent for. Which means that's as much as I got to experience of actual life. I'm a fifth-generation pastor. And now I have the boring, godly life, with the important, godly job, but I don't even have the family life or the community or the miracles to make it worthwhile. I don't feel God close to me. I am no more blessed for following His rules. I just lose. I lose and I lose and I lose. And if I ever want anything else for my life, I'll lose everything.'

I let him get it out. I've never heard anything, *anything* like this from Lucas. He has always maintained the stance of Job.

I will suffer and praise. I will believe harder for the miracle. I will never blame God. I will see the goodness of the Lord in the land of the living.

'Welcome to the dark side,' I say. 'It suits you.'

He laugh-sobs in protest. 'And yet, we're here.' He stares around the terrace, bathed in soft light, clouds floating in the sky like they were painted just for Neve. 'Is it wrong that it doesn't feel like enough? That I feel disappointed?'

'That unless God came up to you on His hands and knees, repenting for the way He has fucked over your life, it might never be enough?'

He nods, swiping at his tears as if they might be acid.

'I don't know what this place is, Lucas. And I don't think it matters how you feel about it. I think we're allowed to feel like shit.'

'Good. I do.'

Lucas cries, and I grip his arm to let him know that *I get it,* and soon he is sobbing into my shoulder, ripping at the air with his grief. He is hurting honestly, openly and all at once. And all at once, I realise I might one day forgive him.

'Mummy, there are some more guests coming to the party but I don't know the letters for their names. I need you to write them.'

Neve sees us with our arms around one another, doesn't frown or question it, just moves through it with a natural ease. She retrieves some of Lucas's invitations, and she gestures to the door we came in through.

'I don't know who they are, my love. I can't write names I don't know.'

'I'll go and ask them.'

She runs off towards the door. I stand to follow, confused, then look back at Lucas. Dog has wandered over and is beginning to chat to him animatedly. My ex-husband gathers himself in order to be vaguely present for the child.

Ahead of me, Neve runs through the exit and into the stairwell. I run after her, anxious at her sudden disappearance. *Not now, not yet.* I too slip through the door.

Neve is nowhere to be seen once I'm inside the stairwell. Across the landing, the locked door stands before me, its handle gleaming in the dim light. I attempt to open it – still no luck. I peer over the railing. There's no sound of four-year-old feet pitter-pattering down the stairs, no blur of lavender tulle. She *must* have gone through the door across the landing.

I knock.

No answer. Or perhaps a sudden quiet?

I knock again.

Nobody comes. There's only silence. As if they're waiting for me to open it myself. Except I can't open it, I haven't been given –

Oh. I open my purse and pull out Jasper's key.

to speak is to be silent is to speak

Letter from Lucas Harkin to Frances Harkin, 16 June 2020

Frances,

I am writing to inform you I have separated our assets – please see the spreadsheet below. I have split our finances as I deemed fair, considering I am the one in full-time employment. If you want to make this decision, you can carry the financial consequences of it.

I reject your claim as 'primary parent'. There is no such thing. I would like 50/50 custody and recognition of my equal role as parent to our child.

I would like to ensure that no medical decision is made without my consent, and no spiritual formation undertaken without my full briefing and consent.

I have informed the church, and the families we are close to, of your betrayal and your abandonment of this family. I've spoken about you with respect and hope you will do the same about me.

You may have left this marriage, but I never will. I will always be your husband under God. I will always be devoted to my vows before Him. I will inform our child of what you have done, so she understands.

Bless you as you go, but remember you are nothing without Jesus. Nothing.

Lucas

The Gospel According to Frances 26:5

The door does not open into a room. I should have expected this, but I did not.

It is a grove of olive trees. *Gethsemane*. They twist and arch over soft grass and dust, their trunks ancient and gnarled. The grove extends as far as the eye can see in the hazy morning light.

Under a nearby tree is Neve, unfazed, chattering incomprehensibly to a woman in a white wedding dress. She has blonde hair, beautiful piercings. A whole, perfect face, lit up with delight at the presence of my child.

Sylvie.

The door closes behind me, and I stumble in my haste to reach them.

'Frances! You took your bloody time!'

Sylvie embraces me, her hair iridescent, her body filled out. She feels quite real, and I flounder internally, trying to piece together where we could possibly be.

'Sylvie has been helping me do stuff here, Mummy. We hang out.' She smiles adoringly at the bride, who in no way resembles a deceased heroin addict. 'We like the same kinds of dresses.'

Sylvie takes my hand and squeezes it, as if to say, *I can explain*. She turns to my daughter, instead: 'I am ready for the party, Nevie.'

Neve gives Sylvie an invitation. Her name has somehow appeared on it without my assistance, in a beautiful cursive hand. I always forget how weird this place gets.

'Where are the others?' Neve asks Sylvie.

Sylvie smiles, gathers up her skirts. 'They're around, don't worry.'

'And the Innkeepers?'

'Later, little one.'

Neve skips back towards the door, which appears in the grove as a whitewashed hut with a thatched roof.

Sylvie and I follow slowly behind her.

'Are you . . . Is this . . .?' I ask tentatively, afraid to say it.

'No, no, nothing like that. This is just part of the Inn. I've passed on to somewhere else entirely, but I lingered for a while, because a part of me is still alive here.'

I falter, then remember: *her liver, in Neve.*

'I'm a visitor, no matter how much I would like to stay,' she adds, with a sadness that catches me off guard. 'I always wanted to be a mother, you know. And now perhaps I understand a little bit of what that feels like. Your soul running around outside of your own body.' She looks at me with gratitude, and it cuts like a knife.

to kiss is to pierce is to kiss

'Sylvie, who are the Innkeepers?'

She pauses, as if solving something in her mind. '*Who* is a complicated question. *Where* is probably the answer you are looking for. Or *when*.'

'I need to know, I need to speak with them.' I am desperate.

She nods, eyeing the key I'm still holding. 'Don't be afraid, Frances.'

Sylvie points to a path through the dense olive trees, obscured by foliage. She presses her palm into my shoulder, as if to say *go*, then turns back to follow my daughter like a shadow. *My daughter*, who skips and twirls through the open door to attend her final party.

The Book of Mary 16:1

I don't have a key, which means I'm not invited to speak with them. I am, however, used to going into places I am not invited. So fuck it.

The child and Sylvie run out full pelt, colours streaming like tulle tornados. They do not see me behind the second door, they do not see me hold it open, or duck into the olive grove. They do not hear Gabriel squeak in his sleep as the cool air settles on his skin.

I know the way from here. The garden of grief is always the same.

The Gospel According to Frances 26:6

The table is set under a clearing in the trees.

It's an exact replica of Neve's party table on the Tuscan terrace – the same branches and plates, the same cake. The same crafted place settings, Neve's same wrapped 'gifts' in the centre of the crowns. However, different people sit around this table, while one person in particular arranges its decor with delicate intention.

In a lavender ball dress, all tulle and lace, with flowers in her long, curly hair, stands a woman, perhaps twenty-five years old. She is radiant. A picture of confidence, strength and beauty. Her eyes are green, kind – she has laugh lines already. She's statuesque. The kind of woman I might be intimidated by, if I did not already understand implicitly that this woman is my daughter.

At the table sit three others. A woman in her forties, with platinum blonde hair, wearing a wedding dress. A man in his fifties, eyes crinkled and hair grey, in a blue shirt with cream pants. And a woman in her fifties, in the peach-coloured satin gown.

The older version of me wears it better, with an ease I admire. Her brown hair is pulled back in a low bun, her collarbones are fine. She looks soft. Softer than I know myself to be.

I take them all in like they are a vision. It isn't until the older Neve speaks that my focus clarifies, and I recall why I have come.

'You wanted to see us, Frances?' she asks, voice like a wind chime.

'Uh . . . yeah. I did.'

The older Frances laughs so heartily I am almost offended.

'You find it quite difficult to receive gifts, don't you?' she says knowingly.

I'm startled by that. 'No. I find it quite difficult to lose and lose and lose, and then be told that loss is a gift I should be grateful for.'

The Innkeepers go silent, the air pulsing between us all. I don't know if they're listening, or preparing to speak. I don't know if I have said the wrong thing. Then I realise the older Frances – so soft, so different – has started to cry.

'What do you want to say?' she asks me, without condescension.

It feels impossible to get the words out. It feels almost wrong to lay it before them like they're judges. I want to know, and of course I do not want to know – I just want it to be different. An answer will not solve it.

'I want to understand why . . . why my child has to die.'

The air ripples. The older Lucas and older Frances nod to the older Neve.

'Because that is her story,' the older Neve answers simply. She reaches for the hand of the elder Lucas, and I flinch involuntarily.

'But isn't that the point?' I ask. 'She doesn't *get* a story anymore.'

I'm aching, hurting, furious that I have to defend my pain.

'Doesn't she?' asks older Neve. The complex, elegant adult straightens her back and looks me in the eye, her face resolute. 'I can assure you that she does.'

The older Lucas stands and walks towards the older Frances. He puts his arms around her as she remains seated.

Is this what would have happened, what could have happened, if I hadn't left, if I hadn't fucked it . . . ?

As if hearing my thoughts, he smiles. 'This is just who we are after it all takes place. After all the ebbs and the flows. Once the dust settles, and everyone has the information they always longed to know.' He speaks to me with such delicacy and tact. Such understanding.

The older Frances glows at him, like a mother proud of a father's evolving parenting. 'She barely recognises you.'

He laughs. 'She barely recognises *you*.'

The older Frances smooths out the satin of her dress and stands. Lucas moves out of the way respectfully. They aren't a couple, I realise with relief. They're *friends*.

The older Sylvie says nothing, just holds her invitation with delight, and smiles as Frances walks towards me like she's walking on water.

'I've been trying so hard to reach you. I have wanted to hold you for so long.'

With strong arms she pulls my hardness into her softness. She smells like jasmine. Like the Inn. Like the dinner, the beach, the dance floor. She smells like the butterfly quilt. She holds me tightly, lets me bury myself in the weight of my future learnings, in my future losses, in my future story. Soft, like moving water. Smooth, like weathered stones.

The person writing my story is me. The person writing my story is me. The person writing my story is me.

The Book of Mary 16:2

I move through the trees. They're all at the table.

Frances is there. *Wow.* Frances.

Our own familiars are missing; they must not have come out yet. They will.

I've come to this table so many times. I came to this table when they told me I would get free. I came to this table when they told me I would get pregnant. I came to this table after I missed the abortion. I came to this table when they told me I needed to find Frances. I came to this table when they told me to go north. The demanding god of the actualised self. The brutally all-knowing, all-seeing *hindsight.*

Well. Now I've come to this table to tell them where to shove it.

The Gospel According to Frances 26:7

Two shapes appear from the trees behind the elders and their table. I pull away from the embrace of my future, distracted. There is a woman in her thirties, with a shaved head. And a boy of twenty or so, lanky, hair black and eyes blue.

'I have questions too.' The teenage voice behind me crackles with an electric anger.

The older Mary whispers something in the ear of the twenty-year-old boy. They walk over to where sixteen-year-old Mary stands behind me. Younger Mary is dressed in pyjamas, hair long and in plaits. She is cradling a perfect, dark-haired baby close to her chest.

I want to scoop her into a post-partum recovery bed immediately, bring her soup and tea and cake. She should be resting, nestling into the hum of newborn bliss. Except this is the Inn, not reality. *So what is she doing here?*

'May I hold him?' asks the boy.

To my surprise, younger Mary shakes her head.

'I want to speak with you.'

She gestures to older Mary, also in pyjamas, who nods in understanding. 'All of you, actually.'

The collection of Innkeepers pull out their chairs and sit at the table, as if preparing themselves to hear her out. The young man stares at his teenage mother, compelled.

The older Mary gestures to her younger self. 'Please. Speak.'

'I don't want this story anymore.'

'Why not?'

'I want to keep him.'

The older Mary looks to the older Frances, as if to exchange generational knowledge, a deeper wisdom.

'We can't keep *anyone*. Least of all children.'

The teenage girl begins to tremble, her body constricted with grief.

'No, no, no. You asked me to trust you. Told me it was worth it. How *dare* you give me this child, then rob me of being his mother.'

The face of older Mary is cracked with compassion and concern. 'I am still asking you to trust me.'

'Well I don't trust you. I hate you. I don't want to do this anymore. I don't want to know the future. I don't want Dog's help. I don't want to visit the Inn. I can do it without you.'

The Innkeepers are still, unreadable.

The older Mary nods, conflicted. 'I love you,' she says softly.

Mary shakes her head. 'You don't know me at all.'

She turns to leave with her baby, the conversation seemingly over.

Then the twenty-year-old boy stands, voice quivering. 'Mum. Please.'

Younger Mary hesitates, and turns back. She looks at his blue eyes, at how his mouth matches hers, how they mirror the best parts of one another.

'Gabriel?'

He walks up, embraces her. 'Thank you.'

Gabriel kisses his tiny infant self, then kisses his mother's cheek again.

'Don't say goodbye,' she pleads. 'Not yet –'

'First just go to the party. Go say goodbye to Neve.'

The older Neve smiles at his words, and I could swear more flowers bloom in her nest of hair with every holy breath she takes.

The Book of Mary 16:3

Frances and I walk back through the trees, away from the Innkeepers. We do not look back.

Neither of us has answers, but we have our babies, for now. I can tell she wants to get back to Neve. Like there's something ticking inside her, urgent, making her legs move faster. I know that feeling now.

She stares at Gabriel, still sleeping in my arms as we walk.

'So, Mary . . .' she says, kind of smiling.

'Yeah?'

'How's your vag?'

I snuggle my baby's milky head closer to my breast. It's getting sore and full now.

'Jasper will never be the same again after what he witnessed.'

We laugh then, like we're crying, because really they're just the same thing. And Gabriel croaks and mews, and Frances calls him *perfect* and we walk through the door, back into the stairwell, then step out into the sweet, sweet air of the rooftop. There are no more questions now, because all the guests have finally arrived, and right in the middle is a giddy, grinning four-year-old girl hugging a cheeky little boy called Dog.

The Gospel According to Frances 26:8

The party has begun. Lucas sits by Sylvie, who chats to him with great enthusiasm, gesturing to Neve and Dog, whose faces are smeared with chocolate. The children explode with excitement at the arrival of the baby, and rush to smother him with sticky fingers and crows of adoration.

Gabriel, Mary tells me she has named him. *Because he is good news.*

We eat cake. It tastes like white chocolate and pink lemonade. We delight in the delight of Neve.

Neve instructs us to open our presents. The others unwrap their drawings and present them to the table in exaggerated astonishment, letting Neve burst with pride at each reveal. Drawings of each of them with crowns upon their heads and flowers at their feet. Drawings of cake, drawings of the Inn, drawings of Neve and Sylvie holding hands.

I open mine last. It is a picture of us together. All of us. And wrapped in the picture is a ring. A tiny crown of thorns, engraved with words.

to hold is to let go is to hold

Lucas sees me lift it into the light and reacts in surprise.

'I thought you got rid of that.'

'I lost it, actually.'

I feel its weight in my left hand beneath the table and slip it into my mesh purse. Neve is waiting patiently for me to present my drawing to the other guests, where it is met with cheers of approval.

Neve points out each character in the drawing.

'That's Mummy, that's Daddy, that's the cake, that's Dog, that's Sylvie, that's Mary and Gabriel . . . I drew him in last minute floating in the sky . . . and that's Big Neve. She's wearing a beautiful dress too.'

Lucas stares at the picture, stricken. I place a hand on his shoulder, urge the warmth from my own beholding of adult Neve to rush into his body. I want to offer him tenderness. I want to acknowledge his loss.

The sun has descended in the sky. It always feels like it goes quicker on the way down.

'It's almost bedtime,' Sylvie announces to the children, and I reach for Neve in protest.

I decide bedtime. And bedtime is never, not ever –

Sylvie's expression is firm. 'Bedtime for everyone, Frances.'

Neve embraces her guests, as if it really is just another night. Just another bedtime, just the end of another big day. She does look tired; I can see she is squinting, her eyes a little red. She kisses Lucas then curls into my lap, ready to be carried.

'Thank you for my party. I love parties. Let's go to bed.'

Dog is almost passed out on Sylvie's lap. Mary is breastfeeding Gabriel, who holds his tiny hands together in contentment. It's peaceful, quiet. Lucas gestures to the stairwell.

I carry her down the stairs with Lucas opening doors for us. Neve murmurs, her crown slightly askew on her head. When we reach the bottom room, *our room,* I place her gently on the soft bed, right in the middle. She smiles, that between-worlds joy and delirium of soft, somnolent children.

'Best day of my whole life.'

She stretches out her arms, grabs us each by the neck and pulls us in, kissing our cheeks.

Then, with her mother and father curled up either side and flowers in her hair, she falls asleep.

The Word of Dog (Revelations)

In their dreams I collect up all the petals and I'm rich in spirit.
I am the bird I am the child I am the hag I am the last train out of hell.
I am the dog without a collar.

I dig up your money to find seeds.
I dig up your gifts. I dig up your bones.
I love you.
I will follow you anywhere.

Don't you get it?

Don't follow me. I just end up following the sacred smell of piss and trash.

I go where you go. Wherever you go. We're a pack. Let's lie down together. Tear up the lawn. Lick a wound.

Tell me where to sleep. Tell me when to sit. I will follow you anywhere.

I love you. I will follow you anywhere.

The Gospel According to Frances 26:9

Bring her back. Please bring her back. Bring her back. I'll do anything, just bring her back.

She's still warm, see? Her skin is –

'The Little Match Girl' by Hans Christian Andersen, translated by H.L. Brækstad

It was terribly cold; the snow was falling, and the dark evening was setting in; it was the last evening of the year – New Year's Eve. In this cold and uncomfortable darkness a poor little girl, bareheaded and barefooted, was walking through the streets. She had certainly had some sort of slippers on when she left her home, but they were not of much use to her, as they were very large slippers. Her mother had used them last, so you can guess they were large ones. As the little girl ran across the street just as two carriages were passing at a terrible rate, she lost the slippers. One of the slippers could not be found, and the other a boy ran away with. He said he would use it for a cradle when he got children of his own.

There was the little girl walking about on her naked little feet; they were red and blue with cold. In an old pinafore she had some bundles of matches, and in her hand she carried one of them. No one had bought anything of her the whole day, and no one had given her a penny. Hungry and shivering, she passed on, poor little girl, looking the very picture of misery. The snowflakes fell on her long yellow hair, which curled itself so beautifully about her neck; but of course she had no thoughts for such vanities. Lights were shining in all the windows, and there was such a delicious smell of roast goose in the street. 'Ah! it is New Year's Eve,' she thought.

Over in a corner between two houses – the one projected a little beyond the other – she crouched down, with her little feet drawn up under her; but she felt colder and colder, and she dared not go home, for she had not sold any matches or got a single penny; her father would beat her, and, besides, it was just as cold at home. They certainly had a roof over their heads, but through this the wind whistled, although they had stopped the largest cracks with rags and straw.

Her little hands were quite benumbed with cold. Ah! a match might do some good. If she only dared to take one out of the bundle and rub it against the wall, and warm her fingers over the flame! She took one out – ratch – how it spurted, how it burned! It was a warm, clear flame, just like a little candle, when she held her hand round it. It was a wonderful light; the little girl thought she was sitting right before a great iron stove with bright brass feet and brass mountings. How beautiful the fire burned! How it warmed her! But what was that? The little girl stretched her feet out to warm them also, and the flame went out – the stove vanished – she had only the small stump of the burned match in her hand.

A new match was rubbed against the wall; it burned, it gave a beautiful light, and where the light fell on the wall it became transparent like a veil. She could see right into the room, where the table was covered with a bright white cloth, and on it a fine china dinner service; the roast goose, stuffed with prunes and apples, was steaming beautifully. But, what was still more delightful, the goose jumped from the dish and waddled along the floor, with knife and fork in its back, straight towards the poor girl, then the match went out, and there was only the thick, cold wall to be seen.

She lighted a new match. Then she was sitting under a beautiful Christmas-tree; it was still larger and more decorated than that she had seen through the glass door at the rich merchant's last Christmas. Thousands of candles burned upon the green branches, and coloured pictures, like those that you see in the shop windows, were looking down upon her. The little girl stretched both her hands towards them – and the match went out.

The light seemed to go farther and farther away from her. She saw now that they were the bright stars. One of them fell down, leaving a long train of fire after it.

'Now someone is dying,' said the little one. Her old grandmother, who was the only one who had been good to her, but was now dead, had told her when a star falls a soul goes to God.

She rubbed a match again on the wall. It gave such a light, and in its lustre stood the old grandmother – so clear, so bright, so mild, so blessed!

'Grandmother,' cried the little one, 'oh, take me with you! I know you will be gone when the match goes out – gone, just like the warm stove, the beautiful roast goose, and the great, beautiful Christmas tree.'

And she rubbed quickly all the remaining matches in the bundle – she would not lose her grandmother – and the matches burned with such a splendour that it was brighter than in the middle of the day. Grandmother had never before been so beautiful, so grand. She took the little girl in her arms, and they flew away in brightness and joy, so high – high, where there was no cold, no hunger, no fear – they were with God!

But, next morning, in the corner by the house sat the little girl with red cheeks and a smile about her mouth, dead – frozen to death on the last evening of the old year. The sun of New Year's morning rose up on the little corpse, with the matches in the pinafore, and one bundle nearly burned. 'She wanted to warm herself,' the people said. No-one imagined what beautiful things she had seen, and how happily she had gone with her old grandmother into the bright New Year.

Letter from Reverend Reg Holland to the congregation of Eternal Fire Christian Church, 29 August 2022

Dear Eternal Fire congregants,

It is with immense sadness I inform you that Neve Harkin passed away last night, surrounded by her parents and grandparents. I understand we all prayed and petitioned for the healing of Neve, and that certain members of our congregation are praying for resurrection. For now, we shall accept the hand of the Lord, that she has been Promoted to Glory, now with Jesus forever. We can praise His name for this.

Lucas Harkin will be taking leave, and has asked not to be contacted at this time.

Who knows why God needed another angel in heaven, but all we can do is lean further into Him and His promise of eternity.

If you would like to make a donation to Lucas, or to the church's healing ministry, please do so via the link here.

Rev. Holland

The Gospel According to Lucas 1:1

It is worse than I ever imagined it could be.
That is all I came here to say.

But I remember the party. I remember the little boy, who told me he was sorry. And in the morning I was wearing the ring, engraved with the words, and I finally took it off.

Frances Kocsmáros's eulogy for her daughter Neve Harkin, 7 September 2022

Hello, everyone. Thank you for coming.

I don't feel comfortable explaining Neve's life as something that has been lived fully, and is now over. She isn't so easily distracted. There is a playground somewhere that she continues to climb, looking for things to collect as treasures. It just isn't here.

I would like to thank everyone for your support in our heartbreak. Thanks to my mother and father for helping me. Thank you to the church community, who have delivered a lot of food to both our homes. Thanks for the flowers and messages. Thanks to the nurses, to the doctors, to the funeral assistants. It has been a very difficult few weeks.

I would like to share a story about my daughter that might be one of my favourites. Neve's most-loved thing in the world was drawing. She drew everything she saw in her imagination, everything she saw with her eyes. She understood this world visually.

This is something that happened during her diagnosis. Everyone who has been through it knows the 'before and after diagnosis' realities: things are remembered more beautifully in the before, of course, because you didn't know; after, everything feels like the last time. But during diagnosis it's like Schrödinger's cat. The uncertainty makes you crazy, and also kind of immortal. Everything is terrible and perfect at once.

Neve would have been two and a half. Lucas, Neve and I were living in the big house that belonged to the church. Neve had been drawing shapes for the first time, and we were finding them on things other than paper – on walls and plates and stuffed toys. She would just find pens and use them, so we had to have a couple of conversations about pens and paper, about not drawing on furniture. Lucas felt a bit more strongly about it than I did, from memory. I kind of liked her interior design instincts.

There wasn't always paper handy, so we'd have to recycle random things quite a bit, or buy her drawing pads. When she was first getting tested and treated, we were really consumed by it, and we didn't always remember little things like that.

One time, we got home from an appointment and just left her in the living room for about an hour, thinking she was watching ABC. We were talking and crying, and then went back downstairs to start dinner and begin on a few of the forms we needed to fill out.

We came down to find Neve on the floor beneath the kitchen table, pens and paper strewn everywhere. On top of the table we had left a whole folder of test results, prescriptions, hospital and chemotherapy information and health insurance sheets. She had found the folder, pulled it down, and decided it was hers. She had drawn these people for the first time – these faces with legs coming out of their heads. 'Mummy, Daddy and Neve' she said they were, just drawn over and over and over again, on twenty pieces of paper. On every single hospital form, medication prescription and induction letter. She had taken the entire pile of cancer paperwork and covered every page with portraits of herself and her family. She'd made us all look so happy. Some pages were so covered in drawings you couldn't see what was beneath them.

She saw us, and just lit up, so proud of herself. 'Look, look, Mummy!'

I found the piece of paper that specifically diagnosed her, the letter that accompanied the biopsy. And on that piece of paper she had drawn another picture of a smiling face with long legs, this time with some kind of crown on its head.

'Who is that?' I asked her.

'That's me, all grown up,' she told me. 'A princess.'

I wish I had kept that picture, to remind me it might just be true. After the first round of chemo failed to halt the cancer, I threw it away. I couldn't bear to look at it anymore.

But I remember her, all grown up. And I want you to remember it too.

Letter from the Department of Children, Youth Justice and Multicultural Affairs, Child Safety to Queensland Police, 9 September 2022

Detective Ramineni,

Thank you for your request for information.

On Sunday, 28/8/2022, Penelope Lingard, also known as Mary, a teenager (16yo) with no fixed address, went missing from her hospital room at BUH in the maternity ward. Shortly after, it was reported that her biological child, who had been in the special care nursery due to his premature birth and had been removed from Penelope's care by the state, had been taken from his crib without permission.

The mother and baby were found on the top level of the car park, both asleep. She was breastfeeding him.

Child Safety have taken the baby back into the special care nursery under statutory supervision, and are allocating him to a foster carer on his release from hospital. The next court date is scheduled for one week's time. Penelope is in significant distress and we are investigating options for her placement.

We are in talks with various welfare organisations to find suitable outcomes for both children.

Regards,
Anneke Dowd

The Gospel According to Frances 27:1

. . .

. . .

. . .

. . .

. . .

. . .

. . .

. . .

. . .

I bury the coin, the thimble, the key, the car and the ring in the soft earth.
I bury the butterfly quilt in the soft earth.
I bury Peach in the soft earth.
I bury the body of the only person I love in the soft earth.
I bury my broken heart like a seed.
I wait to see what will grow.

. . .

. . .

. . .

. . .

to let go is to hold is to let go

Letter from Senior Constable Paul Jacobs to the Presiding Magistrate of the Children's Court of Queensland, 14 September 2022

To the Presiding Magistrate,

It is my position that Miss Penelope Lingard should be given full parental responsibility of her child.

As per the letter from Detective Devi Ramineni, I have been supervising the emancipation of Miss Lingard (also known as 'Mary') from sexual exploitation and directing the ongoing support she has received as a minor. I understand that Eternal Fire Christian Church and Street Aid Mission has been providing ongoing support for Miss Lingard, including housing, supervision and healthcare.

As a professional, I have assessed Penelope as being of sound mind and under the influence of no drugs. She is no longer soliciting underage, now removed from a coercive circumstance that forced it upon her. I believe her transition into motherhood is timely and important, and that she will be a devoted mother.

I have spoken at length to Pastor Lucas Harkin, who has given written confirmation the church will commit to continuing the support of her and of her baby, if you should choose to reunify mother and child.

I would like to also point out that no significant reason was given for the removal of the child, no thorough investigation conducted, and the circumstances of the removal were deeply insensitive. There was never any evidence to substantiate the alleged concerns. I will ensure that Penelope is represented effectively and defended aggressively in court if the Department continues to take this stance, and will personally ensure an appropriate investigation.

Please see the letters from Eternal Fire Christian Church, attached.

Thanks for your time,
Senior Constable Paul Jacobs, with the supervision of Detective Devi Ramineni
Queensland Police Service

The Gospel According to Frances 28:1

I sit in the darkness of the theatre again. This time I am an audience member. The ushers point me to my seat, turning twinkling eyes on Paul as he moves to sit beside me. Only Cressida knows what has taken place. She organised the tickets.

'Whatever you need, love. Whatever you need.'

It is the final performance of Ruairí's play. We have not spoken since the watch house. They still do not know who I am, really. Perhaps I don't know them either. That feels appropriate.

It has been two weeks, and this is the first time I have left the house. I am wearing the pale blue dress, the one from the back of my cupboard. Her favourite. Paul stares at me, sitting beside him in a ballgown, and offers a quiet smile of recognition.

The stage lights go up. The play soars, tumbles. Mary, Sylvie. I tense in grief. No-one has seen Mary in two weeks. We do not know who has Gabriel. Sylvie's funeral was held a week before Neve's. It's a lot. I'm trying to scoop out the ocean with a thimble.

I listen to the stories of other people who have suffered. Names I do not know. People who had car accidents, or lost their homes in floods, or fled from war in Afghanistan. People who have questioned why they should remain alive. Ruairí and the cast work hard, they sweat for us.

The audience gasps and cries and laughs at all the right moments. They receive the horrors of humanity and touches of the divine offered as entertainment. None of it really reaches me tonight. I think it's a good show. But it's only theatre.

The play receives a standing ovation. Vivaldi's 'Spring' plays.

Paul notices me fidgeting while the audience is still applauding.

'Do you want to stay and say hello to them?'

'No, I'll message them later.'

Just as we prepare to leave, the house lights dim again.

Ruairí comes back on stage, now in their civvies, affectations dropped and eyes peering past the fourth wall into the seating bank. I duck, begging not to be seen. They speak into a microphone.

'As tonight is the final performance of *Brightness,* we have the great honour of inviting the writer of this work to the stage – Glenda Lui.'

The audience claps and cheers.

A woman with black hair and a tattooed collarbone leads a second woman, wearing a sharp green suit, onto the stage.

Glenda surveys the audience, nodding vaguely, gripping Anouk's hand for dear life. Anouk takes the microphone from Ruairí, and begins to speak.

'Thank you, everyone. In 2018, Glenda received her diagnosis of early-onset Alzheimer's. I felt our lives were demolished in that moment – lives we'd crafted so lovingly, and so thoughtfully. But Glenda was not so sure. She felt her work was not done, and that her insight into that work had only just begun with what her diagnosis was revealing to her. So before her condition deteriorated too much, she decided to create one last piece. As a revered academic and leader in anthropological survival, she asked associates from around Australia to film the stories of people they knew who had suffered beyond what you might consider fair. They sent these to Glenda for her to edit and mould into a powerful piece of verbatim theatre. This is the play you were able to watch tonight.'

The audience applauds. Anouk is visibly moved. Ruairí gives her a hug, and she composes herself. Glenda looks down, disengaged.

'Glenda no longer recognises that she wrote this play – or at least wove its stories together. But as Ruairí walked off stage from the first scene, tonight, she said to me: "I've been there. That bright place. It's true." And in that moment I felt such relief, and I hugged her so tightly. Even in her disassociation from this work, the essence of its message still reaches her reality. It is my hope that if you ever suffer as we have suffered, you get to experience whatever beauty it is my wife knows to be true.'

Anouk bows her head before Glenda in love and honour, and they walk off stage. Paul reaches over to squeeze my hand – platonic; grounding. I let him.

He drives me home in silence. It is the kind of silence that descends while sipping tea. Silent because we have chosen to be small and still together. Because silence is kindest, tonight.

Eventually he speaks. 'You will sleep again, you know.'

I do not believe him. I stare at the road.

'And one of these days, you will wake up and think: *Wow, what a gorgeous morning.*'

'I won't.' I refuse to.

'You will. Because it will be warm, and you will have slept so well, and the sun will sparkle on the dew, and a butcherbird will be singing. It won't overpower her loss. It will just be a beautiful morning in the midst of her loss. And it will hold you gently.'

Nothing can, Paul. Nothing does.

He drops me out the front of my place. There's no question of lingering chat or coming in, which is a relief to me. He understands. But he stares at my front porch with a bit of confusion, eyes squinting into the darkness.

'What's wrong?'

'Is that a . . . *dog?*'

A scruffy, stray-like animal sits by my front door, tongue lolling. Waiting to be let in.

The Book of Mary (Revelations)

You won't see this for a long time, little one. But it's important to know that the shape of memory changes. Just like we have changed.

I've been in every place we have been and will be, every age we've been and will be, with every bad haircut. I have seen the way life lacerates and crusts and hardens on us, and I know how we wear it like armour, until it falls off to reveal soft, healed skin.

Remember when we had a bedroom? Remember the smell of our mother's laundry, the way it permeated every room in the house? The musky smell of washing detergent, the one that let us know these were our clothes, this was our home, that it was a good week – that this week there would be small kindnesses and cooked meals and conversations about ballet and promises of holidays. Remember the days the house smelled of bodies instead? Of sweat and crumb and mould and old bottles? When we knew it was a bad week, a hard week, with talk of revenge and death and not enough food because she wasn't hungry, and not enough words because she didn't want to speak.

Remember when we would sleep at other girls' houses and hear them talk about brands and boys and social media and blonde highlights and how their mums let them laser their leg hair at thirteen, and we just wanted to know how to blend in with them? How to disappear into the middle of the shoal of fish, so we wouldn't be eaten first?

Remember when it wasn't safe to sleep in a bed anymore?
Remember when the school uniform could no longer be worn?
Remember when the vultures picked at our body like a carcass?

Remember when seventeen different men were told we were a virgin?
Remember when T held the car door open just long enough to let us smell freedom?
Remember when we realised how to survive, a dog in a dark city?
Remember when the men grunted and rolled and we knew it was a dream?
Remember when our jeans did not fit and we did not know why?
Remember when the day came for the appointment but we got lost on the way to Brisbane?
Remember when I whispered a secret into our body, not because we were chosen, not because we were reckless, not because he lied, not because he found us, not because God decided we were special or worthless, not because we were saintly or sinful or suicidal, but because I already knew it would be there?

And remember when I told you. How you did not believe me. You did not believe yourself.

We do not know what will save us, Mary.

We do not know what will lead us into the arms of one another until the very end of the story. We do not know what treasure we have buried until we return to the earth to dig.

A miracle, I said. But the baby was never the miracle. We were.

Dog waits patiently while I check the house. There is no-one inside, and I catch the hope and disappointment sitting like an unflipped coin in my throat.

As if I expected everyone to have come back. As if I was walking into a party on a terrace . . .

I open the door to let the animal in, and wave Paul away like what has just happened is totally normal.

He drives off with a respectful nod.

Dog sits by the front door while I get water for him, and then laps at it thirstily.

'Come inside. Sleep on the couch.'

He doesn't move, stupid animal.
Except he's not an animal, he's –

A shape, by the front gate.

I hesitate. My mind is beaten up by grief. I do not know reality from fantasy. I do not know where I have been the past two weeks. I cannot let myself believe in my own denial.

A small, pierced teenager with an almost bald head walks up the footpath. She has a bag. She has shoes on. She is holding a newborn baby.

I don't know what to do or say.

She puts down her bag.

'Could you hold him for a moment?' she asks me, and I nod, still mute.

She places her child in my empty arms while she bends and embraces Dog, scooping him against her chest. His tail wags frantically.

She lets him go, then fidgets with something in her pocket. Gabriel shivers at being separated from her and begins to cry with full lungs – a universal roaring of his humanity.

I am alive, he cries. *Do not forget.*

Mary pulls out a tiny charm. A dog, in sterling silver. Engraved. I read the words, her unasked question lingering on the doorstep.

to return is to leave is to return

My heart screams along to Gabriel's ancient song. My relief. My loneliness. My future, like jasmine to a shadow.

I do not notice the curlew calling out in vain devotion. I do not notice the child is swaddled in a dirty quilt, embroidered with butterflies.

I do not notice a stray dog wandering back through the front gate, and onwards, onwards into the dark night.

ACKNOWLEDGEMENTS

THIS ISN'T MY STORY, BUT THIS IS A STORY THAT CONTAINS THE TRUTHS of many people I have walked with along the way.

I would like to acknowledge those who continue to navigate the desperate divide between liberation and religion. I would like to acknowledge those in the throes of illness, death and grief. I would like to acknowledge those who have traversed child custody, child services, and separation. You are athletes. Stretch the muscle of the heart and let it rest. It has carried too much today.

When I decided to write this, I did not write it for any other reason but to survive. If you wonder whether life will ever get gentler, I promise you this: the person writing your story is you.

—

Firstly, thank you to the team at Allen & Unwin: my publisher Annette Barlow, my copyeditor Ali Lavau and my editor Christa Munns. Working with you is a dream I have held for my entire life. I never expected it to come true.

Thank you to the Cuthbertson family, who continue to traverse the unthinkable. You welcomed me into your home so many years ago and taught me how to grieve. This book was inspired by your courage.

Thank you to my book midwives and close readers: Daniel, Charlotte, Claudia, Danielle, Hannah, Emily and Jada. Thank you for every suggestion and for all your encouragement. Thank you to Danielle and Hannah for the work we had previously done together in developing the screen concept.

Dan, thank you for believing in magic when I could not.

Thank you to Indigo, at The Viper Room, for your generosity and openness. Thank you to all the girls who introduced themselves to me that night, for the valuable insight and understanding you offered me.

Thank you to my brother and surgeon-on-call, Will, for being specifically equipped to answer every medical question that arose in this.

Thank you to my sister-in-law, Kate, a saint of a social worker, for guiding me through child safety and family violence legalities.

Thank you Liesje – you held my secret and understood its weight completely.

Thank you Mum, for everything, in the hardest year of your life.

Thank you Dad, for reading every word I have ever published. For your eternal presence in me, constantly calling me higher. I hope you get a copy up there.

Thank you to my uncle Andrew, for telling me in his sparse, coy way to 'keep writing'. For showing me what I wanted to be, right from the beginning, and how to tell the truth at all costs. For insisting I was always 'too young' to read *Praise*, which ensured I stole it off the bookshelf aged sixteen. Thank you for your legacy, your defiance, your devotion to story.

Thank you to my daughters, who have been so patient, so demanding, so insistent that we live brightly, even in the shadow of heartache. I know you are still baffled by the thought of a fairy tale not for children.

You can read this when you're sixteen.